JAKE & ELLIE

A NOVEL
BY HAZEL YOUNG

 **FriesenPress**

Suite 300 – 852 Fort Street
Victoria, BC, Canada V8W 1H8
www.friesenpress.com

ISBN
978-1-4602-3004-6 (Hardcover)
978-1-4602-3005-3 (Paperback)
978-1-4602-3006-0 (eBook)

1. Fiction, Romance, General

Distributed to the trade by The Ingram Book Company

ACKNOWLEDGEMENTS

Many thanks to all of you who helped take this story from an idea in my head to the printed page: first, always first, my wonderful husband, Dennis, who literally makes everything possible; my beautiful daughter, Jennifer; my loving and lovable sisters, Betty, Judy, and Brenda; and my generous friends, Marnie, Elizabeth, and Holly. All of you read the first clumsy drafts, loved me anyway, and encouraged me to keep on trying. Elizabeth, you deserve an entire page of gratitude. Thank you, my friend.

I must also thank my talented daughter-in-law, Carla, who allowed me to use her beautiful photograph for the front cover, and my son, Steven, who, perhaps inadvertently, gave me a favourite coming-of-age story. My "oldest" friend, Sheila, holds a special place in my heart for so many reasons but right now in particular for having taught me the "sergeant-major" song over fifty years ago in boarding school. This silly little song (which her mother taught her) has popped into my head at the oddest times in my life and was undoubtedly the seed that grew into the 'Goodnight Gracie' chapter. Thanks to my husband's family, some of whose family stories I have borrowed from and woven into this book. I have heard these stories so often they feel as if they are my own, but they're not, and I thank you for having shared them with me.

Thanks to my editors – Annik Adey-Babinski, and Michael, at First Editing who gave me the confidence to go

ahead with the book and are responsible for helping me to improve it in so many different ways.

This book centres around the mysterious question of illness, something I am familiar with, and I must thank a remarkable doctor, Dr. Francis Kilbertus, who came into my life in 1994. Francis, you are a true healer, and I am so grateful to have known you.

DEDICATION

For Dennis – who stayed.

v

DISCLAIMER

All characters appearing in this work are
fictional. Any resemblance to real persons,
living or dead, is purely coincidental.

JAKE MADISON

CHAPTER ONE
August 31, 1999

Whoa! Where the hell had she come from? A vision of uncommon loveliness had floated through the door of Jake's hospital room – he had opened his eyes and there she was – and now she was hovering beside the bed bathed in a strangely soft, glowing light, a light completely foreign to any hospital light that Jake had ever encountered. Jake was no stranger to hospital lighting. She gestured toward him with an arm so slim and elegant that he could only gaze, awe-struck; such perfection didn't exist in his normal, everyday world. Botticelli's Venus – in scrubs – he was thinking, though it seemed odd that her flowing blonde hair was now short and dark, reminding him of an illustration from a book his mother must have read to him once about pixies – or were they elves? Jake couldn't remember; it had been a long time ago.

"Mr. Madison." Her voice had music in it; he knew it would have, so he wasn't surprised, just smugly pleased that he had nailed it so well.

Again, "Mr. Madison, I believe this is for you." She held in her hand one of the little paper cups that must form the foundation of institutions like this, he thought to himself – millions of them cemented together. A flimsy foundation

even with all that cement, he was thinking, and then his mind did a sharp left turn (it seemed to be doing this more and more frequently these days), and there he was, all muscle and sinew, handsome, young and tanned, sweating in the heat and pushing that damned wheelbarrow filled with cement – dumping it, and filling it, and dumping it again, all the time trying to block out the sound of his uncle's raspy, profane orders to, "Move it you lazy sons o' bitches! Time's money!" But no, not now, he thought, as he clawed his way back to the present. That was then. Right now he had an angel hovering over him wanting to give him something.

Jake smiled, turning his head to look directly into her eyes just as he would have done thirty years ago when a look like this could have been the start of a beautiful thing. Not this time. In the split second it took to refocus, his enchanting, ethereal Venus began to waver and change, in an instant transformed into something glowering and gnome-like. How had this happened? Jake rubbed at his eyes and blinked rapidly. This was crazy.

"Still me, Mr. Madison," she growled, her voice low and gravelly. He rubbed his hands roughly over his face. He was rapidly becoming aware that the idea of a gnome appearing in his hospital room was miles beyond the scope of what anyone would consider normal.

Man! Was he having a day!

It had to be some kind of a nurse, he decided, and from the sound of her voice, one who had sucked back far too many cigarettes in her lifetime. He wondered how she had the time. He pictured her with a cigarette dangling from her lips (those luscious Venus lips that had suddenly become puckered and thinning) from the moment she left the hospital till the moment she returned. He hated how sanctimonious he was becoming about tobacco. His mind was obviously doing another of the unexpected U-turns it had been performing all morning. He remembered how people, during 'the Bert years', used to say his apartment reeked of dead cigarettes, but he also remembered how he would drag himself through the door at the end of a brutal day. He remembered how the stale-smoke smell of his apartment would hit him, and how he would breathe it in, glad to be home.

BERNICE JACKSON

CHAPTER TWO

Bernice glared down at her feet. I swear they're trying to escape these running shoes, she thought. They seemed to be picking a hard way to do it – puffy ankles billowing over the edges of the padded, once brilliantly white, now greying, athletic gear that she didn't think they even called running shoes anymore. Who knew what they called anything anymore? A table of contents was a menu, a cell was a phone and who really knew what Google meant? Her son apparently. Ever since her Sidney had discovered acne and computers, Bernice rarely understood a word he said about anything. She remembered when she had understood everything he said even when no one else seemed to. She knew that a hoing-tatter was a helicopter. K'nook meant come look. Lerve was the most special love anyone could ever have for anyone else. "I lerve you Mamma" – and pudgy little boy arms tight around her neck. Bernice felt a fatigue like the weight of three heavy woollen blankets smothering her. She gave her head a shake and took a long drag from the cigarette she had forgotten was between her fingers. Where was that freakin' bus?

"Hey, Bernice. Kill anyone today?" It was Jerry behind the wheel tonight – skinny, balding with a comb-over glued with great precision to the top of his skull. You had

to admire his relentless denial of the ageing process, and Bernice wondered how much better she might handle having to look in the mirror every day watching her scalp becoming ever more naked with every ticking moment. Ain't life grand, she thought, but hey, no point in letting Jerry know that she felt any sympathy for his particular predicament, and next to the crap she had been dealing with all day, it really was no predicament at all. And there she went again, letting the hospital invade her opinions on everyday life.

"Not yet, Jerry. But I might if you don't get this bus movin'."

"Ah, Bernice you gorgeous thing. Have I ever told you that you remind me of my old drill sergeant?"

"Every time I tell you to move your butt, you jackass." The tired banter was more or less the same every time, but Bernice had to admit that she didn't mind it. At least Jerry wasn't throwing up while he was needling her.

"And a-waay we go," Jerry sang out in his best Jackie Gleason.

Bernice began her cautious shuffle down the centre of the bus, hanging on to the seats as the bus began to accelerate. It wasn't overly crowded tonight, so she was able to lower her ample form into a seat next to the aisle with little difficulty. Once again she looked with irritation at her puffy feet. Maybe she should start walking around the hospital on her hands – now that would make them sit up and pay attention. A choked chuckle erupted from her throat, surprising her as much as it did the wino sitting beside her. That Jake Madison would have a reason to look at her as if she'd just sprouted another head if she could accomplish that. What was that look he had given her today all about anyway? She had jotted down "possibly hallucinating" on his chart but was having trouble dismissing the incident.

There was something about him that wanted to lurk around the edges of her mind – something a little Steve McQueen around his eyes, or maybe it was his mouth. Bernice pondered this for a moment and then abruptly straightened her spine. Was she really mooning about over a patient, which was bad enough, but even worse a patient with perhaps a few marbles missing? "Mercy," she heard herself mutter. "I need a vacation even more badly than I thought."

JAKE

CHAPTER THREE

Jake laid the red Queen on the black King and swore under his breath. Maybe he should try playing this damned game on the computer – he might have better luck. But he knew he never would. He hated computers even more than he hated – what, he thought? What did he hate more than computers? Well, cats of course. His mind travelled back to the apartment and his neighbour Bert's old cat, Mica. He hadn't thought about Mica in years, but that didn't mean he'd forgotten about him – not Mica, who had, at one time or another, peed on every mother-lovin' inch of hallway all the way down to the elevator in his building, and on one very special occasion on Jake's foot. Now that was a moment to treasure. Good neighbour Bert had caught him just as he was about to punch the button that would urge the ageing elevator up to the sixth floor. Something about money Jake owed him – wasn't every conversation with Bert about money Jake owed him? – and that damned cat had started circling Jake's legs the way cats do and then suddenly he was peeing on his boot, right there in the hallway. Jake could hardly believe it. And then Jake was swearing and hollering, and Bert was laughing so hard it was a miracle that he didn't pee his pants, and that

idiot cat was high tailing it back to the safety of Bert's half-open doorway.

Jake took a drink of his lukewarm coffee. Well, it hadn't turned out all bad.

After he finally quit laughing Bert had leaned against the wall to catch his breath. "Okay, Madison, I guess that makes us even this time. Poker's at your place next week, dumb-ass," and still doing little hiccupy hee-hees he had headed back to his apartment. Jake could hear that little baby voice that all cat owners adopt (surely they weren't born with it?): "C'mon Mica, c'mon baby, Daddy's here."

"Oh, kill me now," Jake had muttered. Then he had turned his attention back to the elevator button.

How old had he been then, Jake strained to remember. Ellie had already left him, taking with her the furniture, the good dishes, a painting they had bought at an art fair in the early days of their marriage and their daughter Jenna. Screw the furniture, and, as for the dishes, Jake ate most of his meals alone standing at the kitchen counter anyway. The piece of artwork meant nothing to him as he didn't understand a thing about abstract art except that it made Ellie happy. (Funny thing about the heart – all these years, and he could still remember how happy it had made him to buy that canvas of red and yellow circles that had made Ellie's face light up like Christmas morning.) But, oh man, he had missed Jenna. Ellie was fair about it – he still got to be with his daughter on his days off and holidays – whenever he wanted, really, but it was never the same.

Jake had been shocked when Jenna was born, by how instantly, totally, crazy in love he had felt about her the minute Ellie had put her in his arms. He had never felt this way about anyone, except Ellie of course. He knew he would die for this tiny, red, still wrinkly, cone-headed little person. "Daddy's here, it's okay," he had said over and over again, never realizing he would sound like Bert a few years down the road.

MARTY

CHAPTER FOUR

In the mirror, Marty studied the woman sitting in his chair in the hair salon. The salon was called The Hair Place. Everyone in the shop called the woman Ellie; apparently she had been coming here for years. Marty couldn't guess her age, which was strange because he was usually good at this, but she was one of those women who was still a total fox, even though she was probably his mother's age. Good bones, the girls in the salon told him. There was something fragile about her that made him careful with his language, something that didn't always come easily to him. He wanted to say something so clever she would break out in uncontrollable laughter; she had that kind of a laugh. Fat chance that was going to happen – none of his well-practised lines had produced any effect so far. Marty unhappily decided it was time to throw in the towel as far as Ellie was concerned. What the hell, Lucille had an appointment in half an hour; he'd save his cultivated charm for her. Lucille was the perfect woman from Marty's perspective – older, which equalled grateful in his experience (oh, so grateful), bored with her marriage, and loaded. The guys he hung out with had busted his balls when he had gone into hairdressing, but he had the last laugh. Who got laid more than him?

Ellie began fidgeting, impatiently crossing and uncrossing her legs. Martin, Marty, this new hairdresser seemed to be taking much longer than her regular girl, but June had called in sick today leaving Ellie scrambling to find someone else to highlight her hair in time for the wedding. Edgar's daughter, Karen, was getting married tomorrow. Ellie knew she should have had this done weeks ago, but she had been busy with a project which thankfully she had been able to wrap up two days ago. Marty had stepped in to replace June, and Ellie was grateful to him, but she couldn't wait to get out of his chair. This slightly oily leering Romeo was beginning to make her skin crawl. Still, she would have to remember to be generous with the tip. She fervently wished she were one of those earth-mother women who were able to reach that certain age and say 'to hell with it all' and let her hair grow wild and long and grey, and quit wearing underwire bras, maybe even dump the contents of her make-up drawer into the trash – well, maybe next year. She didn't honestly think she was ready for that yet.

Ellie checked her watch just as Marty was finishing up with a cloud of hairspray. She pressed thirty dollars into his palm, quickly settled her bill at the front and hurried out of the shop knowing Edgar would be waiting for her. After the door closed behind her, Marty checked the tip she had given him. Damn, no slip of paper with a phone number hastily scrawled across it.

Ellie rounded the corner of the building and there he was, waiting in the parking lot just as he had said he would be. Edgar – so trustworthy, so dependable; so why did her jaw clench ever so slightly when she saw him waving from his shiny grey Cadillac? Edgar was a tax attorney, probably the driest, most mind-numbing occupation on the planet, but he loved it, of course he did, and why did that, why had that, always bothered her? It was just a small irritation, like a crooked picture on a wall that you wanted to straighten but for some reason couldn't, so you pretended you didn't notice it – but you did, and it drove you crazy. Yes, exactly like that.

Ellie, you are a crazy lady, she thought, as she waved back at Edgar and rubbed at the crease between her eyebrows. He didn't deserve this attitude. Edgar (she usually called him Eddie – it had seemed so sweet at first – Ellie and Eddie) was a good man, a generous man: steady, trustworthy, dependable, always dependable. But then, totally unbidden, the crazy witch lady who had taken up housekeeping in the back of Ellie's brain cleared her phlegmy throat and started in with her familiar mantra. "And let's not forget boring – bone numbing, sucking the life out of you, boring! Boring, boring, boring!"

Oh Lord, oh Lord, oh Lord – Shut up! Ellie silently screamed at the nagging voice in her head. "Eddie, you're right on time," she called out, trying to smile.

"Of course he is," unwelcome witch woman settled herself a little more deeply into Ellie's brain.

EDGAR

CHAPTER FIVE

Edgar watched as Ellie shifted herself into a comfortable position in the passenger seat. She had smiled at him when she opened the car door, but the corners of her eyes hadn't wrinkled up. They were supposed to wrinkle up if a person was genuinely happy – he had learned that on *Law and Order* last night. That was how Bobber had caught the killer. Bobber wasn't the detective's real name, but he was always bobbing and weaving around as he interrogated his suspects, so that is what Edgar had named him. Perps, that's what they called them – the suspects – Edgar wondered for a moment what it would feel like to be the kind of a man who could throw around a word like 'perps'. Not exactly his style, he thought.

Yes, he watched far too much *Law and Order*, he admitted that, but there were always interesting little pieces of information that you could pick up from it, like this one. Okay, no big surprise. He had known Ellie hadn't been happy for a long time, but what more was he supposed to do about it? He bought her every new thing that came out on the market and could never understand her reluctance to accept these gifts. Her gentle, "Oh Eddie, I don't need this," never failed to surprise him. Isn't that what women wanted – stuff? He always said the right things, asked the

appropriate questions (the Dale Carnegie course had not been money wasted), he certainly never gambled or drank too much, he didn't chase other women – well, there was that one time, but he was certain Ellie didn't know about that – and he tolerated her "artistic" friends with the patience of Job. He would do anything he had to do to hang on to Ellie. Everything he didn't understand about her faded away when he walked into a room filled with his colleagues, her slim arm tucked into the crook of his. These colleagues were mainly men just like him, who lived for information about taxation and dividends and loopholes, and knew little about the inner yearnings of the human heart, and he knew that none of them could figure out why Ellie, lovely, lovely Ellie, was with him. He knew that the more jaded among them thought it was because of his money, but in Ellie's case he felt fairly certain that it wasn't about that. It wasn't her *modus operandi,* so to speak. There was some more *Law and Order* for you. And so, that was the question, wasn't it? Why was Ellie with him?

Edgar glanced at the console clock. He'd better step on it or they'd be late for the rehearsal.

THE REHEARSAL DINNER

CHAPTER SIX

The rehearsal had gone off perfectly, Karen declared over and over again to anyone who would listen, mainly, Ellie thought, to reassure herself. It actually seemed to bob along, furiously treading water, trying somehow to keep its head out of the crashing waves that tomorrow's ceremony would bring down upon all involved.

Did I actually think that? Ellie was shocked. When had she become such a cynic?

She rubbed the small crease in her forehead. What was going on here? Ellie knew she was not a frivolous person. She cared deeply about Edgar's daughter and wanted only the best for her, but there was something about the preparation for this wedding that was really setting her on edge. She didn't like Karen's fiancé, but Karen was twenty-five, the decision was up to her. Obviously it had to be something going on with herself, nobody else, just her. Oh, really! Wasn't she too old for all this soul searching? Give it a rest Ellie, she said to herself and began scanning the room for the waiter with the tray of champagne. Spotting him she raised her hand, and he glided toward her as if on well-oiled wheels – the help Edgar hired had an uncanny knack for doing this. Who was it who had said that the rich

were different from the rest of us? Like his waiters, Edgar's well-oiled lifestyle was proof of that.

Ellie slipped a glass from the waiter's tray, agreeing that it was a delightful party, and, yes, she was having a delightful time, and then looked up to see Jenna weaving her way through the tables and felt her heart begin to melt. It always did this at the sight of her daughter. Jenna was twenty-four now, five foot ten and lovely, but as Ellie watched her cross the room she suspected that in the back of her mind Jenna would always remain six years old. She wiggled her fingers, waving at her and sipped at her wine, her mind sliding back to their mornings from years ago: Jenna climbing into bed with her – skinny, freckled, Band-aids on her knees, her hair shooting up in all directions. Her hair had been a light sandy colour back then and had seemed to take on a life of its own during the night. Jenna would burrow under the blankets and then wrestle her way back to the top, the static in the bedding giving her hair added license to fly wildly around her head – and she would slap at it, pawing it away from her face as she whispered secrets and shared stories about the intrigue that was happening behind the doors of her first grade class room.

"Wanna know somethin' Mamma? . . . "Wanna know somethin' Mamma?" Back then she had always reminded Ellie of a beautiful little colt – all legs, and energy and lightning quick moves.

"Jenna, you kick me one more time and you are out of this bed – forever!" And then Jenna would throw her arms around Ellie's neck and cover her face with wet kisses, sending Ellie ducking for cover. She could never stay angry with that beautiful little face.

Jenna had hit five foot ten and the high school basketball court at about the same time. It had been a case of perfect timing – the gangly teenager had become a high school hero almost overnight. Ellie remembered how grateful she had felt – all that adolescent insecurity and angst magically turned into self-assurance and self-acceptance. Jenna had proven to be a natural athlete, and really, why wouldn't she be? After all … Ellie let that thought dissolve into itself. Not now, she thought, as she put her glass down and put out her arms to let Jenna's arms surround her.

Jenna hugged her tightly and then pulled away, still holding her mother's hands in hers. She seemed to be breathing too quickly, Ellie thought, and when she opened her mouth words began tumbling out randomly. "Honey, honey, slow down. Here, sit down," she eased Jenna into a chair. "Now, start again – and breathe this time."

Jenna began rubbing at her eyes. When she dropped her hands mascara was smudged across her face. Ellie reached toward her to stop her, but there was something about the look on her daughter's face that made her drop her arm.

"Mom, it's Daddy."

Ellie was momentarily confused; the noise level in the room was high, and she was unsure of what Jenna had just said. She leaned closer, "Danny?" she asked, her mind clicking through a mental rolodex. Who was Danny?

"No, Mom – Daddy," Jenna was becoming exasperated, her hands gesturing in the air.

Ellie, who had been standing, suddenly felt the need to sit down as she began to understand what her daughter was saying. Jake, she thought, and then aloud, "Jake? Are you saying something happened to Jake?"

Her daughter nodded, her shoulders slumping. Tears began mixing with the mascara under her eyes. "The hospital has been trying to call you all day – I guess they don't have your cell. I don't know how they got mine."

"What? Why, Jenna? What's wrong? What happened to Jake? He's not …" Ellie couldn't bring herself to finish the sentence, but Jenna understood and began shaking her head emphatically.

"No, Mom, but it might be some kind of head injury. I don't really know. You know how hospitals are – they only tell you enough to scare you."

Oh shit, oh shit, oh shit. Ellie wrapped her arms around her waist and began rocking slightly back and forth. She knew all about these calls. There had been so many of them in the years she and Jake had been married. It was usually Frank, tough as nails Coach Frank Bailey on the other end of the line. "Don't worry Ellie, you know Jake, he's got a head as hard as a rock. We'll have him out of the hospital by tomorrow morning."

And that was why she had finally left him.

JAKE AND BERNICE

Chapter seven

W ell, well, well, so you're still here, Mr. Madison?" Bernice was genuinely surprised. Hospitals shipped patients in and out so quickly these days it made your head spin.

Jake was sitting in the chair beside the bed, his right foot resting on his left knee, his foot jiggling. Impatient. "Yeah, couldn't convince Doogie Howser to let me go." Jake was done. He'd totally had it with this place – just wanted to get the hell out of here. He looked more closely at the nurse who had entered the room and realized she was the one he had labelled "the pill gnome" on that first groggy day. Not so nice, Madison, he realized now. Hell, she was no great beauty, but she didn't deserve the "gnome" title either. He wondered what wild and woolly trip his brain had been on when it had made that observation. In an attempt to make it up to her, he stood and held out his hand. "Thanks for putting up with me," he said, "I know I can be a royal pain in the as ... butt," he corrected himself, "at times."

"No apology needed, Mr. Madison," Bernice waved his hand away. "I assume since you are dressed that you are waiting for someone to pick you up, correct?"

This all sounded so formal that Jake's face split into a grin, and then, remembering who he was waiting for, he

sat back down in the chair. "Yeah, yes I am. She should be here any minute."

"Good then. Take care of yourself." And Bernice was out the door leaving Jake alone to think about what was coming next.

Ellie. He doubted that this was going to go well.

JAKE AND ELLIE

CHAPTER EIGHT

Jake had first met Ellie when he was about thirty thousand feet above the ground. Fitting, he thought now – Ellie had always made him feel like he could fly. He actually was flying this time, though – the team was returning from two games with Boston. Jake had spent most of the second game in and out of the penalty box and had a fresh scar running down his left cheek to prove it. The team was high with the high winning brings, and the stewardesses were kept busy maintaining some sense of order, as the guys were ready to party. It was 1969, and they called them "stewardesses" at the time, Jake remembered – he wasn't quite sure when they morphed into flight attendants. Jake wasn't really in a party mood. His head was throbbing and the pills the team doctor had given him were making him groggy. He leaned his chair back and tried to stretch out his legs. All he really wanted to do was get home and pass out for about eight hours. He was caught up in how much he wanted this when a voice in the aisle interrupted his train of thought. It was a female voice, a nice voice, a soft voice; soft like caramel pudding, Jake thought to himself, and immediately smacked himself on the forehead. Pudding? Where the hell had that come from? He hadn't said it out loud, had he? "I'm sorry, it's the pills," he said to he didn't

know who. He fumbled around trying to get his seat into an upright position. Weren't they always going on about getting your seat in an upright position in case of an emergency? Well, this obviously was one and he couldn't even find the fucking button to get himself there. Then the caramel voice was speaking again, telling him to relax and here, she had some ice for his face. Soft, capable hands placed the ice pack gently on his cheek. Jake didn't really know it yet, but he had just met Ellie. Minutes later he was sound asleep.

The rumble of the landing gear sliding into position finally woke him. There was all the usual milling about that came with landing, and Jake let everyone else exit before he started toward the open curtain at the front of the aircraft. The tiny blonde stewardess was positioned there saying all the thanks and goodbyes that were part of her job during the deplaning process. She was nodding and smiling – the airline should pay her extra for that smile, Jake was thinking. It was hands-down the greatest smile he had ever seen, and she wasn't one of those phony platinum blondes – her hair reminded him of warm honey – it probably smelled as good as it looked. He liked that it was long, and thick, and wavy, and she wore it off of her forehead. It seemed to Jake that the other girls he noticed lately all wore their hair long and poker straight, with bangs cut straight across their eyebrows. Not this one. Jake felt himself wondering what it would feel like to have his hands in that hair.

Hey, slow down Madison. You don't even know this girl.

When he got closer to her he made a production of pulling on his coat – he didn't want her to disappear from his sight – not yet. "Thank you for flying with us, Mr. Madison," her eyes examined the side of his face. "Are you feeling better now?" Her eyes, that were focused on his cheek, made Jake fumble as he pushed his arm into his coat sleeve; her eyes were blue, but a deep blue, not the colour usually used to describe blue eyes. How would he describe them, he wondered? He had seen the sky that shade of blue – sometimes in the fall it would look like that, he was thinking, and nearly laughed out loud. Oh, you're a regular poet, you are, Shakespeare, he said to himself – but damn! Her eyes were really blue! Then he realized that she was still looking at him, a question in those amazing eyes of hers.

Jake nodded, suddenly feeling his six-foot self dwarfing her. "Thanks for helping me out – uh, the ice – you know…" He knew he was babbling, but something about this very pretty girl was making it difficult for him to breathe; a coherent sentence was temporarily out of the question. He put the palm of his big hand on the top of his head and began rubbing his hair, hoping that she had somehow missed this. He glanced down at her and saw that the corners of her eyes were crinkled up, and she was laughing. He had never heard a laugh like hers – this girl just kept getting better.

"I think a bowl of pudding might have done the trick just as well, Mr. Madison." She was still laughing, and Jake felt a wave of relief wash over him. She was flirting with him. Jake knew when he was being flirted with, and this beautiful girl was doing exactly that.

He took a deep breath of stale cabin air, and a smile began to spread across his face. His smile had a way of sneaking up on him – slow and lazy. "You watch that smile," his mother had always warned him. "It's just like your father's – it can get you into a pile of trouble." He remembered his aunts gathered around the kitchen table back home; how they would nudge each other, turning away and laughing when they would hear her say this.

"Please call me Jake," he said, holding out his hand. He was grinning now. "Do you think I could buy you a cup of coffee?"

An hour later they met up at the baggage carousel. And that, thought Jake, was the beginning of that.

ELLIE AND JAKE

CHAPTER NINE

I t was early December in Toronto and, as usual, the weather didn't know which way to turn. Yesterday had brought rain and sleet, streets so icy they would have made the Pope swear, but the sand trucks had been out in full force, and today the city seemed to be returning to normal. Jake proudly pulled his car up to the front of the airport, and Ellie swung into the passenger side, easing herself into the comfort of the leather seat. "Hmmmm, pretty fancy car, Mister Madison," she said, placing extra emphasis on the "Mister."

Jake had the good sense to look embarrassed. "Yeah, yeah, I know. It was the first thing I bought for myself when I signed with the team. You know, it was probably the first thing I'd ever owned that was brand new."

It was Ellie's turn to be embarrassed. "Oh goodness, Jake, I'm sorry" she pushed her hair behind her ears. "Sometimes I say things without thinking. I'm working on it, but it seems like things just keep burbling out of my mouth."

"Burbling?" That lazy smile was starting to play with his face again.

"Yes," Ellie sighed, "I make up words too."

"Oh hey, this is great," Jake hit the steering wheel with the palm of his hand. "Here I was thinking you were so perfect – so perfect I was afraid to even breathe in case I didn't do it right – and now you're telling me you're just as screwed up as the rest of us?"

"Well, it would have been nice if we could have made it out of the parking lot before you found that out," said Ellie, touching his shoulder.

It had gotten late, so coffee turned into dinner at a tucked away restaurant on a side street in Toronto's colourful Yorkville. They had both ordered spaghetti and garlic bread and red wine. Ellie kept picturing the spaghetti scene in *Lady and the Tramp*, and it made her smile. Looking at Jake's face made her smile, as did the warmth and soft lighting in the tiny restaurant. You don't even know this guy, she thought to herself, and then she looked at Jake and smiled again. She liked his sandy coloured hair and his eyes, though she wasn't exactly sure what colour she would use to describe them. They were such nice eyes, though. She liked the way they laughed when he laughed.

They talked about growing up in Northern Canada – Jake in Ontario, Ellie in Saskatchewan – how they had spent their winters skating and tobogganing, and their summers swimming in lakes city people could only dream about; how one of the most exciting days of the year had been the day the Sears Christmas catalogue arrived in the mail. They both laughed about the early days of television in the North: how everyone would gather around the TV on Saturday nights to watch Hockey Night in Canada, but the screens were so snowy you could barely make out the players, let alone the puck. Jake told wonderfully exaggerated stories about how his uncles and his dad would argue about who was really on the ice, and he did a flawless Foster Hewitt that made Ellie laugh so hard tears began streaming down her face. "Stop! Stop!" she was holding up her hands, "My eyes are leaking."

Jake leaned back in his chair, smiling. The fact that he could make this beautiful girl laugh filled his chest with something bubbling, effervescent. He watched as she composed herself and then began talking about her job. She loved flying; meeting people, sometimes even famous people, and she loved the three day layovers in places like England and Paris, the gardens and the museums that she had only read about, growing up. Her face was glowing, and Jake thought he could sit and watch her all night – he couldn't remember when he had been this happy.

They told each other about their families, feeling an immediate connection over their shared Irish background. Ellie told Jake about how she had lost her mother when she was very young leaving her father to raise his two young daughters on his own. Her father had never remarried, claiming there could never be another woman for him. Jake watched her face cloud over as she told him this, and even though they had just barely met he felt an impulse in his gut to put his arms around her and keep her safe. She laughed and shook her head, embarrassed by the emotion that had snuck up on her, and quickly asked Jake about his family. He had been leaning forward listening to her, but now he sat back and began telling her about his parents and younger brother, his many aunts and uncles. His stories about his large clan-like family soon erased the lost look from Ellie's face and she was laughing again. Jake felt his chest expanding. At that moment, being able to make her smile again felt like the most important thing he had ever done.

They talked about the music they liked. Jake said that he loved jazz and country which made Ellie's eyebrows shoot up and she was laughing some more, saying what an odd combination that was, and Jake said he knew – he got bugged about it all the time. But he loved jazz because it had no hard and fast rules, and he loved country because country was all about story telling. His mother used to read to him when he was little, and he could never get enough of it. He grinned and added that there was something about 'cheatin' women and hard drinkin' good ol' boys' that always cheered him up when he was down – and when it came to jazz, a trumpet or a sax could be a powerful thing.

Ellie was laughing again, knowing she should probably stop but not sure she could – she loved the way he put things. She admitted that she didn't know much about jazz, but she did like Dave Brubeck. She was more into folk and loved Joni Mitchell and Joan Baez. They were both big fans of Bob Dylan, and the Beatles and Gordon Lightfoot. Being from the North, Lightfoot's "green, dark forests" resonated with both of them.

The conversation took a more serious turn as they both recalled exactly where they had been when Kennedy was assassinated. They touched on Viet Nam – how glad they both were that they didn't have to deal with those issues.

Jake drained his glass of wine and looked directly at her, "I'd go though – if I had to."

Ellie was shocked to hear this. Nobody she knew talked this way. "There's no way Jake, I'd never go."

Jake took a minute, and his fingers lightly traced the stitches on his cheek. Finally he said quietly, "Sometimes you have to fight, Ellie."

Ellie stiffened in her seat, "Viet Nam's not a game, Jake."

"But that's it," he said. His voice was still quiet. "Hockey's not just a game for me either. It's my whole life. It's all I've ever wanted to do – it's the only thing I can ever imagine myself doing." He stopped: he wanted her to understand this; not everyone did. "And, as it turns out," he continued, "one of the best things I do, when it comes to hockey, is protect the other guys on my team." He paused and rubbed his hand over his hair. "Oh, I'm pretty good with the puck – I get some pretty decent shots away – I don't think they'd keep me around if I didn't, and I'm fast," he ducked his head almost shyly, "but mainly I'm what some people like to call an enforcer." Jake really didn't want to use the word; it scared people off, and that was the last thing he wanted to do with Ellie, but he had grown up playing a rough brand of hockey and he figured he'd better keep things real. He rubbed his hand over his face and tried again. "You see, what I do is make it possible for the guys who are really great at setting up plays, and the big-time goal scorers to get down the ice and do their job. I'm never out to cripple anyone – I couldn't operate like that, but guys on the other team usually know I'm not an easy guy to mess with." He grinned ruefully and shrugged his shoulders. "And then other times it feels like I'm in a fight almost every time I step on the ice." He saw her eyes growing sad, and he quickly added, "But I love it. With a team, everyone has a role to play and this one's mine. The guys count on me, Ellie, and I'm there for them." And then almost pleadingly, "It's what I do, Ellie."

Ellie looked down at the tablecloth. She knew that if this relationship were going to go anywhere, and all of her instincts were telling her that she wanted it to, then this conversation would be sure to come up again.

They were quiet for a few minutes, and then Jake said, "Hey, c'mon puddin' lady, let's order that coffee."

They both ordered espressos, probably to impress each other, and when they came they both sipped at them silently. Finally Jake broke the silence. "Truth, Ellie?"

"Okay," she answered, a little afraid of what was coming next.

"So," he paused, looking down at his cup of espresso, "when you were growing up in Nowheresville, Saskatchewan, did you ever in a million years think that someday you would be sitting in a restaurant in Yorkville, in big old fancy Toronto, laughing at the bad jokes that the guy across the table was telling you, and drinking a cup of coffee that tastes THIS bad, in a cup THIS small?" And then Ellie was laughing and espresso was streaming from her nose, and Jake knew that something in his chest had just taken flight; it would never completely light down again.

ELLIE

CHAPTER TEN

Ellie had decided to spend the night at Edgar's. She had always kept her own apartment and split her time between it and Edgar's home in Toronto's prestigious Rosedale area – his fancy-dancy house, as Jenna had called it. When Jenna was younger she had loved the swimming pool and the grounds around the house where she was free to run wild, but she had never really warmed to Edgar. No one could ever replace Jake in her life, even for a few hours.

Ellie had spent a sleepless night, tossing from one side of the bed to the other until Edgar declared that he'd had it and went off to sleep in one of the guest rooms. After he left she sprawled out diagonally on the king-sized bed, and a restless sleep eventually found her. She had called the hospital as soon as she had pulled herself together. The nurse she had spoken to was all icy professionalism: Mr. Madison was resting comfortably, would be released in the morning, and Dr. Philips would like to meet with them both before signing Jake's release papers. Yes, of course Ellie would be at the hospital by eight am.

It hadn't sounded anywhere near as bad as Ellie had first imagined, and her heart rate had returned to normal though she doubted that her blood pressure had. What was going on? Why did this Dr. Philips want to talk to both of

them? She and Jake hadn't been a "both of them" for years. Her brain spun like a top until she finally dozed off and the alarm woke her at six, just as Edgar poked his head around the door to say he had a seven o'clock tee off. He knew Ellie was headed for the hospital and voiced some vague condolence about how he hoped "that dumb jock hadn't really stepped in it this time" and why the heck had they called Ellie anyway?

"I have no idea, Ed," she replied. She had felt herself bristle at Jake being referred to as a "dumb jock." She remembered the overflowing bookshelves in Jake's apartment; those lazy, rainy afternoons during the off season when he would have his head buried in a book. *Don Quixote* had kept him mesmerized for days. Had Edgar ever read *Don Quixote*? She knew he hadn't.

"Excuse me? He doesn't even know how to pronounce it." Sometimes the voice in Ellie's head was a Black woman from a TV sit-com – her arm extended – "talk to the hand". Other times she reminded her of Carol Burnett's charwoman. Whatever – this time Ellie agreed with her.

She picked up the phone, quickly calling Jenna to reassure her that everything was going to be fine. Such a motherly expression, Ellie was thinking. How many disasters had been averted with that little phrase? She made Jenna a "love swear" promise that she would call her as soon as she had all the details and then headed out the door. "Love swear" had been Ellie and Jake's pinky swear. It was silly, it was sophomoric, but it was theirs. It was a commitment that they would follow through, and after she and Jake had separated, it was a ritual that she had made sure she and Jenna continued. Ellie felt her eyes welling up remembering Jake putting up his big bear of a palm, as if to high-five, and Ellie touching her small hand to his. She wiped at her eyes with the back of her hand and pressed down on the gas, easing the car in the direction of the freeway.

THE HOSPITAL

CHAPTER ELEVEN

Ellie pushed through the doors, found the correct floor, and asked a nurse behind the desk where she could find Jake.

Following the directions she had been given, she walked quickly down the hall to the fifth door on the left, but reaching it she stopped, leaning her back against the wall. What was going on here? Ellie felt as if she had spent the last twelve hours in an emotional mix master. The thought of Jake being hurt had left her floundering. Now, that was a laugh – she had spent most of her life with Jake worrying about him getting hurt, and here she was again – but she knew she couldn't be anywhere else. That was the last thing Jake had said to her as she had slammed out of the apartment. She could hear his voice, husky with the sadness that was swallowing him – "It's the glue factor Ellie. We've got it. You can't stay away forever." Well, she'd certainly been working hard to prove him wrong. It dawned on Ellie that she was weary. That was one of her father's words, and she realized that she only now understood it. It didn't just mean tired, it meant fed up, tired of fighting. But tired of fighting what? Enough of this, she thought to herself. She straightened up and tapped three times on the door.

"Ellie," almost instantly Jake was standing in the open doorway. "You came," he said, quietly.

"Jake," she put her hands on his arms. Her first instinct was a desire to shake him until his teeth rattled. She wasn't exactly sure why: maybe it was the hospital, maybe it was the fact that he was apparently hurt again and all the baggage that came along with that, but then the old familiarity that came flooding back made her simply want to lean into his chest and let him wrap his arms around her. She made herself push this thought aside and reached up and kissed his cheek.

"Here, let me look at you," she said, stepping back and scanning him up and down for bumps or bruises, swellings or new scars. He really didn't look like there was anything seriously wrong with him. She gave a small sigh of relief and then took another step back and just looked at him. He stood there shifting from one foot to the other, obviously unnerved by her scrutiny. He was at least ten years older than the last time she had seen him. That would have been at Maggie's funeral, she remembered, but immediately pushed the thought away, feeling her throat constricting. The crow's-feet around his eyes had deepened slightly and so had the laugh lines around his mouth, but he was still broad-shouldered and flat-bellied. And that face, that wonderful battered face, still had the same delighted look that it had always had when he looked at her.

Ellie let herself bask in this look for a minute. Did Edgar ever look at her like this?

"Okay you. Start talking." It was time to get this straightened out.

Jake motioned for her to take the visitor's chair and brought another one over and sat beside her. He stretched out his long legs and rubbed his hand over his hair, that sweet gesture that Ellie had seen so many times. Then he began to talk. He had been crossing the street, he said, and out of nowhere a motorcycle had come around the corner, and suddenly Jake was on his back, his head hitting the curb.

"Honest to God, Ellie, I haven't gone down that hard since that game in Detroit when their defence took me into the boards."

Ellie nodded, remembering the call from Coach Bailey. Even the unflappable Bailey had sounded concerned that time. "We're in the hospital, Ellie. Jake took his sweet time coming around this time, but no worries, he's looking like his ugly old self now. He'll be home good as new tomorrow." Ellie had hung up and screamed into the sofa cushions for more than an hour.

Jake did come home the next day with two horrendous shiners and seven stitches in the back of his head. The headaches that he had so often became even worse, and Ellie noticed that he spent less time reading. "Just can't concentrate right now, Sugar," he'd said, "but hey, it gives me more time to sit here and look at you." But all his sweet talk – "blarney," her father would have called it – didn't sway her. Their fights began in earnest after that.

She forced herself back to the present. "Okay, what happened next?"

Jake shrugged, "I woke up here. I didn't even know my own name for the first few hours. They've been poking, and prodding and running me under a microscope ever since."

Ellie absorbed all of this then took his big hand in hers, rubbing it gently. "Poor Jake," she murmured. They sat there in silence for a minute, and then Ellie straightened up sharply. "But why does this Dr. Philips want to see me?"

Jake didn't answer right away, and Ellie became aware that he suddenly looked antsy, uncomfortable. "Well,

Ellie," he cleared his throat, not looking directly at her, "it's probably because I still have you down as my next of kin."

"What! You can't be serious!" Ellie was on her feet, "Jake, for crying out loud, what's wrong with you? We haven't been together for twenty years – what were you thinking?" She threw her hands up in the air in frustration and then sank back down in her chair.

Jake was on his feet now, looking as uncomfortable as she'd ever seen him. "Ah Ellie, I don't know... I just never changed it ... we were never officially divorced and unless I missed something, I don't think you and good ol' Ed ever got officially married. It just never seemed like a big deal ... until today I guess." His voice became quieter. "Besides, I knew that if anything ever did happen to me, it would be you I'd want them to call – you and Jenna."

Ellie covered her face with her hands. Jake saw her shoulders beginning to shake, and recognizing what he'd done his remorse began flooding the sterile room. "Oh, Jesus, I'm such a dumb-ass. C'mon, Ellie, please, I never meant to make you cry. I hate it when you cry. Please, Ellie." Jake was squatting down beside her chair now, pleading, desperate to make this better.

Ellie held up her hands to stop him and grabbed a tissue from the bedside table to wipe her eyes. Jake peered up at her, confused.

"Jake! Look at me. I'm not crying – have you forgotten?" She took a breath, still wiping at her face, and then pulled her hair back, holding it behind her head with both hands. She looked down at him, shaking her head, and Jake mentally slammed his head against the nearest wall. Shit! He could be such an idiot. She wasn't crying; of course she wasn't crying. This was Ellie laughing, and he felt his heart quick-step in his chest as he watched her eyes crinkle up at the corners. He loved this look – he had always loved this look. Her laughter was pure music to him: all silver and light, just the way he remembered it. It was as sweet to him as the sound of wind chimes, and it had been such a long time since he had heard it. He stood slowly and slid back into his chair, remembering how she had never been able to laugh without it ending in tears streaming down her cheeks. His mind wound back to that first night at Mamma Rosa's. He remembered her laughing at something he had said, saying, "Stop, stop, my eyes are leaking." She'd had him right there, he realized.

The look of relief on his face started Ellie off again, and this time she did let herself lean into his chest, and this time his arms did go around her. It was so easy, so comfortable. She was still shaking her head, trying to say something. "Oh Jakey," she began, but Jake didn't hear anything more. For a second he was sure he must be having a heart attack his heart was beating so fast. He had his arms around Ellie, and she was calling him Jakey. He didn't want to think past this moment. Freeze me right here, God, he was praying, right here, right now. I don't ever want to be anywhere else.

But, all good things ... as his grandfather would have said. Ellie sat up in her chair and cleared her throat, still wiping at her eyes. "So then, will this Dr. Philips be calling me 'Mrs. Madison,' do you suppose, Jake?"

Oh Christ. Jake rubbed his hair. Dr. Philips. "Ellie, wait till you meet him," he snorted, "Honest to God he looks about twelve years old – it's crazy! When did they start letting kids into medical school?"

"You should see my gynaecologist!" it was Ellie's turn to be outraged, "He doesn't look old enough to know that women have these girly-bits down there."

Jake leaned back in his chair, chuckling. "Girly-bits, that's a new one. Where did you get that one?"

"Jenna I guess," Ellie smiled, thinking of her daughter – their daughter. Jenna was the one certain link that had always kept Jake and Ellie within a memory's reach of each other. They sat quietly, enjoying how it felt to be sitting so close to each other, neither of them too sure that it should.

"Doctors," Jake eventually muttered. "He'll probably leave us sitting here all goddamned morning."

The thought occurred to Ellie that Jake was probably feeling nervous about the upcoming conversation with this Dr. Philips. How stupid of her – of course he was. The laughter she and Jake had been sharing had made her forget that there could be something seriously wrong here. She ran her hand over his arm wishing there were something more she could do. She wanted to take his face in her hands and tell him everything was going to be okay, but that felt too intimate. Jake wasn't hers to touch this way. She clenched her hands in her lap, and then, because she needed to do something, she stood and shrugged off her coat: the weather channel had been calling for rain this morning. Jake had stretched out his legs and crossed his arms over his chest. His eyes had been focused on the window across the room, but as Ellie turned to slip her coat over the back of her chair his gaze shifted and he was staring at her.

Holy shit! When had this happened? Jake straightened up in his chair.

Over the years he had often seen Ellie at Jenna's basketball games and school events, but Edgar had always been with her, which had left Jake prowling around the ends of the bleachers or the seating arrangements. He couldn't stand watching them together. And the funeral didn't count – no one had been seeing straight that day. As a result, it had been years since he had actually gotten a good look at Ellie, and obviously things had changed!

Ellie had always been beautiful, perfect as far as Jake was concerned, but in a tiny, slender, woodlands nymph kind of a way. Twenty years later, she had suddenly become softer and more rounded: curvy seemed like the right word. Jake caught a glimpse of cleavage beneath the v-neck of her dress, and there was a gentle rise to her hips that hadn't been there before. Despite the fact that he was sitting in a cold, sterile hospital room, he suddenly felt himself growing warm – sweaty, in fact.

Judas H. Priest, life really did suck. He got all the Twiggy years, and old Egbert got Sophia-fucking-Loren. Okay, so that was a slight exaggeration, but this had been totally unexpected.

"Jake, you're staring. Is something wrong?" Ellie self-consciously brushed her hands over the front of her dress.

Jake rubbed a hand roughly over his hair and looked down at the floor, forcing a neutral expression onto his face. "I'm sorry, it's nothing," he mumbled. "I was just thinking how nice you look. You really do, El. You look really, really nice." Could he get any lamer than this, he wondered?

Ellie looked at him, not quite sure as to what was going on and started to say something, but a noise at the door stopped her. They both turned their heads toward the sound as Dr. Philips entered the room.

GREGORY PHILIPS

CHAPTER TWELVE

Greg stepped off the elevator onto the Neurology floor. He had three patients to see on the floor, starting with Mr. Madison in Room five. Greg had seen Jake when the ambulance had first brought him in; Jake had been in and out of consciousness at the time, but he had been able to speak with him later and had a nurse take his medical history. There had been something about Jake that had nagged at Greg, and he had ordered a full battery of brain scans and x-rays and kept him in hospital for observation. He was holding the results in a file and paused at the front desk to reacquaint himself with the results. Neurology was a fascinating field, one in which he was pleased he had been able to specialize, but he didn't harbour any illusions that many of the patients with whom he was dealing shared his enthusiasm for his chosen line of work. He felt a twist in his gut remembering the office visit yesterday with a young woman named Anna. She and her husband had stared at him in silence as he had confirmed what he knew was their greatest fear: yes, the MRI had definitely proven the presence of multiple sclerosis. Anna had clutched at her husband's hand. Her mother had lived with MS most of Anna's life; she knew what she was in for.

Greg knew that at terrible moments such as these his patients hated him. Well, why wouldn't they? Later, he knew they would come to trust him and depend on him to help them make sense of the quagmire they would have to learn to live with. He also knew that this wasn't always the case. He knew, even though he couldn't completely understand it, that in order to cope with the job, many of his colleagues completely closed themselves off emotionally. Greg could never do this. Once he took on a patient he was in it all the way. People told him he was going to burn himself out.

Well, he'd have to see about that.

Greg glanced at his reflection as he passed a window. The hospital was discouraging the wearing of ties. It hadn't made his job any easier; a tie automatically gave the wearer an air of authority – maturity. He might need that right now – it wasn't easy to accept news you didn't want to hear from someone who looked like he might not yet be finished high school. Well, there was nothing he could do about that. He reached Jake's room, tapped lightly on the door and walked in.

ELLIE AND JAKE AND GREG

CHAPTER THIRTEEN

Jake stood when he saw Dr. Philips but took Ellie's hand and kept her fingers tightly laced in his. Ellie felt something in her chest growing heavy.

"Mr. Madison," Greg began, but Jake put up his hand to stop him.

"Call me Jake," he said quickly.

"Great. Jake then," he turned to Ellie – "Mrs?"

Ellie also stopped him with a hand. "Ellie, just Ellie. Ellie and Jake. Jake and Ellie." She realized she was sounding like a scene from *Annie Hall* and forced herself to stop.

She sneaked a look at Jake and was surprised to see that his face was trying to control a smile. "She's burbling, Doctor. She does that sometimes." He squeezed Ellie's hand, and for a second a look passed between them.

Greg didn't know what exactly had happened, but the two people in front of him had just visibly relaxed. Well, this was starting out better than he had anticipated. "Let's all sit down," Greg suggested. He waited till they were all settled and then he began. "First of all, Jake, the scans we ran on you didn't really show us too much, one way or another," he clicked his pen a few times and added, "though we are seeing traces . . ." he stopped himself. "You don't box, do you?"

"No," Jake answered, "but I probably got hit in the head almost as often."

A look of recognition suddenly passed over Greg's face. "Jake Madison, for Pete's sake! Of course! I'm sorry I didn't make the connection sooner. I should have, my father was one of your biggest fans." An image flashed across Greg's mind of his father leaping off the couch in his family's basement rec room – 'Je-sus Christ!' his father was yelling. 'Madison's down again!' Greg forced his professional face, which had slipped away for a moment, back in place. "Okay, I understand," he said slowly, and then, "well, Jake, this is what I'm piecing together."

Half an hour later, Jake and Ellie were sitting stiffly in their seats trying to absorb all the medical jargon that was being fed to them. All the fights, all the times he had been slammed into the boards, all the concussions he had suffered might now be taking their toll. Over the years, Jake's brain had suffered serious trauma. It had obviously fought back, healing itself as best it could, but now as Jake was getting older, effects from the damage could possibly start showing. Researchers were finding that brain trauma that happened early in life could sometimes result in problems later on.

"When we spoke yesterday, you told me about the difficulties you have been experiencing lately with your memory, etc." Greg cleared his throat. The mention of memory problems appeared to startle the attractive woman sitting next to Jake. She had said her name was Ellie – that was it, wasn't it? Greg wasn't good with names. It made it easy for him to empathize with many of his patients. For a second he wondered why she was unaware of these issues that Jake was having but reminded himself that it was none of his business and continued on. "It's totally up to you, Jake," he said, "but it might be wise to look into these difficulties more closely." Greg looked down at his notes again, and Ellie turned in her chair.

"Jake? What's going on?"

Jake waved her question away, "Oh, probably nothing – just something they want to check out." But his face had become serious. He crossed his arms over his chest and looked at Greg. He wasn't completely sure that he wanted to look into this 'more closely'. Didn't most things simply disappear if you left them alone? On the other hand, he had never been any good at pussy-footing around things. "You aren't saying that you think I'm likely to turn into a drooling old geezer, overnight, are you?" His hand reached for Ellie's. "What's the bottom line, here? This is hard," his head was down; he was almost talking to himself. "Just what exactly are you telling me?"

Ellie could only sit, looking from Jake to Dr. Philips. She had expected, at worst, the usual concussion story – 'not much we can do about it – just keep moving,' – that was the best they had seemed to be able to offer back in the early years – how many times had they heard it? But this was different. Everything about this was sending a chill through her.

Greg shook his head slightly, sorting through his mind in search of the words to reassure this slightly battered, somehow still boyish-looking man. Jake reminded him of someone he had seen somewhere, but he couldn't put his finger on who. "Neurology is not an exact science, Jake. No two brains are exactly alike. It would take several more tests before we could hazard any kind of diagnosis, and let's bear in mind that it may be nothing at all. In fact, it probably is nothing at all – sometimes stress, or depression or simple overwork can make the brain behave strangely." He stopped and looked down at the notes in his lap. "I know how difficult all this medi-garble is for you to hear, but if you would just let me look on the brighter side for a moment, from what you tell me, your brain has been through a lot but has obviously healed itself in an amazing way. It's a wonderful and mysterious organ, and we should never underestimate what it can do." Greg stopped himself before he launched into a full blown lecture that he knew Jake and Ellie had no interest in hearing right now. "What I'm trying to say is this: yes, something is going on, but from what I can see I'm sure you are nowhere near that worst-case scenario that is probably looping through your head right now."

Ellie could see the fear in Jake's eyes. "Mohammed Ali," he said, his lips tight.

Greg nodded and then shook his head. "Exactly. Ali has been diagnosed with Parkinson's, probably exacerbated by all his years in the ring. Happily, we are not seeing any of these symptoms in you and, hopefully, further tests won't give us any reason to believe otherwise." He pushed up his glasses and looked down briefly at his notes. "Right now we are more concerned with the other symptoms you've described: headaches, loss of concentration, the things you say you've been forgetting – these are the things that we really want to look into. You were hallucinating when you first came in. You took a nasty bump to the head, and it's probably nothing more than that. As you probably know, there really are any number of things that can cause the brain to behave in a slightly wonky manner – to use a highly clinical term," he added, smiling, "but, for your own peace of mind, it might be a good thing to check it all out and be absolutely sure."

Ellie felt the muscles in Jake's arm begin to relax. "Well, shoot," he said, his voice subdued. "I've been handling 'symptoms,' as you call them, like that since the first time I was knocked out cold in Chicago. If that's what it is," he gave a shaky laugh, "I'm pretty sure I can handle it." He looked down at the floor for a minute, thinking, and then raised his head. "Okay," he said, "go for it. Check the hell out of me and let's get to the bottom of this."

"Good, I like your attitude. Keep thinking like that," Greg began to stand. "My receptionist will get back to you about the other tests I'd like to have done, and I'll see you in my office at the end of the month. I'm sorry it can't be sooner, but..." he spread his hands, looking slightly helpless. Jake and Ellie both nodded; everyone knew how slowly the wheels of the Health Care System turned. Greg looked at the two people sitting in front of him, hating the power he knew they felt he had over them. "By the end of the month, this will all just be an unpleasant memory." They all shook hands and Greg quickly headed out the door, his mind already refocusing on his next patient.

Jake had stood, and now he sat back down. "Baby Doc likes my attitude, El. I don't know when I've been so proud . . ." Jake's voice was both annoyed and amused; he was getting that feeling again – that irritating feeling that the world had changed overnight and was suddenly in the hands of a group of over-achieving fifteen year olds. Doctors used to be grey-haired and wise looking . . . ah, better give the kid a chance, he thought, and he probably wasn't anywhere near as young as he looked anyway. He and Ellie remained in their chairs staring at the pale green wall in front of them.

"That's all very easy for him to say," said Ellie.

LEAVING THE HOSPITAL

CHAPTER FOURTEEN

Jake continued to stare at the wall in front of him. He was aware that some strange things had been happening to him for a while. There was the mood thing for starters. He didn't understand why he seemed to lose his cool so much more frequently these days. Off the ice, he had always considered himself a pretty easy going guy, but lately, even his friend Mickey was on his back about how quickly he lost his temper. He was usually able to cover for it, but it was so unlike him to be like this, and he hated how it made him feel. He glanced over at Ellie. Having her sitting here beside him he felt calmer and happier than he had felt in a long time. It would be different, he thought – maybe, just maybe, it would all be different if she were still with him. Well, there was a pipe dream for you!

And then there was this crazy thing with words and names – they just kept slipping out of his grasp. It annoyed the hell out of him, but the office receptionist claimed she had the same problem; they kidded around about it all the time, which was in a way reassuring, but from things she had said Jake was pretty sure she was going through the change, menopause, whatever they called it. This gave her a legitimate excuse – he didn't know what his excuse was.

Then, a few months ago, the real kicker had happened. He had actually found himself lost driving home from work. He had been sure that he should know where he was, but he had driven around for half an hour before he got his bearings straightened around. He had been totally pissed off because it had caused him to miss a night out with Mickey. The two of them had been too busy to get together as often as they usually did, and Jake had been looking forward to the evening out. Jake prided himself on his sense of direction and couldn't figure out why it had happened – ended up blaming it on the on-going road construction and the fact that the day had been so crazy he hadn't eaten lunch – probably simply a case of a drop in blood sugar, he had decided, but the whole thing had been weird and unsettling. And he had been so angry. When he had finally gotten home he had slammed out of the car and kicked at a fire hydrant – ended up hurting his foot – hadn't been able to run for weeks; served him right, he figured. The incident continued to bother him for a few days, but it hadn't happened again, and he had finally been able to shake it off. He had pretty much shaken it all off. Playing hockey, he had learned how to do that. He had told Philips all of this stuff. It had seemed important to him, but what the hell, Jake thought, he wasn't a kid anymore. Everyone his age forgot things every once in a while, didn't they? And most of the time he felt great; these odd things just kept popping up every now and again. Jake had never been much of a worrier – shit happened, good stuff happened – you learned to roll with the punches. Mulling it all over, he felt fairly certain that this, whatever this was, wouldn't amount to much of anything. Hospitals had been patching him up for one thing or another for years. This couldn't be much different, could it?

"Jake? Hello, are you still in there?"

56

JAKE & ELLIE

"Oh, yeah, sorry – just thinking."

"I don't know, Jake . . . this sounds more serious than
the usual concussion- hospital routine – we both know a lot
about that song and dance. And what's all this about you
forgetting things? You were always the one reminding me
about things like birthdays and anniversaries." Ellie's voice
was rising at the end of her sentences. Jake remembered
how it had always sounded like that when she was becoming anxious. "For a few minutes there you actually looked
upset, and you never used to look that way – I'm pretty
sure I'm missing something here."

"Ah, no, I don't think so – you know doctors – they'll
drive you crazy." Jake knew he wasn't being completely
truthful, but he wasn't going to let Ellie get all upset. He
grinned, "It's probably just another variation on the usual
merry-go-round ride that they always put you on."

She didn't answer right away, just sat watching his face.
There was a look of concern in her eyes that Jake wished
he could erase. Her eyes were still so blue, he thought.
Well, naturally they were, but it still took Jake slightly by
surprise. They had always had this effect on him. "Okay, if
you're sure," she finally said but continued to watch him.
His voice sounded forced, somehow, she thought, and his
smile wasn't as easy as she remembered it. She pulled her
hair back looking like she wanted to say something more
but then changed her mind and began pulling on her coat.
"Alright then, let's get out of here before we come down
with something serious." Ellie put her arm around his
shoulder, squeezing him gently.

"Yeah, you're right. Who knows about hospitals? I came
in here a little banged up from taking on a motorcycle and
Phillips has me leaving, a potential zombie." Just shut
up, he told himself. He hadn't been this close to Ellie in
he didn't know how long, and he didn't want to waste

57

however much time he had with her, talking about hospitals or concussions. All he really wanted was to hear her laugh again.

"Let's just get out into the fresh air where we can think." Ellie said, gently rubbing his shoulder, prodding him out of the chair. Jake stood up, a little unsteady, and Ellie grabbed his hand and together they walked out of the antiseptic green room. Minutes later they were standing outside the hospital, breathing in the morning air. Ellie was shocked when she realized it was only nine thirty – it felt like a lifetime since she had stood in front of Jake's hospital door, afraid to knock.

Jake inhaled deeply and stretched his arms above his head. "Where's your car, Sugar?" he asked, falling into old speech patterns as if it had been only yesterday. "Sorry Ellie. Didn't mean to say that."

"That's okay. It's been a crazy morning." But her heart had done an odd little skip when he had said it – "Sugar" – he had always called her that.

"So, do you think you can give me a ride home?"

"Are you crazy?" Ellie gave his arm a backhanded swat, "The only reason I came all the way down here today was because I'd heard that this Dr. Philips was just so darn good lookin'. You, goof! Come on, I'm in parking lot seven."

Jake snorted, but his face had lightened and he headed out in the direction Ellie was pointing, but then stopped, looking at her. "So, if you're no longer going by Mrs. Madison, what are you calling yourself?"

"Oh, it's no big deal. I just dropped the Mrs. for the nowheresland of the politically correct Ms. Actually, I quite like it now."

"Okay," Jake said slowly. "That was quite a mouthful. Now, what does Egghead think about you still wearing your wedding band?"

58

"Edgar," said Ellie. "You know, I doubt if he even real-
izes what it is, and I am wearing it on my right hand, and
no, I don't know why I'm still wearing it, so don't even
ask." She looked up at him, "And you're a fine one to talk
– you're still wearing your ring, and it's still on your left
hand. What's that all about?"

"Just something to scare off the women."

"That's a problem for you, is it?"

"Oh, you don't know the half of it. Hoards of them,
everywhere I go. I literally have to beat them off with a
stick." Ellie had stopped walking and was standing there
laughing now. Here was that thing about Jake again—he
had always been able to make her laugh.

"Come on, you," said Ellie, "I promise I'll protect you
from any marauding females."

"Can I ask you one more thing?" asked Jake, not waiting
for an answer. "I know it's none of my business, but I've
always wondered – whatever made you take up with
Egbert in the first place?"

Ellie had her hands on her hips. "It's Edgar, you impossible twit, and no, it isn't any of your business, but if you
really must know – it's probably because, at work, none of
his colleagues try to mash his head to a pulp!"

"Oh," said Jake.

They had missed the worst of the morning traffic, so
they made it to Jake's apartment with no problem. There
was no difficulty finding it; Ellie and Jake had lived here
together during their entire marriage. Ellie's eyes scanned
the stores and restaurants along the way, noting the
changes. Sometimes only the names on the buildings had
changed, and she wondered how many times that had happened. So many optimistic dreams squashed, she thought.
But then again, maybe not – maybe the owners had retired
and moved to Florida, or won the lottery. She glanced

over at Jake. This morning was obviously leaving her a little unhinged.

She slipped into a vacant parking spot. "Today's not a total write off," said Jake. "At least the parking gods are with you."

They sat in the car not speaking, looking straight ahead. "Thanks for coming Ellie," Jake began cracking his knuckles, always a sign that he was nervous, Ellie remembered. "I know I had no right getting you down there," he stopped and sighed deeply, "but, man, I'm glad you were there." He unbuckled his seatbelt and hastily held up his hand, "Like I said, it's probably nothing – but you being there made it easier to listen to."

Ellie felt her eyes beginning to sting. "Jake, we need some coffee. No, not there, their coffee tastes like dishwater – well, I think it tastes like dishwater." Jake had been pointing to a coffee shop down the street. She looked up at his apartment building. "Don't you have some at your place?"

Jake was laughing at her. "Dishwater, eh?" he said, but then nodded, saying coffee was the only food group he could ever be sure he had in his kitchen, and opened the car door.

HOME AGAIN

Chapter fifteen

Ellie's eyes travelled around the living room as the apartment door closed behind her. This was unbelievable. How could this possibly be the same apartment where she and Jake had spent their entire married life? Only the bookshelves looked the same. "Exactly where are you buying your furniture these days?" She made no attempt to conceal the sarcasm in her voice. "Good grief, Jake! This place looks like a crack-house!"

Jake was already busy in the kitchen but must have heard her because he poked his head around the door – it was one of the swinging types that you seldom saw anymore. Ellie had forgotten that she had loved this door; so silly – it was just a door, but still . . .

"Wow! Somehow I remember you being a little more tactful." Jake watched as she slowly turned, taking in the entire apartment, and then stopped and looked at him. She was shaking her head, but he remembered by the way she was biting down on her bottom lip that she could be laughing in a second if she would let herself. He wished she would let herself. He rubbed the back of his neck and ducked back into the kitchen, refocusing his attention on the coffee maker.

Ellie watched as the kitchen door swung shut behind him then stood very still in the middle of the room. She closed her eyes as shadows from another lifetime jostled for position in her mind. It pleased her, far more than it should she thought, that the windows were still flooding the room with the morning light she had loved. She remembered those days when she and Jake would have time off together – that sensation of lazy luxury she used to feel as they would drink their coffee in this sun washed room. They would lie propped up at opposite ends of the couch, their bare toes occasionally touching, inching up a leg, teasing. They would read different sections of the morning newspaper to each other. This was how Ellie had learned about football, and Jake had come to understand that feminism was more than just a bunch of crazy, bra-burning broads. Jake had never put it this way, but Ellie knew how the guys talked in the dressing room.

"Earth to Ellie! Hey girl, where are you?"

Ellie came back to the present, startled. What was she doing? She wasn't twenty-five anymore. What was all this nostalgia about? She gave Jake a little laugh and told him that yes, she still just took sugar in her coffee, and Jake said how that was a good thing because the milk had gone sour and then disappeared back into the kitchen. Ellie lowered herself onto the lumpy sofa from someone else's lumpy life and attempted to breathe in and out slowly. Minutes later Jake re-appeared holding two mugs of coffee, handed Ellie hers and sat down across from her, placing his coffee on a metal TV tray with a scratched and cigarette-burned mountain view pictured across the top. He rubbed his hands over his face roughly and then looked over at her.

"I guess it doesn't look quite the same as you remember it, right?"

Ellie smiled and gave a little shrug.

"I must have lost my will to decorate after you left," he said.

"How about your will to dust?" Ellie asked, running her fingers over the decrepit coffee table.

"Yeah, that too." He looked around the room, his face registering a look of unexpected surprise. "Christ, this place is a mess. How the hell did that happen?" He looked so bewildered that Ellie felt the laughter beginning to expand inside her chest again.

"Oh, relax, Jake. A good housekeeper could have this place looking like a show home in ... oh ... no more than six months." And then they were both laughing, and it felt so good to be doing that in this musty, run-down room.

They settled back in their places drinking the coffee Jake had made, not speaking. Finally, Jake cleared his throat, "Ellie, I probably shouldn't say this, but no matter how bad this morning was, it was all worth it to get to see you again. Just hearing you laugh makes me feel twenty-five again."

"No Jake, you probably shouldn't say that," Ellie agreed, shaking her head.

She watched as a shadow began to ripple around his eyes and his mouth. It was the first time he had shown any real concern since they had left the hospital. "I guess this might be a rough month to get through," he said, quietly.

"Yes," Ellie answered, barely a whisper. She felt her throat tightening, making it difficult to swallow. She stood up, turned around and then collapsed back onto the sofa. Jake was watching her, a curious expression on his face. She again pushed her thick hair behind her head and held it back with both hands, just as she had done at the hospital, just as Jake had seen her do a thousand times. Watching her, he felt his heart slam against his chest. She was still so beautiful. She looked over at him, blinking, trying to hold back the burning behind her eyes, and then she couldn't keep it together any longer.

This shouldn't be happening, she knew that, but a dam had just broken inside her. The floodgates, that she thought she had successfully slammed shut years ago, had re-opened and all the deeply concealed loneliness and regret that she had been pushing away for too long came rushing to the surface and began pouring out of her. Jake was quickly beside her, burying her face in his chest and making soothing noises, the same ones that Ellie remembered him murmuring to Jenna when she was a baby.

Then Ellie was screaming at him, hitting him with her clenched fists.

"This is it. This is exactly why I left. I couldn't watch you dragging yourself home, all broken and hurting anymore. I was so afraid that someday a doctor was going to say just what we heard today, and I knew I wouldn't be able to do anything to help you. And you would never listen. I tried and I tried to make you see how you were hurting yourself, and you just wouldn't listen. I just couldn't watch it anymore, Jake. I thought if I left it might make you change your mind. And now here's this Dr. Philips – and I'm not falling for your, 'Oh, it's no big deal' routine! There's something wrong here, I can feel it . . ." Her voice was becoming hoarse and rough. She felt as if she had been split wide open.

Jake did not back away, his arms holding her tightly until the ragged crying began to wear itself out. She slowly began to calm down but remained with her face buried in his chest, rocking slightly, and Jake pulled her closer to him repeating, "I know, I know," over and over again. He held her for the longest time, all the old pain and the new fear that the meeting at the hospital had brought to light, settling over them.

"I don't know what to say, Ellie," Jake was trying to wipe her face with a corner of his T-shirt. "Maybe you were right. I guess it's too late for that, isn't it?" He gently pushed her over into the corner of the couch and, putting his hands on his knees, straightened up.

He went back to the chair he had been sitting in. "It just doesn't seem possible to me. I'm having these flashes of old guys in nursing homes, soup dribbling down their chins." For a second the mood lifted as he went into a Foster Hewitt routine – "He's reaching for it folks. He's got it. He aims. He's gonna put it in. It's going in ... Ohhhhh, he misses!" Jake did an imitation of the crowd roaring and even Ellie gave a reluctant laugh.

She picked up a pillow and hugged it to her. She was chewing on her lower lip, her gaze somewhere beyond the walls of Jake's apartment. "You know, Jake, this may be what I've missed about you the most," her voice was quiet, lonely. "You can laugh about anything. You always could. I've never known how you do this."

"Well," Jake sighed, "it's what's got me through my entire life. I don't think I'm likely to change now, not at my ripe old age. Ellie, can you believe that it won't be long before I'm a senior citizen? It'll be great, actually: I'll get to golf tons cheaper and McDonald's will be practically free." He was grinning now, trying to jolly her out of her sadness.

"Ouch, let's not rush things!" Ellie looked slightly horrified – weren't they almost exactly the same age? "I'm pretty sure you've still got almost fifteen years before you hit that landmark," but then she backtracked. "You golf?" Her voice was incredulous.

"Well, I swing a golf club pretty much the same way I hit a puck, but what the hell, it keeps me off the streets."

Ellie sat watching him, listening to his voice. She shifted self-consciously in her seat, becoming aware that her body was reacting in the same way it always had when she had felt his arms around her. "Honestly, Maggie, he touches me and my whole body feels like melted candle wax," she had once confided to her sister after many glasses of red wine. They had been rooming together at the time, both in their early twenties, and with this revelation, both had collapsed on the living room carpet where they had been sitting cross-legged – children again, giggling and whispering secrets to each other under the covers.

All these years later, and Jake still had this warm, melting effect on her. There was a buzz pulsing through her body that was making it difficult to keep her breathing even. She re-crossed her legs and brushed her hands over her skirt. "I don't know if I should say any of this," she stopped, feeling her face becoming warm. "No, I shouldn't," she said, shaking her head, "it would be stupid – after a certain amount of time some things are best left alone."

Jake was leaning forward, looking at her, puzzled. "What's going on Ellie? If there's something you want to say to me, just say it."

Ellie rubbed at her forehead with her finger tips for a second then gestured in the air, a move that suggested futility. "So much water has passed under this bridge, Jake, are you sure you want to get into it again?"

"I guess I won't know till you tell me."

"It's just that I've never had the chance to say this to you. Maybe if I had, everything would be different."

"Ellie, for Christ's sake, what are you trying to say?"

"Sorry, sorry," she shook her head. "I'm not trying to be difficult, it's just that this IS so difficult. God, I wish I still smoked – I'm pretty sure I could use a cigarette right now."

Jake nodded, "I've been having that feeling all morning. Now, do I have to beat this out of you, girl?'

"Okay, okay," she said, giving an odd laugh that Jake thought sounded strangely nervous, and then she began again, "At the hospital, when you asked me why I had 'taken up' with Edgar, I was pretty flip with my answer." She stopped, pushing her hair behind her ears. "It's much more complicated than that." Ellie's eyes found Jake's, and she bit down on her lower lip again. She knew she was at a fork in the road, but she wasn't sure she had the courage to say what needed to be said. She felt so tired though, and she knew that, whatever the consequences, she just wanted it finally to be all out in the open.

She breathed in deeply and continued speaking. "The truth is, after you and I separated I just didn't feel much of anything for the longest time." Ellie rubbed at her forehead, remembering. "I was so hurt by it all, and I didn't want to get involved with anyone who could hurt me like that again. I had loved you so much, and I still did, and I just couldn't risk it. Besides, if I'm really being truthful here, nobody ever came close to you."

"Hey, whoa!" Jake looked like he had just had the wind knocked out of him. "Ellie, are you telling me you still loved me back then? You'd have come back to me if I'd asked you to?"

"Oh Lord no," Ellie shook her head. "Yes, I still loved you, but I hated you at the same time. It wasn't till much later that I began to sort things out. You must remember how I always loved fooling around with our camera?" she asked, seemingly out of nowhere.

Jake nodded, slightly impatient. What did this have to do with anything? But, yes he did remember. He nodded again.

"Well," she continued, "after we split I started taking photography classes, mainly to keep myself sane, but I found out that I loved it – I mean, I really, really loved it. I entered some of the photographs I'd taken in various contests and was shocked to find that there were many people out there who wanted to see more of my work." She made a motion with her hand trying to erase what she had just said, knowing that the term "my work" probably sounded affected. She glanced over at Jake, but he hadn't seemed to have noticed, so she continued.

"I started doing photography as a side line, but before long I realized that it could become a full-time job, maybe even a career. The thing about it was how addicted to it I became." She was leaning forward now, her expression animated. "It didn't matter if it was just a wedding or a birthday party – and there were plenty of those at the start – I couldn't wait to get up in the morning and get to work. Somewhere along the line I had realized that photography was all about capturing the spirit of a thing and bringing this out in the image, and somehow I became very good at doing this. Honestly, Jake, I loved it so much it made me giddy."

Ellie looked at Jake's face. He was listening to every word she was saying, but she knew he was wondering why she was telling him all of this right now. She quit speaking for a few seconds. "I've wanted to tell you this for so long, Jake." She put her arms around herself, hugging her body. "I've just wanted to talk to you about it for so long." Ellie saw that his face was looking both confused and anxious, and she hurried to finish what she was finally getting a chance to say. "The point is – this is what I'm trying to tell you, Jake – I finally realized what being passionate about what you do, actually means. I finally understood what you had been trying to get through my head all those years. I got it. I still hated how your career might be hurting you – that fear never left me – but I finally got it."

Jake was on his feet, staring at her. "Why the hell didn't you tell me?"

"I tried to," she said quietly, feeling her eyes beginning to sting again. "I must have picked up the phone a million times wanting to talk to you, but I just couldn't. Part of me still felt like I'd come in second best – pride, I guess. And then Jenna told me that you were involved with some woman named Sarah, and I guess I figured I really had lost you." Ellie stopped, her eyes on Jake's face wondering what he was thinking. "Edgar came along shortly after that."

"Oh fuck, no." Jake's voice was so low she almost couldn't hear him. He slowly dropped back into his chair and leaned back, putting his hands behind his head. He looked up at the ceiling for a full minute then closed his eyes, and she realized he was working at controlling his breathing. At last he straightened up and gave a snorting kind of laugh. "I am going to go out and find our daughter and paddle her backside." He began speaking quickly perhaps realizing he was finally getting a chance to set things straight. "Sarah never meant anything to me. We were together for a while, but I knew it could never go anywhere. I told her it was over, but she would never accept it. I kept trying to get her to leave, but she would never take the hint." Jake threw up his hands remembering how out of control the situation had felt. "I had to get down and dirty, dressing-room rude before she finally left, but it took forever." Jake looked over at Ellie. It was such a relief to finally be able to tell her this.

He was leaning forward now, his fingers laced together. "After I retired I wanted to call you about a million times too, but I never felt I had the right to. I knew from what Jenna told me that you were with Edgar" – he grimaced unconsciously as he said this – "and even though he seemed all wrong for you I didn't want to do anything that would mess things up for you. I figured I'd screwed things up badly enough the first time around." He was gazing out the windows, his voice and his eyes far away. He rubbed his hand over his hair and cleared his throat, then continued. "Even though it was never like this, I never wanted you to feel that now that I had hockey out of my system I finally had time for you." He stopped, looking down at the floor. "My problem was I wanted both of you, you and hockey, all the time."

Then Jake was looking at Ellie with a look that she couldn't quite decipher. He rubbed his hands over his face almost as if he were trying to erase something. "At Maggie's funeral," he started, but then stopped and his voice became very soft, "I wanted to take you home with me, and put you to bed and let you cry till you cried yourself out. And then I wanted to make you toast and tea, the way you liked when you were sick or sad. And I wanted to take you for walks until you felt like you could smile again." He looked down at his hands, "But I couldn't. You were with Edgar..." He let his words trail off. "Edgar," he said, clearing his throat, "is he important to you?"

"Sweet Jesus, Jake..." Ellie felt his voice moving through her, soothing the memory of the numbness that had filled her during the funeral and dogged her for months after. The fact that Maggie wasn't here anymore tore her to shreds – it always would. Not a day went by that she didn't long to pick up the phone and hear her sister's voice on the other end of the line. She covered her face, her body bending toward her knees. Jake stood, trying to move toward her, but she straightened up, putting her hands out to stop him. "No, Jake, don't – I have to say this." She wiped at her face with her hands, swallowing the burning in her throat.

She couldn't speak as she attempted to gather herself together, and then she forced herself to begin. "I feel uncomfortable saying this," she finally said quietly, hoping Jake would understand. "It sounds so calculating, but the truth is I've never really loved Edgar. Oh, don't worry – he's never really loved me either. I think I'm some kind of trophy girlfriend to him." Ellie shook her head, a distracted look on her face. "Girlfriend – that's such a stupid name for anyone over fifteen, but what other word can I use?" Her shoulders slumped slightly and she smoothed her hands over her skirt, almost brushing something away, and then continued. "What it comes down to is Edgar's a pretty dull guy, but he has a good heart, and he's always been good to me. I knew I was safe with him. My heart," she coughed, embarrassed by her choice of words, "my heart was safe with him because I'd never really let him into it, and he never really tried to find a way in. I could never have stayed with him if he had."

They both sat quietly, not speaking, neither of them sure of what was happening.

"What are we saying, Ellie?"

Ellie's eyes were fixed on his face, watching for the slightest change in his expression. "I'm afraid to say this out loud," she stopped. Her heart was beating so loudly she knew Jake must be able to hear it. "I think I'm saying I love you. I always have. What are you saying, Jake?" Her voice was barely a whisper.

Jake stood and walked over to the couch, sitting down on the edge of the coffee table, taking her hands in his. "Are you serious, El? Don't do this to me if you're not. I've been dreaming some version of this for twenty years."

Ellie leaned forward, taking hold of his arms, "Jake, I can't believe I'm finally saying this to you, and I probably shouldn't be, but I'm so tired of pretending – I just don't care anymore." Her hands squeezed his arms. Her eyes were so sad Jake could hardly look at her. "I'm so lonely,

I'm just so lonely without you. I think I've been lonely since the minute I walked out that door. Every day something will happen to me, and my first thought will be that I want to tell you about it – and then of course I can't ..."

Jake sat completely still, almost afraid to breathe. He reached for her, holding her shoulders, at first just whispering her name over and over, and then, almost unsure whether to say it, "Are you sure, Ellie?"

Ellie's eyes never left his as she nodded.

Then Jake was on the couch beside her, his arms swallowing her up. He was laughing with relief, his voice tender, telling her how much he loved her – how he had never stopped loving her. He pulled her to him and kissed her, his kiss deep and hungry like it had always been. She hadn't been kissed like this in so many years, and she wondered how she had gone this long without the taste of him on her mouth or the feel of his arms around her.

Suddenly Jake stopped and pulled away, "But, this morning Ellie."

"No don't, not right now. Just keep holding me, okay? Please?"

They fell against each other, running their hands over one another – over their faces, across their shoulders, up and down each other's arms as they searched to see one another again – feeling their way back. Ellie felt tears streaming down her face again, but now her tears were as soothing and welcome as rain after a long, choking dry spell. Jake wiped her face with his hands, and they whispered all the words that they had waited so long to say, impatient, trying to say it all – everything, all at once. She wiped her face against his shirt. She was laughing, her voice shaky as she apologized, "Your shirt," she said. "My snotty nose is all over your shirt."

"Fuck that! Use me – I love you – I love your snotty nose," he pushed back her hair, still kissing her face and her neck.

She put her hands on either side of his face the way she had wanted to do earlier. "I don't know how," she said, "but somehow we're going to get through this, whatever it is – together. You and me, okay?"

"Okay," but his voice had changed, and his hands began running down her body. "It's going to kill me if I can't have you right now." Jake could feel a fire smouldering deep in his belly. His voice had become hoarse, and he reached to edge her coat off her shoulders. "I want you so bad, El – you know that, right?"

Ellie ran her hands down his shoulders – she loved the strength in his arms and the warmth of his skin under his shirt. It was a physical ache, this longing she was feeling. She remembered his hands running over her body, sliding up her leg . . . that sweet spot on her inner thigh. She knew he wouldn't have forgotten. It had always been like this, almost a magnetic force pulling her to him. She laid her head against his chest and made herself stop and breathe before things got completely out of control. She frantically searched for a quiet place in her head willing her mind to slow down; she couldn't let herself do this right now, she knew that. As gently as she could, she pushed his hands away from her.

"What, baby? Tell me what you want," Jake's voice was quiet. He took a long breath, trying to slow his heartbeat.

"I can't do it like this, Jake," her hands and her voice were shaking. "I wish I could but I can't . . . you know me – I have to make things right, first." She put her hands on his chest forcing a slice of distance between them. "I'm so sorry, but I have to end things with Edgar, first," Ellie stopped again and stroked his face. "And then there's

73

Karen – we've become close over the years, and she expects me to be at the wedding." Ellie turned her wrist, looking at her watch. She was probably going to be late as it was, she said. "Please, Jake, I have to make it right. I wish I could let myself stay, but I can't – I have to do it this way." Her eyes were begging him to see it her way.

Jake was shaking his head wanting her not to be saying this. Finally he groaned and began nodding reluctantly. He again rubbed his hands over his face and then looked at her. There was the smallest smile playing over his mouth. "Damn, you're hard on a guy," he rubbed his hand against the back of his neck. He pushed himself up from the couch and took her hands and pulled her up with him. He grabbed her shoulders and shook her slightly. "You just come back to me, Ellie, do you hear me? We might have a second chance here." His eyes were filled with such a longing for what might be that Ellie could feel her resolve to leave coming undone. She forced herself to push away from him before she knew she wouldn't be able to.

"I'll be back as soon as I can, I promise. I'll call you tonight and we'll start sorting this out, all right?" She kissed him again and then wrenched herself away. She couldn't allow herself to melt into him again – she would never have been able to leave if she had. She squeezed his arms and not trusting herself to look back was gone from the apartment leaving Jake staring at the back of the closed door.

He felt himself sliding back down onto the couch, and the words 'thank you' began forming in his head. Jake did not consider himself a religious man – maybe at one time he had, not now; however, he was filled with too great a sense of gratitude to keep it bottled up inside.

His second thought was far less complicated. The Leafs could have won the Stanley Cup, the Blue Jays the World Series, cancer could have been eliminated and world peace could be imminent, and he really didn't think that he could be happier than he was right now. It was all of that and more. She was coming back to him. Un-fucking-believable!

You are bat-shit crazy, Madison. He was grinning and shaking his head. He couldn't remember when life had felt this good.

RELIEF

CHAPTER SIXTEEN

Ellie walked quickly down the hallway, punching fiercely three times at the elevator button before giving up and taking the stairs. She didn't want to think until she was safely inside her car, so she flew down the stairs catching her heel once but grabbing the handrail in time to keep herself from falling. The entrance was deserted except for an old fellow pushing a walker. Ellie smiled a quick good morning but averted her eyes as soon as it was politely possible. She couldn't face that image, not right now.

Maggie, I miss you so much . . . I need to talk to you . . . I want to hear you telling me that everything will be okay . . .

She crossed the street, unlocked her car and slid behind the wheel, her brain leaping about like popcorn in a popper. There was so much to think about, so many things to work out, so much that was wrong, so many things that could go wrong. So why was she sitting here – totally frustrated, but virtually vibrating with happiness at the same time? She leaned her head against the window – it wasn't even noon and already today her entire world had been turned on its head. It was almost impossible to process everything that had happened in the last four hours.

Ellie covered her face with her hands as hot tears began rolling down her cheeks. This was the third time today that she had let herself dissolve into a mess of tears. It had been years since this had happened to her. She leaned forward, putting her arms on the steering wheel and then rested her forehead on her arms as she let the confusion she was feeling pour out of her. Initially, a great surge of happiness moved through her as she thought about Jake's arms around her, but it slammed to a stop when it rammed up against the wrenching sensation in the pit of her stomach. The possibility that there could be something wrong with Jake twisted inside her like a knife.

Conflicting emotions collided head-on, smashing into each other, making it difficult for her to catch her breath. She made herself focus on Jake – how he still loved her. She repeated this to herself, hearing the tenderness in his voice as he had said it and felt as if her heart were expanding. During terrible, lonely moments in the past she had often felt as if her body were held together with barbed wire. This new sensation was the polar opposite. It was a soft, sweet thing – like warm syrup flowing through her veins. She wiped at her face, thinking how sentimental this all sounded, but it was true, and the truth of it began to calm her. He still loved her – what else really mattered? Well, many things of course, but right now her tiny corner of the world felt unbelievably sweet. She slowly straightened up, still wiping her face with her hands. It was going to be okay, she thought . . . it had to be . . . he still loved her. Somehow it was all going to work out.

A tapping at the window startled her, and she turned to see a police officer standing at the curb making motions for her to roll down the window. Oh Lord, not now. She grabbed some tissue, hastily blowing her nose and wiping at her face as she turned the key and lowered the window.

"Everything okay, ma'am?"

"Oh yes, yes of course," Ellie tried to give him a reassuring look. "Just something funny that happened today ... I . . . uh, cry when I'm happy. I always have. I know how ridiculous that sounds, but it's just something I do..." Her voice faded off, embarrassed, but it had been the first thing that had jumped into her head and seemed to be as plausible an explanation as any.

The police officer checked her license and registration and peered into the backseat, unconvinced. "You're sure, are you?"

"Oh absolutely," Ellie forced a note of confidence into her voice, wondering where it had come from. She had never experienced law enforcement this close up – she was beginning to feel as guilty as if she were concealing a trunkful of cocaine.

"Okay then, if you're sure." He checked the car over once more and stepped back from the window, "You drive careful, now." He gave her car a friendly tap on the roof and headed back to his cruiser.

Ellie breathed a sigh of relief and leaned back in the seat, rolling her eyes. You twit, she thought, just how old are you, anyway? She covered her face with her fingers as she felt a smile forming around her mouth, and then the smile widened as she realized that, later, she would actually be able to tell Jake about this. A warm, welcome sensation of home-coming crept up through her body. This had been so long-coming and now that it was here her entire body felt weak and wrung out with relief. She was very close to opening the car door and running back up to Jake's apartment when her eye caught the time on the dashboard, and she pulled herself together. She had waited twenty years, she thought, she could wait another day. Well, she couldn't really – but she would have to. She took a quick glimpse in the mirror, pushed her hair back from her face and turned on the ignition. She hardly dared believe it – Jake was back in her life. Two days ago she would have found the very thought completely impossible.

But now she had to hurry. As she had told Jake, there was a wedding she had to be at.

Karen's wedding began at two, and Ellie slipped into the church just minutes after the organist began pumping the wedding march out of the magnificent old organ. She glanced at Edgar as he slowly walked Karen down the aisle. She felt a stab of remorse, knowing that regardless of how lifeless their relationship had turned out to be, Edgar was bound to be hurt by what she was about to tell him. Edgar had never been a man to show much emotion one way or the other; she hoped they could end things without it being too difficult for him.

"Oh please," said the voice in her head, "this is Edgar you're talking about. He'll just be happy there are no pre-nup loopholes to deal with."

CONFRONTATION

CHAPTER SEVENTEEN

All he had said was: "How'd it go with Super Jock?" Except for the cleaning crew, Edgar and Ellie had been alone in the large hall where the reception had been held. Ellie had been her usual self during the wedding ceremony and the reception – gracious, beautiful, charming, everything Edgar had ever wanted in a woman. True, she hadn't spoken to him very much, but that wasn't always a bad thing in a woman, was it? He knew that every man of his age in the room had seen them together and thought what a lucky man he was. He was feeling magnanimous, so he had tipped back in his chair, put his hands behind his head and asked, "So, how'd it go with Super Jock?"

Ellie had rotated slightly in her chair until she was facing him directly. She had looked so happy during the entire evening, but suddenly a veil dropped over her face. "Eddie," she had said. Her voice was gentle but had an edge to it. "We have to talk."

THE CALL

CHAPTER EIGHTEEN

A re you still awake?"
"Still? Are you crazy, girl? It's three o'clock in the morning." Then his voice softened. "I was afraid you might have changed your mind."

"It's been such a long night." She paused, "Oh crap, Jake, this is so hard. I just want to be with you. I wish I were right there lying beside you." She heard his voice catch, "Are you okay?"

Jake groaned into the phone, "Not anymore for Christ's sake. Ellie, don't talk like that. Not unless we're both in the same room."

"Sorry, sorry," she was laughing softly. "I thought men mellowed out a little when they got to be your 'ripe old age.'"

"So did I," he answered. "You're a miracle of modern medicine, Ellie girl."

"Well, that's flattering, I guess," she was laughing again – "I'll take your word for it. If I were twenty years younger I'd hop into a cab and come and see if I could prove this theory of yours, but I'm not, and the only place I'm going is to my own lonely bed." They both stayed on the line, waiting to hear who would speak next.

"Jake, remember Mamma Rosa's ... it's not still open is it?"

"Shee-it," he said – that funny, stretched out way he sometimes said it. Ellie could picture him lying back on the bed, his shoulder raised, his arm across his forehead – that smile on his face. "I've made it my private mission in life to make sure it does stay open." She could hear the laughter under his words. "I eat there at least three times a week. I drag all my friends there. I send strangers there," he let the laughter into the open. "In short, yes, it's still open."

Ellie felt a bubbling sensation filling her chest as she remembered all the evenings they had spent at the tiny restaurant – Rosa's big warm arms, open, welcoming them; her husband, Lou, with his old-world charm, showing them to their table. They agreed to meet for dinner at eight and then reluctantly decided to say good night.

"I love you, Jake," Ellie whispered into the phone.

"You're killing me girl. G'night," Jake replied, gently replacing the receiver.

MAKING IT RIGHT

Chapter nineteen

Most of the breakfast crowd had thinned out by the time Ellie entered the restaurant. She knew that this wasn't going to be easy, but she felt that she owed Edgar more of an explanation than he had wanted to hear last night and was grateful that he had agreed to meet with her. She had suggested a restaurant that she knew Edgar liked, hoping familiar surroundings would make things less difficult. She had spotted his Cadillac in the restaurant parking lot, but as her eyes moved around the dining room she was unable to pick him out. She was just about to signal a waiter to find her a table when she turned and saw him moving toward her, starched and pressed, ready for a day at the office – only his eyes gave away any evidence that he might have spent a restless night.

"I suppose I'm glad you came," he said, gruffly. "I'm at the back, by the window."

He put his hand on the small of her back, and they moved through the room toward the window, not speaking. When they sat down a waiter appeared, filling their coffee cups and offering them menus which they both refused.

"Your timing was lousy," said Edgar, not wasting any time with small talk.

"I know, Eddie, and I'm so sorry. You have to know that nothing about this was planned – I'm as shocked by it all as you are."

"Not quite, I don't think." His voice was clipped and bruised sounding.

He was right, of course. She hated this. Ellie knew there was really very little she could do to make this easier. Who hadn't been on the painful receiving end of a conversation like this?

"Okay, so your knight in shining armour has come back to you," Edgar was avoiding her eyes. "I won't pretend that I didn't know that he was always hanging around somewhere in the back of your head." He stopped. He looked out the window and his voice became cold and quiet. "Was he always there? All the time? Even while we were having sex?"

His words sent Ellie's mind racing back to that night with Maggie – sitting on the living room rug, drinking wine. "So, what do you think, Maggie – is there a difference between having sex and making love?"

"Oh, I don't know, just semantics maybe," Maggie had said, but then she had changed her mind, "No, that might not be true. Maybe you have sex with your body, but you make love with your heart. How about that?" At the time they had both groaned and dissolved limply into another spasm of laughter, but right now Ellie realized that her sister had probably been right. *Damn it, Maggie – even when you were pie-eyed you were brilliant.*

This had been the whole crux of the problem with Edgar, hadn't it? She looked up from the table, shaking her head. "No," she said, quietly. "Jake was never in my head while we were having sex."

"Well, that's something," Edgar shrugged, not really understanding what she was saying but his pride feeling marginally less wounded. He moved the salt and pepper shakers around on the table. "I'm not an idiot. I know this was no crazy, passionate love affair, but we had some good times – at least I thought we did – didn't we?"

Ellie shook her head again, her imagination wanting to fast-forward Edgar into a future where he would be wildly, madly loved but knew that anything she would say could only come across badly. "Eddie, you're such a good man." She was acutely aware that women always said things like this and hoped that somehow he could hear it as more than just a line. "We had some wonderful times. Remember our trips through Europe – all those beautiful castles?" Ellie was close to tears. There was nothing in her that enjoyed watching another person's pain.

Edgar looked down at the table. "I know I'm not a touchy-feely guy. I've never been good on an emotional level – I like things in black and white, I guess I've always been like that. Our arrangement, or whatever you want to call it, always felt good enough for me. I never really kidded myself, you know, Ellie. I was always fairly sure that you only stayed with me because it felt like a safe place to be. I knew how badly you had been hurt." His eyes finally did meet hers, and there was something defiant in them – something in him wanting her to realize that he had known what had been going on.

Ellie stared at him, astonished by how much she had underestimated him. "Eddie, I don't know what to say. Thank you for telling me this ..." she held up her hands, flustered.

Edgar looked at her across the table. "Yes, well let's not get all sentimental about this. Right now, my pride is hurt, but I'm a big boy – I'll get over it." He stopped and looked around the room, and then he shrugged again. "There's no changing your mind about this, I don't suppose?"

Ellie shook her head. She knew that saying anything more would only make things worse.

"The heart wants what the heart wants..." Edgar barked a hard laugh. "I've never really understood that, but . . ." he left it there. "Okay, let's not belabour this – as you know, I'm no good at the big dramatic gesture. He pushed his chair back and stood up. She watched as he straightened his tie, and then he turned and walked back through the restaurant and out of her life.

Ellie put her face in her hands, her fingertips rubbing her forehead. She was fifty-two years old. Did you ever really understand what was going on in your life, she wondered?

MAMMA ROSA'S

CHAPTER TWENTY

Mamma Rosa's was only four blocks away from Jake's apartment, but he was there half an hour early anyway.

After Ellie had left, after that crazy, unbelievable morning, Jake had swung into action cleaning months of debris and neglect from the walls and floors of his apartment. He had wondered how long it had been since he'd had a cleaning service in here. So long he didn't remember exactly – not a good sign. He knew one thing for sure, though: he wasn't going to let Ellie see it that way again, and he felt fairly sure that Ellie would be seeing it again. Don't get too cocky, you idiot, he had warned himself – but goddamn it, he felt like a teenager again, and right now he wasn't going to let anything rain on his parade.

He hadn't known what he should wear tonight – was this a date? Even the word made him uncomfortable. He showered and pulled on a clean pair of jeans and a long-sleeved shirt, turning up his shirt-cuffs. He rubbed his hand over his chin, feeling for stubble, and felt a smile move over his face as he remembered that Ellie had sometimes liked that. She had also liked the way he looked with his cuffs turned up. Sometimes she had *really* liked it. He wasn't completely sure why that was, but he didn't really care; sometimes the

craziest things had turned that girl on. He remembered something about ball caps, but he couldn't recall exactly what that had been about – what the hell – it was all good.

He studied himself in the mirror, glad that his mornings at the gym had kept him in shape. After he had hung up his skates for good, his mornings at the gym had kept him connected to his former life. Most of the men at the run-down, sweat-soaked gym that he called his second home were guys just like him, former athletes from the days before you could win a race by a millionth of a second. There was no high-tech at Aldo's Gym – just guys who liked to work and sweat and feel their bodies responding to what they demanded of them. Many of them would meet on Friday nights for pizza at Rosa's, then a few beers at Zack's just two doors down. It hadn't been a bad life. While Jenna was in high school and university she would often come and spend her weekends with him. He missed those days. Jake always teased Jenna that she was way more of a jock than he had ever been. She had won a basketball scholarship, and her stories about her teammates echoed so many of Jake's that he could often stop her in mid-story and tell her how the story ended. She accused him of stealing her thunder, but he'd say, "No way baby-girl, we just share the same thunder cloud." It was true; she was so much like him. But then there was the other side of her, the Ellie side. Jenna was quick and funny, like Ellie, but there was also Ellie's gentleness in her. That softness would often catch him off guard when he heard it in her voice as she said good bye at the end of a phone call or a visit.

Ellie. He had never wanted anyone but Ellie. All the conflict, all the fights, all the tears; all the attempted reconciliations, all the apologies, and then more tears, and then Ellie was gone. There was no reason to try any more, she had said. He remembered her voice, cold and clipped,

"You've made your choice Jake. You've decided what you want, and I can't be a part of it. There's nothing more to say." And that was it. He had to let her go.

Jake could never put his finger on exactly when it was that he knew he was going to lose Ellie. It was an impossible situation. He had grown up in Sudbury, a hard-rock mining town where hockey was the only game worth playing. Since the age of five, hockey had been the centre of his entire life. His mother told stories about how, as a little boy, he would wear his hockey equipment around the house – he never wanted to take it off. His bedroom was plastered with photos cut from the newspaper, of players like Frank Mahovlich, Johnny Bower, Gordie Howe, Rocket Richard, and his brother, Henri, "The Pocket". Jake, his dad, and his brother, Bobby, would listen to every game they could pick up on the radio, picturing the action in their minds as clearly as they would someday see it on TV. Foster Hewitt's iconic, "He shoots. He scores", still echoed in his head. Jake lived, talked, breathed hockey, and just like every other Canadian boy who ever laced on a pair of skates, he dreamed of the day when he would play in the NHL.

The thing was, Jake was good; most of the time he was much better than good, and as he got older he became faster, and stronger, smarter; a force to be reckoned with. The Sudbury team had an unlikely fan base that attended every game. They were a group of tough, retired miners whose greatest kick in life was to come down to the rink and watch the lads – they always called them the lads – as they charged out onto the ice, deking and diving, stopping in a flash of shaved ice, turning on a dime, power sprinting – storming up and down the length of the rink. To a man, the old-timers had all played hockey when they were youngsters, and the games took them back to their glory days when they could skate for hours and not get winded and crash to the ice, not worrying about arthritic knees or broken hips. Claude Dufresne and Gus Lozinski were the most vocal of this grizzled group. They had separate favourites, but they both agreed that Jake was a level above everyone else. Claude loved the hard knocks of the game and Gus the stickhandling and finesse. Jake fit all of these categories. They would cheer him on, stamping their feet as they tried to stay warm in the cold. They would pull down their ear flaps and pour themselves coffee from a booze laced thermos.

"Butch Bouchard," Claude would say, slapping his leather mitts together. "Don' Jake jus' remine' you of dat crazy guy?" And Gus would nod and cheer even louder. Ten years ago they had watched Bouchard perform his magic on the ice at the Montreal Forum. Jake was so much like him.

And eventually the right people began paying attention. Several scouts began poking around, asking Jake and his dad a lot of questions, raising a lot of hope and causing Jake serious pre-game jitters if he knew one of them would be in the crowd for a particular game. But nothing definite had happened until a day at the end of June. It was a day that would be forever etched – hell, forget etched, branded was more like it – in his memory. High School had just ended, but he hadn't yet begun his summer job, and he and his dad had been at the picnic table in the back yard; his dad was scheduled to work the graveyard shift at the mine that night and had been at home for lunch. The previous day had been Jake's birthday, so they had taken the left-over chocolate cake out to the back yard and were finishing it off sitting at the picnic table – swatting at black flies and planning a trip up to the cabin to do some fishing. Bobby was done with his cake and had been slamming a basketball against the side of the garage.

"Bobby, cut it out – you're driving me nuts," his dad had yelled, and Bobby had ignored him, knowing his father would yell twice more before he was in serious trouble.

His mother had swung open the screen door and stepped onto the back stoop. "A letter for you, Jake," she had said, waving an envelope in the air.

"Ooh, it's probably a love letter from Janet Kowalski," Bobby had said, momentarily losing interest in the basketball.

"Shut-up," Jake had swung at him as he took the envelope from his mother. The letter was addressed to him, and he could see the words, "The Toronto Maple Leafs", neatly typed in the upper left hand corner. Jake couldn't breathe. He was sure his heart quit beating for a second. He had ripped the letter out of the envelope, scanned the page and then looked at his dad. He remembered that for a moment everything had seemed to become very quiet – it probably hadn't, but that was how he always remembered it.

"They want me to try out," he had said, and then he was yelling. "They want me to try out!" He was jumping, waving the envelope over his head.

"Who?" asked Bobby, and then, catching on, he was hammering on Jake's back, yelling, "Which team, which team?"

"The Leafs! The fucking Toronto Maple Leafs!" Jake had yelled, and then, "Oh, shoot, sorry, Mom." She had begun to shake her finger at him, but then she was laughing and hugging him, and Bobby was racing around the yard yelling at the top of his lungs. Jake's father had stood and looked at the letter and then jumped up the back steps and gone into the house, returning with two bottles of beer.

"Oh, Thomas," his mother had said. "Do you think that's wise?"

"I hardly think it's the first one he's ever had, Mary," his father had said, brushing the back of his hand against her cheek. "It's a big day for the boy. He's old enough to join the military – he's old enough to lift a pint with his old dad." Jake had loved it when his dad slipped into 'old Irish'. That's what he and Bobby had always called it when their father's speech would occasionally dip into his Irish roots. And then his father had handed Jake the beer and they had sat there, grinning at each other. Jake would have to go alone, his father had told him, he wouldn't be able to get the time off, maybe his Uncle Kev could go with him; and Jake had scoffed, trying to look cool, reminding his dad that he wasn't a little kid anymore.

Jake had tipped the bottle back and taken a drink. Following the chocolate cake the beer had felt strange and bitter in his mouth, but in another way it was maybe the best beer he had ever had. He knew it was one he would never forget. Two months later he was on a bus headed for the city, scared shit-less and more excited than he had ever been in his life. Jake could remember every minute of that week – how the tension had built, stretching every nerve to the max, finally ending in that adrenalin racing day when he had made the cut. It had almost felt as if it couldn't really be happening to him – almost an out-of-body experience, though he wasn't familiar with that term at the time. The Toronto Maple Leafs had decided that he was good enough! Jake was floundering, trying to put what he was feeling into words: 'unbelievable, un-fucking-believable,' were pretty much the only words that were circling through his brain. But there were sports writers around, and he knew that his mother, a teacher, would be mortified to read that this was the most eloquent thing her son had been able to come up with, so he leaned on the clichés he'd been using for years –'just here to help the team . . . I'll give it a hundred and ten per cent,' the rote phrases they had all learned to say. In the next few years he would develop the skills that would enable him to give an excellent interview. The reporters grew to love him – but right now he was just stumbling along trying not to let his mouth get him into any trouble. He remembered forcing himself to get it together so that he was able call home that night. He called from the pay phone in the lobby, a dozen quarters stacked on the ledge below the phone. He'd had to wait until after six when the rates were cheaper.

"Tell Dad to get out the beer and chocolate cake," he had said. "I made the cut." It became a family expression after that. Anything worth celebrating became a 'beer and chocolate cake' moment.

Later Jake returned to his hotel room, too excited to sleep and too happy to care. Sometime after midnight he threw on his clothes and wandered down to the Coke machine, running into another of the guys who had made it through also prowling the halls.

"Can't sleep either, eh?" said Jake.

"Hell, no! Fuckin' unbelievable, right?"

Jake was laughing, slamming his hand against the pop machine, "That's what I keep saying! You're Michael, right?"

"Yeah, officially," the kid had a big, easy grin, "but my friends all call me Mickey," he had added, holding out his hand.

The next day had been a circus, and after that – well, the rest was history.

To Jake, stepping out onto the ice had always felt like suddenly being infused with pure oxygen. Feeling the ice under his skates made him feel totally alive and centred and somehow free. All the years he played, he never lost this sensation of being exactly where he should be when he was on the ice. There was a joy to it that he couldn't imagine finding anywhere else. Years later he discovered Joseph Campbell's advice to "follow your bliss". Campbell's words resonated within every bone in his body, and it was at that moment that he finally realized why he had made the decision he had. How could he have left the game? It would have been like asking him to quit breathing. The violence that Ellie had hated so much was just a part of it. To Jake, and everyone he played with at the time, it was just the price you had to pay for the privilege of being allowed to play this glorious game. He could never make Ellie understand this, and eventually realized he would never be able to.

And so that had been it. Jake loved Ellie more than he had ever thought it possible to love another human being – that part never stopped, it never even wavered – but he had to be able to breathe. She said she couldn't handle it anymore, she had to get out, and so in the end he had no choice, he had to watch her walk away.

He had dated a few women off and on over the next few years but nothing ever came of any of it. If he was honest with himself, it all boiled down to someone every once in a while who would get him through the night. There had to be a country song in there somewhere – or was there already? There were always so many willing and eager young women hanging around in those days. Jake was no saint: he took advantage of it – of them, he now realized – but eventually it got old, and he began spending his off time playing pool or poker instead, definitely a low point in his life – his Bert Period, as he thought of it now. Bert and that damned cat. It made him laugh thinking about that stupid cat – now. At the time, though, he had spent many of his sleepless nights joyfully plotting Mica's demise. He had been drifting, he knew that. He had even had dreams about rowing a boat on the Niagara River, drifting closer and closer to the Falls. You didn't have to be a genius to figure that one out.

Without Ellie, he felt as if he were sleepwalking through life. Oh, he still worked out, still went to every required practice, still played his heart out – not even Coach could find fault with him, not then. But at the end of the day he still had to go home. And Ellie wasn't there. And Jenna wasn't there.

So what does a guy from Northern Ontario do when the realization finally sinks in that he's lost the two people he loves most in the world? Jake smiled a sour smile. Well, that was a no-brainer. He drank, of course, anything he could get his hands on, while still trying to convince Coach that he was operating at optimum efficiency. This worked for way longer than he ever dreamed possible, but of course the day came when they called his bluff. He was a hair's breadth away from being shipped down to the minors. This finally shook Jake out of the fog he'd been living in. He had lost Ellie because of hockey. He wasn't going to lose hockey to a goddamned bottle of rot-gut whiskey.

He stood in the shower for as long as the hot water held out that night. When he finally stepped out and dried off, he had decided that the rest of his life might be miserable, but he wasn't going to live it as a drunk. He decided to make a clean sweep of things and dumped the remainder of a carton of cigarettes down the garbage chute, praying that he wouldn't be rooting through the dumpster in the morning. After that night, things gradually got a little better.

Jake was sitting on the edge of the bed letting these memories wander through his head. He glanced over at the clock. It spooked him to even think about what this evening might bring. He had held Ellie in his arms yester-day; that alone was unbelievable, but then the unimagina-ble had happened – Ellie had kissed him and told him she still loved him. How was this even possible? The thought that she could possibly become part of his life again was way too raw to even let it linger there. And what about the circumstances that had brought her back to him? He felt something huge and black clawing at his gut. He forced the sensation away by concentrating on his breathing. "You wuss," he muttered to himself, "cut the crap and get your game face on."

Jake walked to the door and pulled on his shoes. He grabbed his leather jacket from the closet; you could already feel the fall chill in the air when the sun went down. He stepped out of the apartment door and locked it behind him. Here goes, he thought to himself, it is what it is. But what had Clinton just said, something about it all depends on what "is" is? He grinned, recalling that little bit of looney toons. Even total, nutso craziness sometimes worked itself out.

HE PASSES TO ELLIE

CHAPTER TWENTY-ONE

Ellie turned her Volkswagen into the alley that led to the tiny parking lot behind Mamma Rosa's. There were only a dozen parking spots here, she remembered, but with any luck her little car would be able to squeeze into one of them. Nothing on the right, but then something caught her eye over in the far left corner. Bright red and yellow streamers were flying in the evening breeze, looped in crazy patterns from the low hanging boughs of the trees that surrounded the parking lot. Nailed to the trunk of the tree directly in front of one parking spot was a large sign with bright glow in the dark lettering that read, RESERVED FOR BELLA ELLIE. Ellie put her hands over her face feeling a great rush of love and gratitude wash over her. When was the last time she had felt so unconditionally special? She didn't have to think very long – it would have been on her last birthday with Jake.

She remembered how she had arrived home late that night. The December wind had been icy and raw, and she had pushed her way into the building exhausted from a gruesome flight where every possible thing had gone wrong. She had just dropped her bag inside the door of the dark apartment when suddenly Jake was all over her, yelling "Happy Birthday." She remembered him refusing

to let her talk, wrapping her in coats and scarves, even pulling an old fur hat down over her ears and then making her close her eyes while he had led her out onto the balcony. When he finally commanded her to open her eyes, Ellie had stood staring in disbelief. Jake had transformed their tiny, dark balcony into a mini fiesta with candles everywhere and tiny white lights and strings of silver Christmas beads laced through the railings. He had pulled her down into a summer lawn chair, covering her with blankets, all the time singing Happy Birthday, dancing and clowning. He had poured them mugs of hot coffee from a steaming thermos, lacing them liberally with rum and brown sugar. He was beaming and kissing her, and then he was running back into the apartment and returning, his arms loaded with gifts. Ellie remembered her younger self swaddled in blankets in the rickety old lawn chair, shrieking with laughter and delight.

"Oh, Jakey," she whispered, as she stared at the flowing streamers. It had always been so strange. She had never been able to reconcile the Jake she had known with the Jake everyone saw on the ice.

"Don't let it get to you, Ellie." It had been Jake's team mate Mickey speaking. A brawl had broken out on the ice one night during a home game with Jake at the centre of it all. "Jake's tough – when he checks a guy, the guy knows he's been hit, that's just the way it is. Jake, on the ice, is a pit bull. Don't get me wrong – he plays clean – he's never vicious, but the crazy bugger's unrelenting. Off the ice he's a teddy bear. Don't mistake what he does with the guy he is." Mickey had slung his arm around her shoulders. "And when it comes to the two of you – trust me – no one will ever love you as much as he does."

Ellie pulled down the visor to check her make-up. It was quarter past eight; she was already late and she didn't want to keep Jake waiting any longer. She quickly slid out of the car, her charm bracelet tinkling as she slipped her purse strap onto her shoulder. When Jenna was little she had always claimed that only good things would happen to Ellie while she was wearing her lucky bracelet, placing all of her childish faith in the silver charms that fascinated her. Ellie began walking quickly toward the restaurant, hoping her daughter's faith in her bracelet had not been unfounded.

REUNION

CHAPTER TWENTY-TWO

J ake nervously checked his watch and rubbed the back of his neck. He glanced around the restaurant, checking the tables to see if he recognized anyone. He ate here so often it was quite possible that he might. Not tonight, though; no one looked familiar except old Lou, tucked away at a small table in the back next to the swinging kitchen doors. Lou must have felt him looking at him, because he looked up from his newspaper and gave Jake a big A-ok sign. Jake grinned back at him, and then, grabbing a bread stick, leaned back in the booth and again concentrated his attention on the door.

Ellie had never kept him waiting very long. Maybe the only time had been on their wedding day.

They were married outdoors, in a park, on the river. Well, Jake thought to himself, it was 1972 – everyone got married outdoors, in a park, in 1972. It really had been beautiful, though. It was June, and the weather had not yet turned into the oppressive heat that everyone who lived in Toronto knew would follow in July and August. The sky was a soft spring blue, the sun warm and mellow. Jake and his brother, Bobby, had chatted nervously with the small group of maybe twenty friends and family who were gathered on the grass, not yet seated on the white

chairs his buddies Gopher and Mickey had set up earlier that day. Jake and Bobby were resplendent in their white tuxedo jackets, frilly mauve shirts, black bell-bottom pants and requisite platform shoes. Jake snorted out loud at the memory and then remembered again that it had been 1972. Even Jake, who knew next to nothing about fashion, knew that the seventies had not been kind to men. Now women, women with their short little miniskirts and knee high boots – that was a different story.

The wedding was scheduled to begin at four o'clock, but it was quarter past four and there was no sign of Ellie. Jake kept nervously rubbing the hair on the top of his head until Bobby came up behind him, poking him in the back.

"Remember Uncle Liam?" Bobby had asked.

"Yeah," said Jake, "what about him?"

"Well," said Bobby, "I don't know if you know this story, but when that man was young he had a head of hair you wouldn't believe."

"What the fuck..." said Jake.

Bobby put up his hands. "Just let me finish – this is a story you need to hear. So," he continued, "from what I've heard, people used to come by dogsled all the way up to Sudbury just to marvel at Uncle Liam's wonderful head of hair. If he had charged admission, he could have been a millionaire. And then he met Aunt Franny, and something about that woman made him so nervous he started rubbing the top of his head – just like you're doing – and now, here he is today," Bobby had paused for dramatic effect, spreading out his arms, "bald as a billiard ball."

Jake had stared at Bobby. "By dogsled..." he'd said.

"Yep," said Bobby, chewing on the corner of his mouth, and then, "THAT'S the part you don't believe?"

Jake had grabbed Bobby around the shoulders and they had swung haphazardly at each other, hooting and laughing, wishing they could fall down wrestling on the park grass like they would have done when they were kids. They had controlled themselves, though, pounding each other on the back and swearing good naturedly, the way men do to show they care. Then finally – finally – Ellie's father's car had rounded the curve with Ellie and Maggie in the back seat.

Jake had felt his legs go weak with relief. Ellie hadn't waited for anyone to open the car door for her. She had jumped out – her dad always claimed that the car was still moving – running as fast as she could in her platform heels on the slippery grass, directly toward Jake. She was screaming, "I'm sorry, I'm sorry, the traffic…" Jake was laughing, his arms wide open, ready to scoop her up, and people were clapping, and the minister was coughing discreetly and pointing at his watch. At last, when everyone had finally taken their places, the cellist and the violinist began playing, and as the sweet strains of Pachelbel's Canon filled the air, Ellie and Jake were married.

Jake was sitting in the booth smiling. Ellie had been so beautiful, dressed all in white – something flowing and gauzy. Those had been her fringe-hippy years, Jake had always teased her. She'd had a wreath of baby's breath in her hair; just looking at her had made it difficult for him to breathe.

It was all so clear to him, as if it had been just yesterday. Why were old memories always so rich and real, he wondered idly. Sometimes this wasn't such a good thing; he chuckled quietly to himself as he recalled some of the blow by blow fights he'd been in. Then there were other times when he couldn't remember what he'd eaten for breakfast, or his own phone number. He had actually been unable to remember his own phone number last week. Craziness! Off to the side a flash of colour caught the corner of his eye, and he realized that someone was standing beside the booth.

"Hey, Sailor, you in town for long?"

Jake shook himself out of his reverie. God, he was getting soft in his old age. He looked up and there she was, his beautiful Ellie. He literally leapt out of the booth and grabbed her, and they were both laughing and talking at the same time. Ellie was here, and he was here, and everything, every-single-fucking-thing, was right with the world.

TALKING

CHAPTER TWENTY-THREE

S it, sit," said Jake, urging her into the booth. "God, I'm happy to see you. I was afraid…" he let his sentence trail off. "Just let me look at you – sweet Jesus, you look prettier every time I see you."

Ellie shook her head and rolled her eyes looking embarrassed, but she looked pleased at the same time. "Still sweet-talkin' the ladies are you, Jake?" her voice was teasing. "Remember your Dad?" She deepened her voice in an imitation of Jake's dad, "that boy's silver tongue could charm the heart of a wheelbarrow." They both laughed recalling his father's unorthodox way of putting things.

"Yep, that man has a way with the English language," Jake agreed, "but, just for the record, we both know that all my so-called sweet talk was reserved strictly for you."

"I know that," Ellie smiled shyly at him. "The sign and the streamers, I love them so much. You did that, didn't you?"

"Well, yeah." Was he blushing? "And Lou helped. He insisted on the 'Bella' part, but if that's the part you like best then I'm taking all the credit for it." He grinned at her and looked back at Lou. "He wants to be sure he gets a chance to say hello." He caught Lou's eye and motioned for him to come over. He lowered his voice, "Rosa passed

on three years ago, and their kids have taken over the business. Lou tells me they're doing a great job. He's big time, Italian-famiglia proud of them."

Ellie watched the silver haired, old-worldly gentleman crossing the room toward them. He was leaning heavily on a cane now, but the broad smile on his face telegraphed his happiness at seeing them. She stood as he came closer and held out her arms. Their greetings intermingled, both talking at the same time – "Ellie ... Bella ... Lou ... so good ... how are you ... you look wonderful ... Rosa ... so, so sorry" – all the words old friends say, wanting to say more, not quite knowing how. They hugged, and kissed once on both cheeks and then again.

Finally, Lou pulled a big square handkerchief from his pocket and mopped his face. "Okay, now you two order whatever you like, tonight is on the house." Ellie and Jake tried to refuse his generosity, but he would have none of it. His slight Italian accent, which they had usually barely noticed, suddenly found itself rolling around on his tongue: "Shuta-up shuta-up." He was hugging Ellie again. "Is what my Rosa woulda wanted." They thanked him again and again. There was no arguing with Rosa.

They settled back into the booth breathing in the heady aroma of garlic and fresh bread. The familiar dining room glowed with soft light, keeping out the dark that was beginning to settle over the city. Ellie's eyes rested on Jake. It could have been thirty years ago: here she was in the same place, with the same man whom she had fallen in love with all those years ago. She put her hand across the table, and he laced his big fingers through hers. "Jake, I'm so happy. I don't know what else to say, I just want to keep saying it – I'm just so unbelievably happy."

Happy was nowhere near big enough a word for what Jake was feeling. "Edgar . . ." he said. "You're okay with all of that now?"

"Yes," she smiled at him and tightened her fingers in his. "It was important for me to talk to him – everything's . . ." she stopped, looked at the table and back at Jake. "It's all okay, Jake. Everything's okay."

Jake felt as if his heart were about to explode. "Ellie, we're ordering right now. Lasagna, that's fast. Is that okay with you?" He began waving furiously at the waiter. Ellie was smiling and nodding, but her mind could not find one appropriate thing to say.

They barely spoke during the meal. They ate quickly, and when they could no longer pretend that the food held any interest for them they pushed their plates away, dropped their napkins on the table and eased themselves out of the booth. They waved at Lou as they stood and quickly headed for the door.

Lou watched them as they left, their arms twined around each other. He sighed and shook his head, remembering the beautiful dark haired girl who had loved him so long and so well.

BACK AT THE APARTMENT

CHAPTER TWENTY-FOUR

The chill in the air hit them as soon as they stepped out of the restaurant. Jake slipped his leather jacket around Ellie's shoulders, pulling her close to him. It only took them minutes to reach the car, but Jake stopped Ellie before she could put her key in the lock. He took her by the shoulders and turned her so that she was looking directly up at him. "Are you sure about this, Ellie? It's your call. Either way, whatever you say."

"For Christ's sake, shut up Jake," she handed him the keys. "Here, you drive. You know where the parking spots are."

Ellie could feel the tension between them rippling in the air – like cartoon heat, she thought. A warm, static buzz began moving through her body, and she stretched out her hand, almost certain that touching something metal could send sparks shooting from her fingertips. She had spent years analyzing her every move, but right now she wanted to be completely in the moment. Jake was the only thing she wanted right now. She wanted to fill herself with the smell of him, the feel of him. She switched off that part of her brain that was always dictating what was right and what was wrong; right here and right now were all that mattered to her.

The lights were with them, and in minutes Jake pulled into a neighbour's parking spot. "Spending the summer out of the country," he explained, pushing the car door open.

Ellie was out of her door just as quickly, and they grabbed hands, almost running toward the back of the apartment building. Jake fumbled as he tried to unlock the door, and suddenly the craziness of it all hit Ellie and she was laughing, leaning into Jake's arm. Jake glanced down at her, then grabbed her around the hips and threw her, screaming, over his shoulder. Curves be damned; she was still no bigger than a minute. "Come on, funny lady – just six floors to go."

In the elevator, she slid herself down until her legs wound themselves around his waist. Every nerve in Jake's body wanted her, right there, but he forced himself to push this thought away and leaned back against the elevator wall pulling her body to his as tightly as he could, kissing her mouth and her neck, saying her name over and over as the elevator creaked and groaned, rising to the sixth floor, eventually slamming to a stop. The door slid open, and they were out of the elevator, sprinting down the hallway until they reached the apartment, and then Jake was cursing as he again fumbled trying to unlock the door. Finally, they stood inside the apartment, silent now, staring at each other. Ellie's arms reached for him, and Jake grabbed her, kicking the door shut behind them.

"Jakey, Jakey, Jakey."

REMEMBERING

CHAPTER TWENTY-FIVE

W ell, we made it to the sofa," Ellie whispered softly into Jake's ear. The early morning light had wakened her, and she had turned as quietly as she could so that she was facing him, examining every inch of his face. She had softly kissed the scars on his forehead and his cheek. It was that scar, she had thought, remembering that afternoon flight from Boston. He was awake now too, smiling at her, that same lazy smile that had been haunting her for years. Nobody could smile like that. Now his hands were running down her body again, but slowly this time, remembering. Last night had been all fire and urgency. This morning was slow and sweet, teasing and gentle. I love you, I love you, I love you.

BREAKFAST

CHAPTER TWENTY-SIX

Ellie sat at the kitchen table wearing one of Jake's old team jerseys that almost reached her knees. She felt a contentment she hadn't felt in years – it felt almost as if she were wrapped in soft gauze. She had showered and pulled her hair back because, as she should have known, Jake didn't own a hairdryer.

"Are you kidding girl? Real men don't use hairdryers." He had been laughing, all fake machismo, but he really didn't own a dryer so she had rummaged through her purse until she found a stray elastic and secured her hair at the nape of her neck.

"I have a skate lace that could have done that – it would have been the envy of every other lace in the house." Jake had stepped behind her, putting his arms around her.

Ellie had given her hair a tug and then turned and slipped her arms around his neck. "You know what my Dad would say about that, right?"

"Yeah, yeah – blarney. But he should talk! He's the original, eighty year old blarney-meister."

Ellie couldn't argue with that. When she thought about it, maybe it had been what had attracted her to Jake in the first place. In a moment of unexpected insight she suddenly realized that her father had probably spoken to her mother

in the same endearingly exaggerated way that Jake often spoke to her; the two men were alike in so many ways. Ellie had never really known her mother – she had been much too young when she had died – but for a moment she felt a warm sense of connection that had never occurred to her before.

It's in our blood, Dad, she thought. *We'll fall for you blarney spewing types every time.* And she had missed it so much. She had given her hair another tug and moved out to the kitchen where Jake was preparing breakfast. She just wanted to be close to him.

A dish towel draped ceremoniously over his arm, Jake was now bringing the coffee pot over to the table. "Coffee for the lady?" he asked.

Ellie nodded and stretched an arm around his neck as he bent to pour, kissing his cheek. "I'm finding the total service package that you offer around here completely amazing."

"We aim to please, ma'am. Now, eat your eggs before they get cold."

And so they ate breakfast, sometimes laughing and teasing, sometimes a little shyly, not quite fitting into an easy groove yet, but never feeling awkward. It felt exactly the way it should feel, and they sat back in their chairs loving this rite of becoming reacquainted until the last of the coffee in the pot had been poured.

Jake had put on some music. Carmen McCrae was singing "God Bless the Child", the best version ever, he had always claimed, and the apartment seemed to lift and soar to the rhythm of her amazing voice. "She's something, isn't she?" he said softly. Then he pushed his chair back from the table and stood up. Ellie saw the lightness beginning to slip from his face, and she felt something cold grabbing at her heart.

"It's time, Ellie. There's an elephant in this room, and we have to talk about it." Jake began moving their chairs so that he and Ellie were sitting directly across from each other, their knees almost touching. He leaned forward, putting his elbows on his knees, taking her small hands in his.

"I love you so much, El." He lifted one of her hands and kissed her palm, still looking straight at her. His voice was cracking, "You know how much, don't you?"

Ellie was nodding rapidly, her eyes beginning to well up. She was stroking his arms and his face.

"I want to spend every second I've got with you. I don't ever want to let you go." Jake stopped for a second, rubbing his arm over his eyes. He coughed and cleared his throat.

"But, Ellie, there's this thing," he gestured in the air, unsure of what he wanted to portray, "this Dr. Philips thing. I know I always go on about how much I hate computers, and basically I do, but even I have to admit that when you need information fast, it's the only way to go." Ellie sat, her breathing shallow as he continued speaking. He had searched the web for information about how concussions that athletes sustained during their careers could impact their lives years after the fact. "We didn't know anything about concussions back then, Ellie. If we were still moving, Coach would say, 'Walk it off you pussy,' and most of the time that's exactly what we did. We just kept walking it off." His voice faltered slightly. "Now they're telling us that all these 'concussions,'" he was spitting the words out now, "can bring on Alzheimer-like diseases–fucking Alzheimer's for Christ's sake." One hand rubbed roughly at his forehead, and then he dropped both hands limply into his lap. "You knew, didn't you Ellie? That's why you were always on my case. But I didn't listen, did I? Not me, not Mr. Tough Guy, Jake Madison."

"No Jake!" Ellie was suddenly behind him, her arms around him, her face against the side of his neck. "I didn't know anything for sure," she was crying now, her breathing ragged, "I just loved you, and I was afraid for you." She stayed like this, holding him as tightly as she could until Jake pulled her down into his lap, both of them feeling this new fear swamping them like some monstrous, unstoppable tsunami.

Eventually, Jake took her hand and led her to the sofa. They lay down, Jake fitting himself around the curve of her back. They whispered words to each other, more sounds than words, and the warmth from their skin helped to ease the feeling of helplessness that was threatening to overwhelm them.

LATER

CHAPTER TWENTY-SEVEN

Jake had pulled Ellie close to him, his mouth against her ear. Tell me a story he had urged her – a story about Jenna when she was growing up. Tell me things I don't know, he had said, and Ellie had searched through her mind, finding stories that she thought she had forgotten. She had merged one into another until after a time she had felt his body begin to relax against her. She had turned until she was facing him and kissed him, her hand lightly touching his face. I love you so much, I just love you so much . . . had been all she could think to say.

Jake ran his hand slowly down the length of her body and then pushed himself over her and off the couch. He stood and rubbed his hands impatiently over his face. "This is bullshit, Ellie – this isn't me." He kicked lightly at the base of the coffee table. "Since when do I get all in a sweat about things before I have all the facts?" He walked over to the windows and looked out over the street, not saying anything, and then he looked at her and walked back toward the couch. Ellie scanned his face and saw with a huge sense of relief that some light had returned to his eyes, and his mouth had lost the grimness that had been there earlier.

He pushed her legs over and sat back down beside her, rubbing his hands up and down her arms. He sat there, saying nothing for a moment, just looking at her.

"Okay baby, we've gotten a look at the monster," he finally began. "We won't know anything for sure until Philips gets the results from his tests. That's a month away and fuck this! I'm not going to spend one more goddamned minute what-iffing myself! I've never done that in my life, and I'm sure as hell not going to start now." He put his hands on her shoulders, and his voice became soft. "I want this month with you, El, free and clear. Could you do that? Would you come and spend this month with me?" His eyes never left her face. "We'll go into a state of total denial. We won't let one negative thought ruin it. There's nothing sensible or realistic about it, I realize that," he stopped in mid-sentence – "oh, fuck it, Ellie – who gives a shit? C'mon," he had his hands under her ribs now, "let's just give ourselves this month. Come on baby, come and play with me."

Ellie was shrieking, trying to squirm away from his fingers. She fell back on the couch, pulling him down on top of her, "Do you really think we could do that? Push it all away and not think about it, I mean?"

"Absolutely," he said. "Look at us here in this room together again – who would ever have thought that was possible? Right now I think we can do anything."

Ellie tightened her arms around him, burrowing into his neck. She felt as if there were no way she could get close enough to him right now, and she also knew whatever happened she would never leave him. He had said Sarah had been hard to get rid of . . . Ha! She thought. He hadn't seen anything!

"All right then, I'm in," she said, pushing back a bit and nodding. She shifted her hips on the couch, grimacing, "on one condition."

"Name it," said Jake.

"Enough of this whining over the small stuff! We have got to get our priorities straight," her voice had become light, doing her part to dispel whatever heaviness still hung in the room. "Important things first, which means that first thing tomorrow we get rid of this lumpy, god-awful sofa. Make your choice, tough guy. It's either me, or the couch." Ellie's eyes were too bright, Jake thought. He saw that she was fighting back tears and loved her for it. She was too much, this beautiful girl. He felt himself wondering for a second if she minded that he still used the word, girl. This was a sore spot with women, he knew that. Screw that! She had been his girl when he had first fallen in love with her. She would always be his girl.

"No question there. Priority number one." The lines in Jake's face had relaxed, and he was grinning as he straightened up, his knees on either side of her hips. With one hand he reached behind him and pulled his T-shirt over his head then put his arms under the old jersey Ellie was wearing and slowly began inching it up her body.

THE OATH

Chapter twenty-eight

It was as if an oath had been taken. Starting right then the mood changed. They had a month to live one moment at a time, and they promised each other that this was exactly what they were going to do.

"Swear?" asked Ellie putting up her hand.

Jake put his big palm up in the air. "You do realize that we're way too old for this, don't you?"

"Yes," said Ellie, softly touching her palm to his. She forced her brain to ignore that side of her that wanted to worry every detail to death. She crammed all of that into a tiny box, far in the back of her mind.

She kissed Jake goodbye with a promise to be back in no more than three hours and flew down the stairs and out to her car. She felt like a window had been thrown open in a stuffy room. She felt like she used to when she was a little girl and had been allowed to wear running shoes instead of heavy winter boots to school on that first really warm spring day – that feeling that she was light enough to fly.

She immediately called Jenna when she arrived at her apartment. She had called her earlier to assure her that Jake was fine, just an age thing, he had to have a few more tests done, nothing to worry about. She knew she had been lying through her teeth, but now she was glad of it. With this call

she asked Jenna to come to Jake's for dinner. Jenna was free – dying to see Daddy – they blew kisses goodbye – love you, see you at six.

Ellie hung up and quickly began packing for a month of living out of a suitcase. When she finished she took a final tour of the apartment, throwing in extras as they caught her eye: books, perfumed soaps and bubble bath, a bag of cashews, a bottle of her favourite wine; good enough. Ellie zipped the suit cases shut, grabbed her laptop and a bag of camera equipment and headed out to her car. It was only four thirty, plenty of time to pick up the Thai food she had promised Jake and be back at his apartment before Jenna turned up.

THE COUNT

CHAPTER TWENTY-NINE

Bernice sat on the bus, wanting a cigarette. She was dressed in a brown floral dress, heading to her sister's – a family birthday dinner. She wouldn't be able to smoke there either, she was thinking. She remembered when her sister used to smoke like a chimney – they used to smoke and drink beer all night. Good times! Not anymore. Now her sister was her own private smoke-free zone. Bernice's thoughts, which were becoming increasingly more irritated, were interrupted as a young woman moved onto the seat beside her. The girl smiled and Bernice nodded. The girl looked to be in her early twenties. At first appearance she seemed to be one of those types – one of those annoying attractive, cheerful types. Bernice saw a lot of that kind at the hospital – young, all bright-eyed and bushy-tailed. It made Bernice tired just thinking about them. Bernice was sure that this girl didn't smoke either; no one smoked anymore. The girl was carrying a back pack.

"University?" Bernice asked.

"First year teaching," the girl said. "Just beginning to get myself organized."

She had sounded proud, verging on excited. Bernice had felt herself recoil slightly. She couldn't imagine facing a classroom of Sidneys every day.

HAZEL YOUNG

"Well, good luck," she said, reaching to ring the bell, "this is my stop."

Jenna moved her legs aside to let the woman pass and then slid over to the window seat and watched the city roll by. There were a dozen more blocks before her stop. She had been coming here on the bus since her parents had agreed that she was old enough to travel by herself. She loved this part of town. She and Ron should start thinking about renting around here until they had saved up enough money for a down payment on a house. It was such a friendly place for a child. Jenna felt a tingle in her chest. She put her head down and put her hand over her mouth.

There was a favourite park directly behind her dad's apartment and an ice cream shop with the best milkshakes in the city. There was a sporting goods store where she and her dad had hung out for hours and a library where Jake had always taken her for story time when she had been little.

The call from the hospital had been shocking and frightening. She couldn't imagine anything being wrong with her father. He was a rock. Nothing seemed to be able to shake him. She'd seen him black-eyed and bandaged many times before, but he had always laughed it off.

"Just part of the job, kiddo," he had always said.

Jake had always had time for her when she was growing up. As an adult, she now realized how much effort he had put into being available to her. He wasn't always able to be physically present, but she had been able to call him anytime she needed him. She had loved hearing his voice on the phone: "What's up baby-girl?" And then he would have her laughing, making everything okay. Jake had a wonderful ability to laugh at life's speed bumps and potholes, and as a result she had learned how to laugh as well.

Her mother had sounded good when she had called earlier – happy and something else. Jenna wasn't sure what that had been about. Her mother? – well it was hard to describe how she felt about her mother. They were closer than any mother and daughter that Jenna had ever known. There had never been anything she hadn't been able to tell her; Ellie had always been there with her arms wide open, saying all the things that Jenna had needed to hear. Her love was blatantly obvious and totally unconditional. Technically, Jenna had come from a broken home, but she had never felt broken. She had felt loved and lucky.

It was going to be so good and a little strange to sit down to a meal with the two of them. She had been surprised when Ellie had said that she would also be at Jake's for dinner. Jenna had wondered why, but she hadn't had the time to get into it. The last time they had all eaten a meal together Jenna would have been too young to remember.

She rang the bell and stepped off the bus into the late afternoon sun. At this time of year the light was always golden and hazy. There really couldn't be a better season, she had always thought – autumn in the city filled her senses to overflowing. To Jenna, September had always felt like the real beginning to a new year. Like the newness of an unopened notebook on the first day of school, September always felt fresh, and unspoiled and teeming with possibility. She crossed at the crosswalk in front of Jake's apartment and hurried into the building. She pushed the elevator button and waited for the elevator to descend to the lobby. She couldn't wait to see her parents together again. It had been a long time.

Jake swung the door open almost before Ellie knocked.

"Jake, you goof, you're beginning to remind me of a golden retriever we had when I was a kid." Ellie was trying to gather together her bags and the take-out that she had just put down in the hallway. "Harvey was equally happy to see us if we'd been away six months or fifteen minutes. It always seemed to me that he lacked a certain degree of discernment."

"Really? You're comparing me to poor old Harvey?" Jake had heard about Harvey before. He had been leaning in the doorway and now he threw his arms in the air, "Women! You're crazy! Okay lady, you want discernment? I'll give you discernment! I am zee Count of Dee-scernment! This is zee House of Dee-scernment!" And he lunged at her – a vampire overcome with blood lust.

"Jake, I swear, you give me a hickey and I'll kill you!" Ellie was shrieking, backing away from him, and Jake was about to plunge into her neck when over her shoulder he saw Jenna standing in the open doorway. Her eyes were as wide as they had sometimes looked when she had been five years old.

"Oh shit!" He grabbed Ellie's shoulders and turned her toward the door.

129

DINNER WITH JENNA

CHAPTER THIRTY

M om? Daddy? What's going on?" Jenna stared at them, astonished.

Ellie jumped back pushing her hair away from her face, and Jake slid down onto the floor, his back against the wall. Jenna's eyes travelled back and forth between her two oddly guilty looking parents and her mother's bags strewn across the entrance floor.

"You two – no – you're not. Are you? You're not. Oh my God, you are." Jenna was jumping up and down now, pulling her mother into a hug and grabbing for Jake's hand. "Do you know how many years I've been hoping for this? How did this happen? Mom, give it up. Come here and tell me everything."

Ellie let herself be dragged over to the table, and, peering at her daughter from between her fingers, began the abridged version of what was going on. Yes, she and Daddy were giving it a trial month. Yes, they were extremely happy, (well, Jenna could see that) and yes they had planned to tell her tonight – just not quite like this. Then Ellie was laughing, and Jake was leaning against the dining room wall, grinning, almost embarrassed.

Jenna jumped up and pulled him into a chair at the table. "Oh no, mister. I want to hear your side too." So the

three of them settled themselves at the table, talking, laughing, explaining what they could and leaving the rest alone. Finally, Jenna sat back in her chair and crossed her arms over her chest. "Well, you two take the cake! Here I was thinking I was the one with all the big news tonight. See Daddy, I always said you stole my thunder."

Ellie stared at her daughter.

"You're not," said Ellie.

"I am," said Jenna, beaming.

"Not what?" asked Jake.

"Pregnant," said Ellie, grabbing her daughter's hand. "Jake, you are going to be a granddaddy!"

Jake poured glasses of wine for himself and Ellie and juice for Jenna. They toasted Jenna and Ron, and the baby, and themselves, and babies, and parents and grandparents everywhere. It could have gone on forever, but Jenna stopped them, yelling, "time-out you crazies, I promised Ron I'd call when I got here." And Jake and Ellie moved over to the sofa.

"How long have Jenna and Ron been together?" Jake asked, suddenly feeling some primal, paternal instinct to protect his daughter.

"Are you planning on hauling out the shotgun, Grandpa Walton?" Ellie started to laugh, but then realized he had an expression of genuine concern on his face. "They're fine, Jake. They've been together for over two years, and you know Ron – he's terrific. He's crazy about Jenna – you can see it every time he looks at her. Honestly, you don't have to worry about that for a minute."

Jake looked across the room at Jenna, trying to remember what life had felt like at her age and then shrugged his shoulders. "Sorry, I think I just turned into my father for a second." Ellie put her hand on his. No matter what had happened between Jake and herself, he and Jenna had never lost the bond that had formed the moment his baby girl had been born.

133

BABY JAKE

CHAPTER THIRTY-ONE

They all agreed that the long forgotten Thai food no longer held any appeal, so Jake made up some grilled cheese sandwiches, and then more sandwiches. "Look at this girl, Ellie, she's eating like a lumberjack. This baby is going to weigh twenty pounds."

Ellie reminded him of all the chocolate shakes she had gone through when she was pregnant.

"That's why I'm the shrimp I am today," said Jenna, flinging out her arms.

"Do you know yet – boy or girl?" asked Jake.

"No, it's too early for that, and neither of us really wants to know. We both figure it's one of the last really great surprises in life – but I have to tell you, we both already refer to this little bump as Baby Jake all the time." Jenna smoothed her hands over her belly, that gentle, protective movement that all pregnant women instinctively adopt.

Her father did a victory fist pump and then, almost ashamed of himself, tried to take it back. "No, I don't mean that. A little girl would be wonderful. You know what I mean, healthy first and everything else is gravy."

"Gravy," Jenna moaned, "gravy and French fries, and deep fried zucchini, and honey glazed doughnuts."

"Stop, you're giving me heartburn," Ellie put her hand over Jenna's mouth.

They were all on the couch now, talking about the house Jenna and Ron were hoping to buy, how Jenna's job was shaping up, how Ron, an engineer, liked the new firm he had joined. Ellie filled them in on how her little business was still doing well, despite the lousy economy, and Jake agreed that there must still be a shitload of money in Toronto because his construction firm had more work than it could handle.

"'Shitload, Daddy? Lovely description."

"And he's on his best behaviour tonight," said Ellie, poking Jake in the ribs.

They sat quietly for a few minutes listening to the street sounds that were finding their way into the apartment through an open window.

"Why now, Jenna? Did it just feel right?" Ellie squeezed her daughter's hand.

"Actually, Mamma, this little peanut is a bit of a surprise," Jenna again rested her hand on her belly. She still occasionally used the childhood 'mamma' when she was excited, or happy or sad about a thing. It warmed Ellie to her very toes whenever she heard her say it. "But when we got thinking about it," she continued, "it seemed like the perfect time – brand new century, brand new baby. Ron would like to have about six kids – I keep telling him to let me get through this one first, and then we'll see."

"So, when's he going to make an honest woman out of you?" Jake asked, ducking behind Ellie. It didn't help. They both jumped on him, forcing him to take it back. Jenna eventually quit punching at him, assuring him that there would be a wedding a few months after the baby was born.

"I don't know – it all sounds a little too Hollywood for a dinosaur like me," Jake's voice was teasing as he pulled Jenna into a hug.

The talk continued, relaxed and comfortable until Jenna began stretching and yawning, signalling that it was time to call it a night. Jake refused to listen to her when she insisted that it wasn't far and she could take the bus home. "I'm driving you," he declared, "end of discussion." She and Jake pulled on their jackets and after many more hugs and kisses headed out into the cool autumn evening.

"Your news couldn't have come at a better time, baby-girl," Jake pulled out his keys, jingling them in his hand, and then unlocked the car door for her. Jenna looked up at him, something uncertain in her eyes – there was a tone in his voice that sounded slightly off. Noticing the look that had flashed across her face, Jake mentally kicked himself and quickly added, "I just mean with your mom and me trying to work things out and everything – it's all good. Hell, it's all great." He watched her face relax and thought to himself, Watch it, Madison.

MORNING

CHAPTER THIRTY-TWO

E llie woke to the feeling of Jake's index finger tracing patterns over her face. His finger gently followed the curve of her eyebrow, over her cheekbone, down her nose. She opened her eyes and looked over at him lying on his side, propped up on one elbow. "Jake, my love," she said, slowly, "if you don't stop this right now, I promise you, I will smother you." She swooped up a pillow, intent on pummelling him with it, but he was laughing, shouting, "No way lady," and blocked the shot with his left arm while his right arm slid under her, pulling her on top of him.

"God, I've missed you, Sugar," his hands were on either side of her face, pushing back her hair.

"The way you smile makes me crazy," she said. "It always has."

"I'll remember that," he said, as he put his arm around her waist and flipped the two of them back over on the bed.

TIBETAN MONKS

CHAPTER THIRTY-THREE

S o, we're looking for a new couch are we?"
"Well, that would be a start."
"New coffee table? End tables? Chairs? Fancy eatin' table?" – His Beverly Hillbillies voice.

"Check, check, check, check and check."

"Okay," he finished tying his shoe lace, "I'm ready, let's go."

Ellie put her hands in her coat pockets and stood looking at him.

"What's the problem?"

"Jake, I don't want to be indelicate," her eyes wandered around the dilapidated apartment, "but are you sure ..." She paused, looking uncomfortable.

"What? What? What the hell is the matter with you, Ellie?"

"Are you sure – I mean really sure – that you can afford to do this?"

Jake stayed seated on the hallway bench staring at her, and then he threw his head back and he was laughing, roaring, slapping his hand on his knee.

"What is so funny, you maniac?" She flung her hands up in the air, exasperated.

"God, Ellie, look at this place." He was still laughing as he let his eyes travel around the apartment. "I haven't bought one new thing in at least ten years. There are Tibetan monks who live better than I do. I didn't care what this place looked like, and I didn't have anyone to buy anything for. I always made sure Jenna had everything she needed," he looked at Ellie. "Didn't I?"

Ellie was nodding, yes, yes.

"Playing hockey was quite a ride. I mean, even when you and I were together the money was pretty good, but after a while it seemed crazy how much they were paying us. I mean, it was just hockey not brain surgery. It's nowhere near what those lucky bastards are getting today, but for a kid from Sudbury, back then it was a fortune. Bobby has turned out to be a financial genius – he works for a hot shot investment firm here in Toronto now. Jenna must have told you that, right?" Ellie was nodding. "Little brother Bobby hit the big time." Jake leaned back against the wall. He was smiling proudly as he thought about his brother's success. "Anyway, he's put my money into some amazing invest-ments, and ... I guess what I'm trying to say, Ellie is, yes, I can afford to buy a new couch." He was laughing again, and Ellie had turned and was banging her head lightly on the wall. "C'mon baby, you had no way of knowing. You would never take a cent from me – I tried to get you to, remember?"

Ellie nodded again. At the beginning, before she could afford it, Jake had insisted on paying for the apartment for Jenna and herself. He had said that it was his responsibility to make sure that Jenna had a good, safe place in which to grow up, and she was grateful for this, but she would never take anything from him for herself. She remembered how she would rip up the cheques he sent her through Jenna.

"God, I was an idiot," she muttered, shaking her head. "Well, this changes things, doesn't it? Come on Daddy Warbucks – we are off to buy one mind-blowing sofa."

"You know you're going to miss the lumps in the old one," Jake warned her as he followed her out the door.

"Thems the chances ya gotta take," said Ellie reaching up and cuffing him lightly across the back of the head.

MICHAEL'S

CHAPTER THIRTY-FOUR

J ake drove through the city with the car windows partly down ignoring both the traffic and Ellie's efforts to get him to stop at different places along the way. "Too fancy," "too country," "too modern," and, "No way I'm going to own furniture that I have to screw together like a fucking Mechano set." Ellie eventually gave up – Jake obviously had plans of his own. He finally made a turn, pulling into a store parking lot with "Michael's" written across the front of the building.

Ellie's eyes moved from the store front to Jake's face, "Yikes, Jake, isn't this just a little chichi?" She was flabbergasted. Michael's was about as high-end as they came.

Jake had turned off the ignition and was sitting back. "Yeah, well, the thing is, I'm pretty tight with the owner." He was watching her, waiting for the penny to drop.

"No!" Ellie stared at him, mentally connecting the dots. "You're not serious! Mickey? Our Mickey?"

"Yup, that's him – Mickey Goldman – Toronto's Furniture King!"

Ellie continued to stare at the building and then back at Jake. "I can't believe it," she started to laugh, and Jake saw tears beginning to make their way from the corners of her eyes and knew that this laughing jag wasn't going to end

quickly. "Oh my God, this is too funny – do you remember his apartment?" Ellie had her hands in her hair. Mickey's idea of furniture had been two ratty bean bag chairs and a suspicious looking futon on his bedroom floor.

"I know, I know," Jake was rubbing the back of his neck. He didn't want to appear disloyal, but it had also often occurred to him that the idea of Mickey owning one of the highest rated furniture stores in the city was easily an inch or two beyond ironic. "Well, it's like this," he was laughing now too; you couldn't NOT laugh when Ellie got really wound up. "Mickey is basically just the money behind it – the head honcho – he's got people who do everything else."

"Oh lord, this is too much – we've all gotten so . . . I don't know . . . sophisticated? Mickey has "people" for crying out loud?" And then Ellie quit laughing as the realization hit her of how much time had passed, and she reached over and squeezed Jake's hand. She felt a tremendous longing to claw it all back, wanting to return to a time before everything had broken. She thought again about the night Mickey had hugged her and reminded her of how much Jake loved her. He and Jake had been friends for years, and she and Mickey had connected immediately as well. He had crashed on their couch on so many nights back in the early years; the three of them, along with Gopher, had spent hours together playing euchre, or hearts, or watching TV. There had always been a new woman in Mickey's life – women loved him and he loved them back. It had been hard keeping up with him.

"Why didn't you tell me? Oh, forget that, we really haven't had a lot of time to talk, have we? Will I get to see him?"

"Absolutely," Jake answered. "He practically lives at the store. Funny thing about Mickey – he's never gotten serious about any of the women in his life. There's always someone new and better around the next corner. Best friend a guy could ask for though." He hesitated, and then he added, "You know, he had a crush on you once – maybe no one else ever measured up."

"Oh, Jake, come on – Mickey?"

"Hell yes, Mickey! In fact, half the team was in love with you when I first started bringing you around." Jake had leaned his head against the car window, remembering. "You women just about kill us poor, dumb-assed guys – you're like the Queen of Hearts yelling, 'off with their heads', while us poor clowns dance around doing all our fancy card tricks trying to impress you. And while you're deciding whether we'll live or die we're yelling, Pick me! Pick me!"

"You are crazy! I don't remember it like that at all – you're exaggerating," Ellie's eyes were starting to do that thing again.

"Oh, don't you kid yourself – it was even worse than that," Jake reached over and put his arm around her neck. "But then you picked me, and life became as it should be, and Mickey, and Gopher, and you and I became the four musketeers and . . . end of story. Any questions?"

She pulled his big palm over her face, trying to smother her laughter as she attempted to apologize for having given him such a hard time, and then they just sat, looking out over the parking lot. "I love you, you pitiful, dumb-assed clown," she said.

"You damn well better – I had the best card tricks," said Jake, rubbing his knuckle against her cheek. "Come on, let's go find Mickey."

The reunion with Mickey happened within minutes after they entered the store. Suddenly he was standing right there in the aisle in front of them, and Ellie threw herself at him wrapping her arms around him; and then

Mickey was hugging both of them, saying how good it was to see them together again, wanting to know how it had happened, and the three of them were off and running. He pulled them into his office and they settled themselves in his plush seating all of them talking at the same time. They hadn't been much more than kids when they had first been together, and now, as they sat there remembering, they felt like kids again. They leaned forward in their chairs finishing each other's sentences and stopping one another in mid-story to add their own details. It felt like only weeks, not years, since they had all been together.

They had been talking for a while, catching up, and Jake was in the middle of a winding story, fully animated, his hands gesturing, when a young woman entered the office, a coffee tray in her hands. Jake let his story hang half-told in the air and openly stared at her.

"Ho-ly shit!" He hadn't meant to say it, but suddenly there it was, and he immediately knew that it shouldn't be. And then he felt Ellie's hand clamp over his mouth – hard – and he knew that he *really* shouldn't have said it.

He looked at Ellie and then back at the woman. She was a knock-out, as his father would say. Not that this was anything new – Mickey had always been surrounded by beautiful women, but Jake hadn't been expecting this at the office. He and Ellie watched as she crossed the room. It was almost impossible not to – she had the legs of a Las Vegas show girl. Stiletto heels and a skirt – so short it had even caused Ellie's eyebrows to shoot up – didn't hurt either. They avoided each other's eyes as they accepted the coffee she offered, neither saying anything until the door closed behind her leaving them staring into their coffee cups.

Ellie was concentrating on her fingernails. "I can't believe they still do this," she said, searching for something safe to say.

"Do what?" asked Mickey.

"Bring you coffee."

"She offered," said Mickey. He was grinning, but he knew the world had changed – he had learned the new rules.

"Good on the computer, is she Mick?" Jake asked. He was slouched in his chair, still trying not to look at Ellie.

Mickey gave him a sideways look, "Jake, old lad, she has talents you can only dream about." He was chewing on his cheek.

"Stop!" Ellie slammed her hands over her ears as Jake and Mickey sprawled back in their chairs, twenty-one again. "Honest to God! Have you two turkeys learned nothing over the last thirty years?"

Jake pushed himself out of his slouch and reached out his arm, placing his big hand on the back of her neck, "Ellie, baby, calm down," he and Mickey were still laughing, but Ellie looked at them more closely and realized that their laughter was aimed at her. "How have you managed to forget how much we love to torment you? This is us, remember? Holy crap, El, even old-school hockey-jocks like us don't talk like that anymore . . . well, certainly not around anyone female."

"Well, aren't you two just a couple of sweethearts?" Ellie's eyebrows were shooting up her forehead. "I can't tell you how much better that makes me feel."

"Mickey, help! I'm losing her!"

Mickey sat forward, leaning his arms on the desk. "Ellie," he began, his face a mask of pure innocence. Ellie remembered this look and put her fingers over her face. "I haven't had a chance to tell you how wonderful you look," and Ellie sank down in her chair. "Honestly, you look even younger than you did twenty years ago, and thinner, probably ten pounds thinner, and I think you're most likely even smarter – oh, and taller – wouldn't you say, Jake? I'd say four, five, maybe six inches taller. Don't you think?" He showed no sign of stopping, and Ellie pressed her face into Jake's arm, weakly waving Mickey away. This was his gift, Jake had always said. Mickey could take the normal and ordinary and turn it into the ridiculous and absurd without missing a beat.

Ellie felt herself falling back into the comfortable space that had always been there when the three of them had been together, and she stayed with her head against Jake's shoulder. Some things never changed; they had always laughed like this. Eventually the laughter petered out in little bursts and gasps, and Mickey stood, searching to regain some remnant of his professional self which had disappeared when his friends had entered the room. Jake and Ellie stood too, brushing out the creases and straightening themselves around.

"God, we look like a bunch of drunks trying to sober up before we hit the front door," said Mickey, which started them all off again, and then he began propelling them out of his office. "Now, get out of here, you two," he was clearing his throat. "I'm getting a call in about five minutes from someone who expects to speak with an actual grown-up – it would work out real nice if that grown-up could be me." The phone on his desk began to buzz as he said this, and as he picked it up his tone changed, his voice becoming strictly business. Ellie and Jake waved and moved toward the door.

"Don't you just hate how they grow up so fast?" asked Jake, cheerfully flipping his friend the bird before the door closed. They stepped out into the hallway passing Mickey's alarmingly attractive assistant who looked up at them, flashing an impossibly white smile.

"I believe we have just cracked the case of why Mickey lives at the store, my dear Watson," Ellie whispered to Jake.

He elbowed her lightly. "But, you know what, Sugar? I've got old photos of you in skirts even shorter than hers." Ellie felt her face growing warm as she followed him down the hallway toward the show rooms.

OLD DEBTS

CHAPTER THIRTY-FIVE

As they had walked into the store, Jake had whispered to Ellie that Mickey's place was the kind of furniture store that interior designers had wet dreams about.

"Really, Jake?" Ellie had said. "And do you think you could have put that any more poetically?" But, as crudely as he had put it, Ellie had to admit that the store was astounding. It was huge and filled to the rafters with the kind of comfort and elegance that was usually only seen in designer magazines, all of it beautiful and luxurious – so much to look at and run your hands over.

Jake planted himself in a leather recliner and refused to move. "You've seen how bad my taste is, Ellie. Now you go for it – do your worst."

Three hours later and the salesman was totalling up the damage: a sage green sofa, rounded and comfortable, two rich, brown leather chairs – Jake-sized – a square iron coffee table with beige marbled tiles for a top, a carpet Ellie had loved the moment she had set eyes on it, its watery shades of green and blue reminding her of the days they had spent at Jake's cabin on Whiskey Lake. The list went on and on, with white blinds for the windows and filmy sheer curtains to catch the breeze; a dining room table with hidden leaves

that let it stretch forever, made of wood so smoothly finished it felt like satin, and comfortable chairs where Ellie could picture friends and family sitting for hours, eating and drinking and talking. There was nothing Jake and Ellie had loved more than to sit around a table swapping stories with the people they loved, even stories they had heard a hundred times before.

Ellie fell into the chair beside Jake. "I'm pretty sure we just made Mickey's day," she said as she pushed the recliner back as far as it could go and stretched out.

"Okay," said Jake, "my turn."

He stood up, stretching his long legs, and began walking back in the direction of Mickey's office. Now he had to convince his old friend to let them walk away with the floor models. It didn't take much. Mickey looked at Jake's face as he tried to explain, without explaining, that he needed everything right away; that he didn't want to wait for an order to come in. There was an odd, uncertain look on Jake's face that never used to be there. Mickey's mind swung back to the many times his old friend had appeared out of nowhere, sprinting toward him across the ice, watching out for him. Mickey knew from Jake's expression that something was going on but what it was really didn't matter; if Jake said he needed the stuff right now, no questions asked, he needed the stuff right now.

"No problem, buddy, we do this all the time." They both knew the store never did this. "I'll have it delivered by seven tonight." They shook hands, clapping each other on the back, and made a date for dinner at Rosa's.

"Thanks again Mick," Jake started. "Someday..."

Mickey didn't let him finish. "Get out of here, you asshole. Some of us still have to work for a living. Come on, I'll walk you out." They stepped out into the showroom, and Mickey moved over to where Ellie was waiting while

Jake pulled out his credit card and began settling up at the front desk.

"It's so great to see you again, Gorgeous," the happiness Mickey was feeling was all over his face. "I don't know how this happened, but I haven't seen old Madison this happy in ages." Mickey slung his arm over her shoulder, turning them so that their backs were to Jake, and then the lightness left his voice and his tone became serious. "I'm worried about him, El," he said, quietly. "Have you noticed anything different about him? Somehow, he's just not acting like himself lately."

Ellie felt her stomach sink. It seemed twice as frightening to hear that Mickey had noticed something as well. She stepped back from him a bit. "How do you mean?" she asked, not sure she wanted to hear the answer.

"Well, he's just different, moodier. Sometimes he gets so freakin' angry! Last month he nearly got mixed up in a bar fight, can you believe that?" Mickey shoved his hands in his pockets. "He's usually fine when he's with me. We've been friends for so long we kind of share a brain, but I just can't seem to get a handle on what's going on with him right now. And you know us – we're not real good at talking about this stuff." His face had such a concerned expression it made Ellie's heart hurt. She knew that Jake was like family to him.

His words had sent an electrical jolt through her. "Do things like this happen often?" Her voice had become scratchy; she didn't want to push the words into the room. Maybe she wouldn't be able to shove everything to the back of her mind.

"Oh, hell no – I didn't mean that, and I'm not trying to scare you," Mickey again put his arm around her shoulders. "Most of the time he's great – but then sometimes the craziest thing can set him off and he'll flip out. He just never used to be like that." Mickey kicked his foot against a loose floorboard. He'd have to see about having this fixed.

Ellie ran her fingernails through her hair. She didn't know what to say, or where to begin. Mickey was truly one of the good guys; next to Jake, the sweetest man she had ever known, and she knew that all he wanted to do was help. She longed to be back sitting in his office where everything had felt so easy and normal.

"He's seeing a doctor, Mickey. He knows something's not quite right – it could just be a blood-sugar thing of some kind. We're going to get this fixed, one way or another, whatever it is, okay?" She was trying to put on the bravest front she could, but all she really wanted was for Mickey to laugh it off and say that Jake had handled tougher situations than this.

But he didn't. He continued to look at her, his eyes reminding her of a child who was hurting for some reason that he couldn't understand. "Are you planning on sticking around?" he asked.

Ellie breathed a deep sigh; despite what they were discussing there was relief in her voice, "I feel like I've just finally found my way back home, Mickey," she said. "Trust me, okay? I'll always be here. I'm never going anywhere."

"Come here," Mickey's voice was low as he pulled her into a clumsy hug. "Honest, El, you are probably the best thing that could happen to him right now. He never got over you, you know." He held her at arm's length. "I always thought that someday he would – but he never did." A smile started to move across his face again. "Having you back in his life might be exactly what he needs," he nodded, convincing himself, and his whole body seemed to ease and loosen.

Jake had finished up and was sauntering over, yelling at Mickey to get his paws off his woman. Mickey put up a hand to high-five Jake and for a second tightened his arm around Ellie. "Just take care of our boy, okay?" he said in her ear as he opened the door for them. "See you two at Rosa's," he reminded them as they left the store, heading back to their car. Maybe everything did work out in the end.

CHAPTER THIRTY-SIX

The ride home from Mickey's had been strained. Jake had been in a great mood, laughing and teasing, but Ellie couldn't get into it; her conversation with Mickey still weighed heavily on her. They pulled into the apartment parking lot, but Jake put his arm in front of her before she could open the car door. "Okay, what's up, babe? You came out of the store a different person than when you went in. What happened?"

Ellie clenched her hands in her lap and stared down at them. "He knows there's something wrong," she finally said. "He's worried about you."

"What!" Jake's neck snapped around and he was staring at her. "He said that to you? Shit! That ass-hole! What the hell is the matter with him? He should never have said anything to you!" He slammed his hand down hard on the steering wheel, his voice angry and ragged.

"Jake, stop," Ellie kept her voice soft. "This is Mickey we're talking about – you know he would never do any-thing to hurt you. He's just concerned. You know how he feels about you."

Jake threw his head back against the head-rest, and Ellie watched him fight to slow his breathing, forcing himself to calm down. Eventually he rubbed his hands over his face

and looked over at her. "I'm sorry, baby . . . Sometimes it feels like I've got dynamite going off in my head." He gave a hard laugh. "Philips better come up with some kind of space-age bomb diffuser that he can feed me." He waited for a minute, and then he reached over and put his hand on the back of her neck. "Actually Ellie, that's what you do for me – with the exception of the last two minutes, I mean," he ducked his head, embarrassed. "When I look at you, or pull you close to me, all the raw nerve endings in my body feel as if they're being coated with something soft and warm." He laughed out loud – "It's that caramel pudding thing again," he said, remembering the Boston flight. "You, my beautiful Ellie Madison, are the amazing "Caramel Pudding Effect".

Ellie was surprised to feel herself wanting to smile. Remembering that first meeting with Jake always filled her with an easy, uncomplicated happiness. She remembered how she had anxiously waited for him to exit the aircraft – flirting casually with his team mates, expertly side-stepping and deflecting their pick-up lines as they had passed by, and then the pleasure that had shot through her when she had seen him walking toward her. She sat for a moment trying to find the right words. "We said we were going to give it a month," she finally said, turning in her seat so that she was facing him. "It's my fault – I'm sorry – I blew it." She held up her hand. "Swear again," she said. "Until Philips tells us anything definite, it's just you and me doing our own thing in any way we need to do it, and whatever happens, we'll deal with it. You okay with that?"

The lines that had formed on Jake's forehead began to relax as he again leaned his head back against the head rest. "Oh, yeah," he said slowly. "I am so fucking okay with that." He looked out the window – "baby, I'm so afraid I'm going to blow this, and you'll disappear from my life again.

Sometimes this seems so impossible – the fact that you're here with me, I mean . . ."

Ellie cut him off. "Do you know how much I hate bucket seats?" she asked.

"What?"

"I want to slide over there and smack you for talking like that, but how can I do that with all this stuff in the way?" She flung her hands impatiently at the console and the gear shift.

Jake's smile crept over his face, slow and easy the way it did, and then he vaulted over the console and slid into her seat, ignoring her flailing efforts to stop him as he wrestled her on top of him and pulled her legs around him. "Better?" he asked.

"Much," said Ellie, burying her face in his chest. She had almost forgotten how easily Jake was able to do whatever came into his head – he had never lost the ability to respond to a situation in the same way a ten year old might do. She had always loved this about him, right from the start. She pulled her hair back from her face and then slid her arms inside his jacket.

"You know, El," he had his arms under her sweater and was running his hands up and down her back, "laughing with you is magic. When we're laughing I know that every-thing is going to be okay."

She moved her head against his shoulder. "It's funny how my father has kept popping into my head over the last couple days," she said, "but, wise old guy that he is, he always claims that laughter is some kind of a gift. He says that the way Maggie and I could make him laugh – we were so little, and you know how funny little kids can be – anyway, he always says that the way we made him laugh back then . . . that was the only thing that got him through the first year after my mother died."

Jake nodded; her father was probably right. Laughter released something inside of him the way nothing else could. Ellie sat back on his knees and put her hands on either side of his face; "I love you, Jake. Absolutely no more talk like that, okay? I love you – I'm not going anywhere. Now, have you got that through your thick skull, you big dummy?" She was laughing again, pounding on his chest.

He tightened his arms around her. "I don't deserve you. Never have, never will, but I love you, and I love you and I love you. Let's get home. I promise you, I'll make up for this sad-sack routine," he was grinning, his old self again as he pushed open the car door.

"You know, you took your sweet time getting to the front of that aircraft."

"What?"

"I must have turned down at least five other dinner invitations from the rest of the team before you finally got there."

Jake sat looking at her, and then he was roaring laughing, "Those buggers . . . you know, I was concentrating so hard on how I could get you to go out with me that I completely forgot that every other guy on the team was probably thinking the same thing." He had stopped laughing, but his smile was still playing around his mouth. "So, funny lady, why didn't you take any of them up on their invitations?"

Ellie sat back on his knees, and then she leaned into him again. "I was waiting for you, Jake," she said. "I think I had always been waiting for you."

SEPTEMBER

CHAPTER THIRTY-SEVEN

E llie stretched out on their cushy new sofa. She was still in her terry bathrobe, her face scrubbed, her hair pulled back in a loose knot. Jake had just left for the gym and she was feeling lazy and peaceful. The last two days had been a roller-coaster ride, starting with the stressful visit to the store and everything that happened after that. Well, it hadn't been all bad, she thought, smiling to herself. The new furniture arrived right when Mickey had promised accompanied by two burly men who had heaved and hoisted it into the apartment. The next day Jake had made a call down to his office, and an hour later one of the construction company trucks appeared to haul away all the pathetic pieces of furniture that had filled the apartment for the last two decades. "It's good to be king," Jake had laughed, as they watched the truck pull up in front of the apartment. He made a huge fuss about how much he was going to miss his lumpy sofa, his duct taped vinyl chairs, his precious TV trays. Ellie had sat on the floor laughing at him, promising to find him a dead-furniture councillor to help him handle his grief.

They spent the next few hours moving things around. Ellie was in charge here. "A little more to the left, Jake. No,

it was better before. No, let's try it against the wall," and then back to the way it had been in the first place.

Jake had marvelled at his own patience, but then again, why not? He had to admit that Ellie could have told him to do anything. He would never be able to say this to anyone, he knew that, but there was no getting around it. Having this beautiful woman he loved so much standing here in the middle of his apartment, ordering him around, telling him what to do, filled him with more pleasure than he had ever thought he deserved.

"Okay, crazy boss lady. It's three o'clock, way past beer-break time. Give me a beer or you'll be hearing from my union."

"Oh God, not the union," Ellie covered her face in mock horror and pushed through the kitchen door. She returned holding two cold beer and a bag of ripple chips. "Health food! Do I know my way around a kitchen, or what?"

"Aaah, definitely my kind of serving wench." Jake pulled her down on the carpet beside him.

They settled with their backs against the sofa, Jake's arm over Ellie's shoulders. They sighed in unison and then laughed and pushed at each other, playing. Ellie knew they were both wondering why this had taken so long; she desperately wished it hadn't – she loved him so much it made her heart hurt. She felt something catch in her throat as she realized again that she wouldn't be here today if Jenna hadn't received the call from the hospital. She stopped herself before she could think any further. They had promised themselves a month.

"Here's to beer, miracle medicine of the masses, liquid penicillin, elixir of the gods." She held up her bottle, and Jake touched the side of it with the base of his.

"Let's hear an Amen for Sister Ellie," he drawled, imitating an old time radio preacher they used to hear occasionally late at night from somewhere in West Virginia. "Get your itty-bitty gold trimmed bibles right here folks," he continued, his Southern drawl becoming thicker by the second. They leaned back against the sofa laughing over a memory that hadn't crossed their minds in years.

"Ellie-darlin," Jake said, a trace of Southern accent still lingering, "we share one shitload of history."

"Yep, we do," she agreed, "but don't let Jenna hear you put it that way."

"Amen to that!" He grinned, tipped his bottle back and took a long, thirsty drink.

MISS KITTY

CHAPTER THIRTY-EIGHT

Ellie was asleep on the couch, an afghan pulled over her when Jake returned from the gym. He padded silently over to the couch and, trying not to wake her, pulled the afghan more snugly around her shoulders. But Ellie had mamma ears. She bolted straight up into a sitting position, startling both of them.

"Sorry, baby, sorry," Jake apologized, "I was trying not to wake you."

"Jake, you scared me," she put her arms out, and Jake, seeing he was forgiven, began to slide his arms inside her robe.

"Holy crap, Jake," Ellie pushed him away, "you smell like a bloody horse."

"Right. . . sorry, the gym showers were out of commission today." Then he was teasing her, "Oh, c'mon baby, you love it, admit it." Ellie was screaming for him to get away from her, and he was ignoring her, pulling her closer.

"Okay, cowboy, how about this?" she quit swinging at him and made an effort to smile, she hoped seductively. She doubted that she had ever known how to smile seductively. "Miss Kitty is going to draw you and your horse a bubble bath . . . and then, Sheriff Dillon, after you are all cleaned up we'll see what happens next."

Jake shoved himself over to the other end of the couch. "Eleanor Madison, I am totally shocked at you. For your information, Miss Kitty and Matt Dillon had the only, I repeat, only, truly platonic relationship between hooker and cowboy in the entire history of the wild west. I just may have to wash your mouth out with soap."

Ellie slipped herself down further on the couch. "Well, lucky for you I'm not really Miss Kitty. I'm Miss Kitty's evil twin, Miss Lulu-bell. So what do you think about that, cowboy?" By now she was laughing, curled up in a ball.

"Come on, you shrimpy little harlet – this cowboy needs his back scrubbed."

"Oh no! You didn't just say that! Shrimpy? Did you really just say shrimpy?" Ellie was pitching couch cushions at him.

"Perfect, I meant perfect! You're an absolutely perfect little harlet!" Jake was pulling her feet off the couch. "Move it, woman. I can't even stand the smell of myself anymore!"

TIME PASSES

CHAPTER THIRTY-NINE

A nd so that September eased along to the rhythm that Ellie and Jake had set. Not once did they mention the term "brain trauma" or anything to do with it. Mercifully, Ellie thought, Jake's tests and appointments were all completed within days after they had initially seen Dr. Philips. She never quite knew how this stroke of luck had occurred, but she was incredibly grateful for it. After the last afternoon of testing Jake arrived home holding a damp newspaper filled with sweet smelling sweet peas.

"How did things go?" Ellie was at the door as soon as she heard his key in the lock.

"Who knows? A bunch of word quizzes, idiot pictures of squares, and triangles and clocks. These people look just as happy if you give the wrong answer as the right one. They're all smiley, and 'That was great Jake,' like I'm some demented four year old."

"You gave the wrong answers on purpose?"

"Well, only a couple of times." Ellie's eyes were shooting daggers at him. "Hey, they were starting to piss me off. I just wanted to see if I could get a rise out of them . . . I couldn't." Jake sighed, "I think that place is run by a bunch of robots. What-ever!" he ended, dismissively. "We'll know the results in a month. Now, discussion closed, okay?" He

held out the sweet peas, "Here. I stopped at the Farmer's Market – you said you like these, right?"

Ellie buried her face in the flowers. "Absolutely the best," she nodded, completely delighted. As far as Ellie was concerned, sweet peas and carnations were the only flowers she had any time for anymore. She understood and appreciated the beauty of the displays in the florist's windows, but she sadly objected to the fact that many flowers simply didn't have any scent to them any longer. Just yesterday a sidewalk vendor had handed her a rose to smell. She had willingly obliged, but then turned back to Jake, her face so screwed up that Jake had almost laughed until he heard a sad note slip into her voice. "Jake, I honestly think they have bred the soul right out of them," she had said.

Now she picked a sweet-pea from the bunch and tucked it into her hair. "So much better than roses – you remembered," she said, putting her free arm around him.

Roses. Something rolled over in Jake's brain. Ellie was standing in the middle of the kitchen, but it wasn't today's kitchen – it was their kitchen from the seventies. She was holding the roses Jake had brought home in hopes of appeasing her after a brutal night on the ice. Things were getting worse between them. Ellie couldn't watch him play at all anymore. She had thanked him, her eyes down, not looking at him, quickly putting the flowers into a vase. Jake had rubbed his big hands over his face and then placed them palm down on the table. He stood like this, still in his long black overcoat, leaning heavily on the old arborite kitchen table long after Ellie left the room. He didn't have any idea what he should do. How could he give up the one thing he had worked his whole life for? On the other hand, how could he give up Ellie? There was no answer to either question.

Jake remembered that the table top had been blue with silver specks in it. Ellie had been wearing jeans and a red and blue plaid blouse. Her hair had recently been permed, and it curled tightly around her face. Neither of them were too sure whether or not they liked it.

Jake gave his head a quick shake. What was going on here? Why were these images from so long ago so Technicolor vivid? He could remember that there had been dishes in the sink, the white ones with the blue flowers around the edges, and a broom was leaning against the wall.

"Are you okay, Jake? You look a little pale." Ellie was rubbing his arm.

Jake shook his head again, "Yeah, no problem. I just need … I just have to get some Aspirin," he stammered, backing out of the kitchen. He blindly found his way into the bathroom and stood with his forehead against the cool wall tile.

No. Not now, Madison, you've got three weeks left – just leave it alone.

He pushed the panic that was clawing at his throat back down inside him, trying to take slow, even breaths. He made himself move over to the sink and let the water run until it was icy cold and began splashing it on his face and neck. Finally he sank down on the floor putting his head between his knees.

"Jake, are you okay?" Ellie was knocking on the door.

Jake filled his lungs with air. There was no way Ellie was going to see him like this, especially not after his rant in the car. "For Christ's sake woman, can't a man have a little privacy around here without someone asking what he's up to?" He coughed, making his voice as gruff as he could.

Apparently it worked because he could hear Ellie backing away from the door, laughing, "Sorry, sorry."

Watch it Madison, he said again silently, the second time in less than a week.

THE GYM

CHAPTER FORTY

Jake headed for the gym first thing in the morning, intent on working all of the strangeness he had been feeling out of his system. A kick-ass workout had always been the one thing he could count on to get himself out of his own head; a sure-fire way to refocus and clear out the mental garbage. As he had hoped, two hours later he felt himself beginning to relax. Relieved to be feeling a sense of normalcy returning, he showered and joined his friend, Red, for coffee. They avoided the trendy coffee shops that had been popping up everywhere, heading instead to a diner a few doors down where they sat in a vinyl booth and drank their coffee, black, from heavy cups and saucers, talking about the Jays, and the weather and The Leafs' prospects in the upcoming hockey season.

"Those boys are breaking my heart," said Red.

"Tell me about it," groaned Jake.

Red was motioning the waitress over to refill their cups. "Somebody said they saw you and Ellie together at Rosa's." There was a question in his voice.

"Yeah, I guess they did," Jake was looking down at the table.

"Well, that's something. Everything good?"

"So far, so good."

"Good. That's good," Red reached across the table and punched Jake in the arm. "So, how's life in the construction business?"

They sat back in the booth as the waitress poured them another cup of coffee, both comfortable in the understanding that their lack of communication had communicated everything they needed to know at the moment. They finished their coffee, talking shop.

"I haven't seen you around much this summer," said Jake. "Still flying tourists around the great white north?"

"You bet. It'll never make me rich, but you know what I'm like – as long as I've got enough change in my jeans to keep the plane fuelled up and operational, I'm happy." Red slapped himself lightly on the forehead with the palm of his hand. "Shit, that's what I wanted to talk to you about – you still have your place up on Whiskey Lake, right?"

Jake nodded, and Red slammed his fist on the table. "There ya go. I knew there was a reason why I felt like coming to the gym today."

Jake tilted his head to the side and frowned, not following him.

"I've been meaning to call you all week. I'm flying supplies into a fishing camp up that way this afternoon, and I plan on taking a few days off while I'm up there. Feel like spending a few nights at the lake?" Knowing how much Jake loved getting back to the cabin, Red knew he wouldn't refuse the offer.

"Fuck, yes!" Jake punched his fist in the air. "Are you serious?"

"Yeah, well it's not all fun and games. I have supplies for the marina on Whiskey Lake, and the owner is getting a little old to be doing much heavy lifting, so you'd be helping me out too."

"I'm your man," said Jake happily, but then his face slipped into a frown. "Would you have room for Ellie?"

"Are you trying to insult my baby?" Red bellowed, putting on a show of being highly wounded by Jake's question. "When's the last time I had you up in my plane? It ain't no piss-ant glider, you jackass – of course I have room for that little bit of a thing. She hasn't gained four hundred pounds, has she?"

"No problem there," Jake was trying to picture Ellie four hundred pounds heavier but couldn't quite get an image in his head. They stood up, digging some change out of their pockets to pay for the coffee, and headed out into the sunlight.

"Great talkin' with you, buddy."

"You too, Red. Ellie's going to love this. You watch out – she's going to be all over you, she'll be so excited."

"I'll be counting on it," Red clapped Jake on the back. "With your luck, I'll bet she's as good lookin' now as she was back then."

"Even better," Jake was grinning. Those curves, he thought. He had no idea what happened to a woman's body as she got older. They would talk about it someday, he was sure, but for now he was happy to accept that every once in a while the planets were simply aligned in your favour. He waved to Red then loped across the street, dodging traffic, not waiting for the light.

CHAPTER FORTY-ONE

Pack your gear, Ellie girl – we're going to Whiskey Lake." Ellie could hear Jake yelling as he came through the door.

She was working on her laptop when Jake burst into the apartment. Regardless of what was happening in her personal life, her small business still demanded her attention. "I'm in here," she yelled back.

"So," he was standing in the doorway, "feeling up for a little Whiskey Lake magic?"

Ellie looked up, surprised, and then a smile crossed her face. It was true – the lake was magical. She sighed. It was a long sigh, so filled with pleasure and memories that hearing it Jake leaned his shoulder against the door and for a minute was lost in his own memories. Ellie sat back in her chair recalling the many summers they had spent at their cabin on the lake. Most people in Ontario referred to their summer getaways as cottages, but their little place on Whiskey Lake could only be called a cabin. It was the kind of place where if you needed another coat hook you could simply hammer another nail in the wall. There was no pretence to it, no lah-di-dah. It had kerosene lamps, oilcloth on the table, sagging furniture, and God forbid, an outhouse. And they loved it. No electricity, no television, no

telephones, just the sweet sound of waves lapping on the rocks, the wind in the pines, and at night the eerie, plaintiff cry of loons far out on the lake.

They used to spend at least three weeks at the cabin every summer. In shallow spots the water often became as warm as bathwater. They lived in the lake, only crawling out when they were completely waterlogged.

Every morning, before Jenna had come into their lives, she and Jake would swim out to the point. That was as far as common sense dictated anyone should swim; any further and the swimmer would probably become too exhausted to make it back to the safety of the island. The rocks on the point shot straight up from the water, too steep to even consider climbing, but she and Jake were young and healthy, both strong swimmers, and their ability to make it to the point and back was a matter of pride. After their swim they would clamber back up the rocks at the cabin and lie there soaking up the sun. Aah, thought Ellie, the good old days, when the sun was still a friend. She remembered the smell of baby oil, their bodies slick and slippery, sliding and grinding against each other, their knees and elbows skinned raw from the granite beneath them.

Jake came over to where she was sitting at the computer and put his arms around her. "What do you think, babe? Red has offered to fly us up there, which means it will take less than half the time it would take if we drove."

Ellie glanced down at her laptop – there had to be twenty new emails in her in-box. Jake began gently massaging her neck. "Screw it," Ellie said quietly, almost to herself. "As of right now I am taking some time off. I haven't taken a holiday in years. I'll have to make a few arrangements, switch a few things around, but," she looked up at Jake, "right now the lake is exactly what we need. Give me an hour, and I'll be right with you." She jumped up and hugged him and then sat back down and her fingers began racing over the keyboard. She could almost feel the cool green of the island surrounding them again.

PACKING

CHAPTER FORTY-TWO

J ake pulled an old duffel bag from the back of a closet, and they began throwing things into it – jeans, T-shirts, socks, underwear. "Jake, I don't have a bathing suit," Ellie suddenly realized and then covered her face because she knew what was coming next.

Jake stopped what he was doing and stood looking at her, the muscles in his right cheek twitching from the effort of keeping a straight face. "Well, Lulu-bell," he drawled, "whatever will we do about that?"

Ellie groaned, falling back on the bed. "Jake, you have to understand. For a woman, being naked out in the sunlight for all the world to see when you're anywhere over forty-five, is an entirely different thing than it is when you're twenty-one. It's just not ... comfortable." She knew "not comfortable" didn't begin to explain it, but she also knew that she could continue trying to explain it to Jake for the next six years and he still wouldn't get it.

She sat up on the bed, "Oh, forget about it. I'll work something out."

"God, I hope not," Jake was no longer trying to control his face.

THE LADY OF THE LAKE

CHAPTER FORTY-THREE

W hen were you here last?" Ellie yelled over the roar of the outboard they had rented at the marina.

"In the spring. Bob and I always come up in May or June to check out how the old girl has wintered. She seems to be hanging in there pretty well."

A shiver shot up Ellie's spine as they rounded the point and the welcome sight of the cabin began to appear. It was a glorious September afternoon, the sun high in the sky. A soft breeze rippling the water caused the lake to shimmer, dancing in the sunlight.

"The Lady of The Lake offering up her diamonds," Jake had said to her, referring to the sun on the water. It had been the first time he had brought her up here, and Ellie remembered how she had loved this phrase he had used. They had been sitting on the dock dangling their feet in the water, watching the light catch the waves. Jake had leaned back on one elbow and told her about the first time he had heard his mother use this expression. He had just been a little tadpole of a kid, he had said, and Ellie had loved that expression too.

"The Lady's diamonds – you like that, don't you, Jake?" his mother had said at the time, catching him up and dancing

him over the dock. *"You've got a wee bit of the poet in you, I think."* A grin had spread over Jake's face as he had imitated his mother's voice that still flirted with traces of Ireland.

"Sir Walter Scott's Lady of the Lake?" Ellie had asked

"Could be," Jake had agreed, "but I always preferred the mother of Sir Lancelot story. That story satisfied my imagination way more than Scott's ever could."

Ellie had fallen over sideways into Jake's lap. "You just constantly amaze me, Mr. Tough Guy," she had finally said. "I've never even heard of the Sir Lancelot's mother story. Are you sure you didn't just make that up?" And then of course he had picked her up and thrown her into the lake. But – Ellie smiled to herself, remembering – that was a whole other story.

Jake pulled up beside the dock and tied up as if he did it every day.

"Have I ever told you how sexy you look when you do that?"

"No," said Jake, "how sexy do I look when I do that?"

"Steve McQueen, Robert Redford in *The Way we Were*, Paul Newman in anything. Shall I go on?"

"And I always thought I was more of an Incredible Hulk kind of guy." Jake jumped back on the dock roaring, going into an Incredible Hulk pose.

Ellie held up her hands, "Help me out of this boat, Hulk. We'll talk about how cute you are later."

Jake held out his hand, helping her onto the dock, and they began hauling their gear and the supplies they had picked up at the marina up to the cabin.

"I feel like a teenager sneaking off without permission," said Ellie, picking up a box of groceries.

"Yeah, weird isn't it?" Jake threw his duffle bag over his shoulder and picked up a gas can. "Boys oh boys! There'll be heck to pay if my Dad catches us – I've got his beer stashed in my duffle. . ."

"Boys oh boys?" Ellie was giggling, totally giddy, and Jake couldn't wipe the grin off his face.

RENEWAL

CHAPTER FORTY-FOUR

For supper Jake built a fire, and they roasted wieners on willow sticks he had cut from the trees behind the cabin. Ellie opened a can of beans which they devoured cold, and Jake poured red wine into the old tumblers with ducks painted on the sides. They sat in aluminium lawn chairs, congratulating each other on their haute cuisine – hot dogs had never been so delicious, beans so delectable, wine so mellow.

Remember when Bobby caught that six pound trout?

Remember when we held the first Whiskey Lake Olympic Games?

Remember Jenna's first time in the lake? The list of memories stretched on forever.

The fire had burned down to glowing coals now, and they took turns stirring it, watching the sparks scatter. Night was closing in around them, the evening air turning cool. Jake went inside and came back out pulling on a jacket and bringing an old plaid blanket to tuck around Ellie.

They sat watching as the fire burned itself out, cheering quietly when an ember would break loose and explode in the air. "Its last hurrah," Jake murmured. Ellie wriggled a little more deeply under the blanket and leaned back, closing her eyes, letting her head fill with island music. The

night was full with the high pitched chirp of crickets. The water in the lake licked at the rocks – a constant, gentle . . . *slap* . . . *slap* . . . *slap*. The island's bullfrogs that you never heard until the light began to fade had come alive croaking their deep, throaty greetings to each other. "It's a freakin' symphony," said Jake. He was laughing quietly but then held up his hand. "Listen, there's a whippoorwill." And then from across the lake came the chilling, lonesome wail of a loon.

"Oh God, Jake," Ellie whispered.

"I know," he whispered back, "You never get used to it, do you? My dad always said they were calling out to each other. They say they mate for life – did you know that? Dad always claimed that when they call out, they're saying, 'I'm here, where are you?' I always loved it when the old man got all poetic on me."

"I love that," Ellie fought her way out from under the blanket. She grabbed his hands and squeezed them tightly. She inched her chair a little closer to his, and his arm slid around her shoulders. She could feel the warmth of his skin through his jacket; she wanted to crawl inside his jacket; she wanted to crawl inside his skin. She felt her breathing quickening, and looked up to see Jake staring over at her. Then, they were both on their feet.

"I'll douse the fire. You go get those sheets warmed up," He grabbed her shoulders and pointed her toward the cabin then pulled her back and kissed her so hard and long she had to push him away to catch her breath. "Go, go," he yelled, as he grabbed a pail and began leaping down the rocks to the lake.

Afterward, they lay together, their arms and legs still wound around each other, Ellie with her head on Jake's chest listening as his heartbeat gradually slowed while Jake ran his hand up and down her back.

186

"Remember, the other day when you asked me why I was still wearing my wedding band?" he asked, as he gently pushed his fingers up through her hair. Ellie nodded and Jake continued. "Well, actually I did take it off for a while, but then I put it back on. I decided I would think of us as being on some kind of an extended break." He pushed himself up onto his elbow, "I always let myself think – somewhere in the back of my head I guess, that someday we'd get back together again." He smiled, embarrassed, and rubbed his hand over his hair, "Unfortunately, I failed to inform you about that part."

"Yes, that seems to have been the flaw in the plan," Ellie was laughing at him, running her hand over his chest. She put her hand on the back of his neck and pulled his face down to hers. "I don't know what to say, Jake – but I'm here now and I love you forever. Can that make up for it?"

"We'll have to keep working on it," he was reaching to pull her on top of him again.

"Yep, yes, we definitely will," Ellie was swatting at him, laughing as she pushed him away from her, "just not right now. Get away from me you crazy man – I need sleep – I'm old, for God's sake – my poor body doesn't know what's happening to it." She rolled him onto his side. "Now go to sleep," she kissed his cheek, "everything will be better in the morning."

"Alright! Now you're talkin'. Mornings are good!"

"Go to sleep!"

"How can I, now that you've got me thinking about the morning?"

"I give up," Ellie pulled a pillow over her head. "Sweet dreams – don't wear yourself out."

"You are one nasty woman," Jake grumbled, but he was grinning as he flipped onto his back and lay with his arms behind his head staring up at the ceiling. He had missed the easy laughter that had always followed making love to Ellie, almost as much as he had missed the love-making itself. Yeah, well almost.

Something about this jogged a memory that lay hibernating in the back of his mind. He would have been about sixteen or so, playing Juvenile D at the time, he remembered. He and another kid, Smitty – yeah, that was his name – had been waiting for their practice time to start; just sitting around banging their sticks on the benches and chewing the fat, talking about sex – what else? Jake laughed to himself thinking about that. It would be impossible, he thought, for two sixteen year old boys to be together and not be talking about sex. He remembered that they had been laughing, hitting at each other, trying to decide which could guarantee greater satisfaction – sex, or sliding a puck into the net. At sixteen, sex had been such a blitzkrieg kind of a thing, and, factoring in the odds of actually finding someone who might possibly WANT to have sex with them, they had agreed that the glory they were able to chalk up by scoring a goal far outweighed anything that sex would probably ever be able to offer either of them. Jake was snorting into his pillow remembering the crazy, exhilarating, terrifying, completely out of control experience that being a teenager had been.

"What's up with you?" Ellie mumbled, her voice sleepy.

"Just wait," he said. "Tomorrow I'll take you on a guided tour through a teenage boy's psyche, but it can wait." He reached out his hand and touched her arm, "I love you, El."

"Me too, Jakey," she whispered back.

MORNING

CHAPTER FORTY-FIVE

Ellie woke the next morning to the smell of coffee and frying bacon. Where there was bacon there had to be pancakes; she knew Jake's cooking habits well enough to know that. She pushed herself out of the deep groove the soft, old mattress had formed around her in the night and slipped on Jake's T-shirt that lay discarded beside the bed. She covered her face with her hands and let last night's heat flow through her for a moment as she remembered him feverishly trying to pull his shirt over his head. It had stuck somewhere on his shoulders, and she'd had to help him untangle himself. God, he was cute – older, true, but still so bloody cute. She found him standing in front of the wood burning cook stove and stole up behind him, putting her arms around his waist. She pressed her cheek against his back loving the feel of him – strong and muscled, just as she remembered.

"Well, good morning, lazy-bones," Jake turned around and rubbed his knuckles on the top of her head. Didn't they used to call this a noogie? "It's about time you woke up – the day's half over." Ellie looked around for a clock but of course there wasn't one.

She gingerly rubbed the top of her head where his knuckles had been. "Jeez, you're rough on a girl first thing in the morning – and you're supposed to like me."

"LIKE you?" Jake flipped four pancakes onto a plate. "I love you, I adore you, I worship the ground you walk on." He picked her up and deposited her on a chair at the table. "Now sit here and eat until you're as fat as a pig, and no man will ever want to look at you again, and you'll be mine, all mine," he threw his head back and cackled fiendishly, "FOREVER."

"Well, since you put it that way, you sweet talker you. Bring it on."

Jake brought over two heaping plates and they dug in, Ellie not thinking about carbs or calories, and Jake not thinking about anything except Ellie. They were both blissfully happy.

THE HAMMOCK

CHAPTER FORTY-SIX

That's what's missing – the hammock." Ellie was sitting on the cabin's front step, looking out over the lake and finishing her coffee. The stillness of the lake was surreal, the reflection of the trees in the water so clear it was difficult to say which was real and which the mirror image. The woods around the lake were waking now, with squirrels chattering madly as they chased each other in circles up and down the pines.

"What do you suppose those crazy squirrels are going on about?" Jake asked lazily, leaning back against the old wooden picnic table.

"Oh, she's probably reminding him to pick up milk on his way home from work, and he's telling her to get off his back and quit nagging him – just the usual stuff."

"Yeah, you're probably right. Come here, crazy lady." She moved over to the table where he was sitting, climbing into his lap, her legs around him and her arms tight around his neck.

"Let's stay here forever. We'll become The Weird Old Wild People of Whiskey Lake," Ellie conspired. "You can make us clothes out of wolf pelts, I'll knit us hats and mitts out of wild grass, and we'll live on roots and berries. How's that for a plan?"

"Amazing," said Jake, "except that there are no wolves on the island, you don't know how to knit and I've seen you eat. You'd be dead in two days if you had to live on roots and berries."

"Details, details. How about this?" Ellie kissed him, sucking on his bottom lip tasting coffee and syrup. "Could you live on that?"

"Try me," said Jake, sliding his hands under her T-shirt. That smile that had always turned Ellie's veins to butter was tugging at the corners of his mouth. "That's just an appetizer, Sugar," he said, "what have you got for a main course?"

Ellie's brain searched for a response but then gave up, "I'll think of something brilliant later," she promised, and then she let her body begin its slow melt.

THE SWIM

CHAPTER FORTY-SEVEN

It wasn't until later that morning that they remembered the missing hammock and went in search of it, finding it in the back shed under the canoe, a little the worse for wear but still all in one piece. They cheered as if they had found buried treasure and set about slinging it between the two maples that stood in front of the cabin, exactly where it had always been hung. The trees had grown so much since the last time Ellie had been here. She knew they would soon become a part of the dizzying colour that hit Ontario in the fall. "I wish I could be here to see them change," her voice sounded wistful.

Jake pulled her close, giving her a sympathetic hug. "Next year," he promised, then looking up at the clear sky added, "You know, I wouldn't be surprised if we got a frost tonight." He stopped, looking down at her, and something in his voice changed, "And if we get a frost tonight, today is as warm as the lake is going to be, at least for this year." He leaned an arm far too casually against the maple. "So, what do you say? Are we going in for that swim?" His eyes had become suspiciously blank, seeing how far he could push this.

Ellie didn't allow herself to stop to think. With a sweeping motion, so perfect it almost looked practiced, she

pulled Jake's T-shirt over her head and threw it in his face, "Geronimo!" – And she was racing down the dock and off the end – her knees up, her arms wrapped around her legs, her chin tucked in. She had been cannon-balling into lakes since she had been six years old, but this flashback from her girlhood was a masterpiece. Her head bobbed up in seconds in a great swoosh of water, "O m'god, O m'god, I'm dying. It's freezing. Jake, help!" And then Jake was racing for the dock shucking off his clothes as he ran, diving in and shooting up seconds later shouting and gasping from the cold. They thrashed about frantically until their bodies adjusted to the temperature, and then, becoming accustomed to the water, they revelled in it, striking out in a crawl or back stroke then circling back around, diving under water, returning. They filled their lungs with air and dived down as far as they dared, a minute later catapulting back to the surface, their lungs bursting. Finally they lay back in the lake letting the sun beat down on their faces.

"It's too cold to try for the point," Ellie said.

"You got that right," said Jake, "but, man, isn't this great?" He cupped his hand, sending water shooting at Ellie's face.

"You, jerk." Ellie cupped her hand, spraying him back.

They managed to stay in the water for a while longer, but reason finally got the better of them, and they decided they had better get out while they still could.

"I'll run up and get some towels. I'll be back in two minutes."

Ellie watched Jake pulling himself up on the dock, knowing without a doubt that she was freezing to death, but oh my, he still had a great butt. She also knew with a certain amount of pride that she had just now become a part of Whiskey Lake folk lore: the day that Grammy Ellie went skinny dipping. It would probably end up having happened in January, probably through a hole in the ice. These stories did get embroidered upon with time, she knew that, but that was just fine with her.

Jake was back in seconds, helping her up onto the dock, wrapping her in towels mummy-like, roughly rubbing her arms and legs bringing back the circulation. "You really are the craziest broad I've ever known. I would never have gone in first. There's no way I would have jumped in like you did. I was just bugging you, you lunatic."

"Guess I called your bluff, didn't I, Sheriff," she stood on tiptoe nuzzling into his neck.

"Yep, you sure did, little lady," he played along. "Now let's go find some goddamned clothes before we really do freeze to death."

The rest of the day moved along at its own leisurely pace. The lake had its own way of keeping time. They woke when the sun came up, ate lunch when it was at its highest point in the sky and went to bed when it disappeared behind the rocky point. At nightfall the sunset silhouetted the pines on the top of the rocky cliff. They jutted upwards, black in silhouette, straight and stiff as soldiers, sentinels standing on guard. Ellie loved this image of the pines guarding the lake and the Lady's diamonds, and all the secrets the island held.

That night she pulled herself into the warmth of Jake's body and whispered to him how grateful she was to be here.

197

HIGHLAND HILL

CHAPTER FORTY-EIGHT

T hey did get a killing frost that night; Jake had been
right. The maples had taken on a hint of pink, and
there was the thinnest layer of ice over a pail of water that
had been left outside.

"It's still warm enough to take the canoe out," said Jake,
"We haven't done that yet."

"Love that idea," Ellie was standing in front of the mirror
weaving her thick hair into a braid. Jake watched as her
fingers wove the strands of hair neatly into place, smooth-
ing in any loose ends as she worked. How she could do
this was totally mysterious to him. He loved watching her
fingers fly through her hair turning what at first appeared
to be chaos into a honey coloured rope of perfect order.
Ellie glanced at him over her shoulder. "Are you sure you
trust me? It's been a while since I've been in a canoe."

"What's the worst that can happen? We've already been
in for a swim," Jake shook himself out of the daze he had
slipped into while watching her.

She wasn't looking directly at him, but she knew from
his voice that he was trying to control the grin that wanted
to spread across his face. "Have I told you, lately, what an
insufferable jerk you are?" she twisted an elastic around her

braid and then grabbed a towel and began slowly moving toward him flicking the towel.

Jake leaned against the doorframe watching her advance on him, observing her as if she were a tiny, annoying black fly. And then he jumped into a crouch, pretending to drop his gloves and throw his stick on the ice. He held his palms out, his hands motioning for her to come and get him. "You want a piece of me, girlie? C'mon, c'mon chicken-shit, bring it on – show me whatcha got!" Then he was yelling and charging at her, catching her at the waist and throwing her over his shoulder.

"Jake!" Ellie was pounding on his back, "You've got to quit doing this to me!"

He was laughing as he lowered her onto the floor. She loved his laugh – it was a big, open, full throttle kind of a laugh that rolled out of him with no embarrassment or self-consciousness. He knelt over her legs as she swung at him until she gave up and slid her arms around his neck. She pulled his face close to hers and rubbed her cheek against his, feeling the scratch of stubble – she liked the feel of it. She loved his eyes. She had loved his eyes from that first night, she remembered. She loved the way playing came as naturally to him as not playing came to most people. She was so tired of being sensible, mature, responsible – all the things that were expected of a woman her age. She put her mouth close to his ear, "You're crazy and I love you . . . maybe I love you because you are so crazy."

"Now, that's more like it," he sat back on his heels and watched her face, wondering if it might not be a better idea to stay right here. "You coming on to me, girl? Oh, come on, humour me. Tell me you're coming on to me."

"Just a little bit," she began to wriggle out from under him. "We are never going to get out on the lake if we don't quit messing around. Come on now, focus! We can do this!" She was laughing at both of them, knowing that they would not get out of the cabin if she felt his hand begin to inch up her leg.

Jake was grumbling as he pushed himself up off the floor, sounding like a ten year old as he pulled her up with him, complaining that it was her fault, that she had started it.

"Oh God, you really are an insufferable jerk," she pushed at his chest. "A big, sweet, insufferable jerk," she added, holding up her hands and backing away as Jake again went into a crouch.

They hauled the canoe out of the back shed and carried it down to the water's edge, slipped it into the lake, then cautiously took their places – Jake near the back, Ellie in the front. They pushed off, sticking close to the shoreline until the paddle's familiar rhythm returned, and then moved out into open water, digging in, heading over to one of their favourite spots – an elevated piece of land jutting out from the mainland that the locals called Highland Hill. The hill was famous for the overabundance of wild blueberries that grew on the sunny side of the far slope. Ellie remembered Jake and herself filling plastic ice-cream pails to overflowing, their fingers becoming stained purple as they picked. Returning to the cabin later, they would fill soup bowls with this embarrassment of riches, drowning the berries in cream and brown sugar.

The hill's name had always intrigued her. She had never been able to say it without picturing Scots in kilts with bagpipes skirling marching over the crest. Years ago she had mentioned this to Jake causing him to stagger about laughing, not the reaction she had expected. "Ellie, you gorgeous Romantic," he had said, tousling her hair as if she had been a five year old. "It's called Highland Hill because it's a high piece of land." But then, seeing how her face had dropped, he had leaped onto the dock, planted his legs wide apart, spread out his arms, and, as she watched, had begun belting out the old Scottish tune, "My Bonnie Lies Over the Ocean" as loudly as he could – playing to the cheap seats in some cheesy off-Broadway theatre. His performance had brought her to the ground, tears streaming from the corners of her eyes.

"Where did THAT come from, you lunatic?" she remembered that she had felt as if she were sputtering like some cartoon character.

"Miss Larson, Grade six music teacher, greatest rack you've ever seen in your life!" Jake was by then sprawled on his back on the dock, the memory rolling up through him, "Every one of us boys in Grades five and six joined junior choir that year. God, I wish you could have seen us!" Jake had been waving his arms weakly in the air. "Half of us didn't even know why we were there, and we sure as hell couldn't sing, but Miss Larson's amazing boobs were this magnificent, incomprehensible magnet drawing us all in." He had finally rolled over onto his side. "Top that one, babe," he had yelled, as he had pushed himself up.

"Can't. I was taught by nuns – boobs – that just wasn't a word that ever came up. So, what else did she teach you, this amazing Miss Larson?"

"Oh, just the usual – you know, the hole in the bucket thing, and the Aunt Rhody thing," and then he stopped. "OH! You should have seen us doing her Waltzing Matilda thing. She even had us dancing to that one."

"Do it!"

"Nah. Only one performance per day. Always leave 'em wanting more." Jake had jumped up and was standing with his hands on his hips. That smile of his had been moving over his face.

"Do it, or sleep alone forever!"

200

"What! Tough talk like that coming from those lips?" Jake had his hands over his heart, mortally wounded. "Are you nuts, girl? You really want to see me do this?"

"You said it, baby!" Ellie had pointed to her watch. "Move it, sweet-cakes! As of right now you're on the clock."

"Unbelievable! Okay, okay . . . but, just so you know . . . you, girl, are going to owe me – big time!"

Jake had adjusted his ball cap – he always did this with both hands, the way ball players do. It was a move that Ellie found irresistible. She had shaken her head: how did he do this to her? She had known him for over two years, and he could still make her squirm like a thirteen year old on her first date. She had forced her attention back to the lake just as he had begun doing a slow soft shoe. And then he was hamming it up as he moved up and down the dock . . . "Once a jolly swagman camped by a billabong . . . under the shade of a coolibah tree . . ."

Ellie had sunk down onto the rocks laughing until she couldn't breathe.

He finished up and climbed up on the rocks beside her. "So, where's my reward?" he had asked, butting up against her, pushing his head up under her T-shirt.

Ellie was wiping her face on his shirt as she had tried to get him out from under her clothes, "THAT, my love, is your permanent 'Get Out of Jail, Free' card. You're a free man – I'll never be able to refuse you anything, ever again."

"Music teachers don't get paid nearly enough," Jake had said.

"Hey, you in the front! Have you decided to quit paddling entirely?" Jake was yelling at her from behind her in the canoe, bringing her back to today

"Sorry, just day-dreaming." Ellie slammed her paddle down hard on the surface of the lake sending water shooting backwards soaking him to the skin.

"Oh, lady! You are in SO much trouble!" But for the next few minutes Jake was too busy steadying the canoe to carry through with his threat.

There were so many memories, Ellie was thinking as they eased toward the hill. They tied up in the bay where they had always left the canoe and hiked up through the trails, stopping for lunch on a flat sunny rock that over-looked the water.

"Aah, life is good, Sugar," Jake said as he lay back on the old plaid blanket, an arm under his head. "And you know what the best part is?" He was teasing her face with a long piece of wild grass.

Ellie stretched out beside him. "What's the best part, Jakey?" she murmured.

"No goddamned mosquitoes," he yelled triumphantly, sitting straight up and shaking his fists at the sky. "We beat them Ellie, we actually waited them out!" He was on his feet now doing a victorious war dance, whooping like a banshee.

The voice in Ellie's head suddenly woke up. "See – told you so," was all it said.

THE HARMONICA

CHAPTER FORTY-NINE

Rain pounding on the cabin's metal roof woke them the following morning. They wandered out to the shelter of the overhang, drinking their coffee, watching as the rain churned up the lake. Yesterday's glassy smooth water was menacing today, dark and wild with white caps pounding on the rocks. They spent the day reading and napping, the warmth from the wood stove making it difficult to finish a page before they found themselves nodding off. Later they played cribbage using matchsticks for pegs, because, of course, the pegs had been lost years ago, and then crazy eights, and finally a game of Clue, where again they had to improvise with some of the weapons. Ellie howled every time she heard Jake proclaim, "Colonel Mustard with a toothpick, or Miss Scarlet with a bird feather."

By evening the storm had blown itself out, leaving a sunset of golden pinks and mauves trailing behind it. "Jake, I think I could die happy right now," Ellie stood transfixed by the shifting colours. Jake unsnapped his jacket pulling her inside it and kept his arms tight around her until the sunset gave way to a blue black darkness. They stretched out on the dock, watching as pin points of light winked into view in the night sky.

"I see the Big Dipper," Ellie pointed upward, "and there's the Little Dipper."

"Yep, and that's it," Jake moved his arm under her shoulders. "All the time I've spent out here staring up at the sky and those are the only two constellations I'm ever really sure of. I think they're just inventing the others to make the rest of us feel stupid. 'The Great Orion's Belt Conspiracy' is what I've decided to name it – how's that for a conspiracy theory that you can really sink your teeth into?"

Ellie shifted her body toward him. "Just who are 'they', Oh Brilliant One?"

"Oh, you know . . . they, them, the According-to-the-Experts guys," he was laughing and pulled her closer to him. "Okay, next time we come up here we'll bring a book and see if we can improve our star tracking abilities – you with me here?"

"Absolutely," Ellie agreed, burying her face in his jacket as she moved in closer to his warmth.

They lay back staring up at the sky until the dock and reality began digging into Ellie's back, and she reluctantly sat up stretching out the kinks.

"Hey Jake, look what I found," she rooted around in her jacket pocket, producing Jake's father's old harmonica. "Do you still try to play this thing?" Ellie found that she was whispering, not wanting to disturb the calm that lay over the lake.

"Try?" asked Jake, his voice hushed but indignant. "Did you really just say 'try'?" He grabbed at the harmonica in her hand. "Here, give me that damned thing. I'll show you a thing or two."

"Really?" asked Ellie, sceptical. "Last time I heard you play, you seemed to be a little stuck on Old MacDonald's Farm."

"Impressed the hell out of Jenna, didn't it?" Jake was laughing and trying to blow into the harmonica at the same time. "All right lady, stand back and be prepared to be amazed."

Ellie leaned back on her elbows, "Okay, go for it. I'm waiting. Impress me.

And then he did. Ellie was astounded at what she was hearing as suddenly the silence around them was filled with something low and bluesy, sexy and sweet; and as the last quavering note echoed across the water she threw her arms around him. "Jake, I don't know how you did it, but you have just taken a giant leap from Sesame Street to Bourbon Street. How did you do that? I don't care how you did it – I just love it – I just love you. Now, play some more."

"Ha! And you doubted me!" He was trying to appear threatening but then pulled her toward him and continued to play until she fell asleep with her head in his lap. Eventually, the night air began to creep through his jacket, and he glanced at his watch and slipped the harmonica into his pocket. "Hey, you, let's go to bed," he gently pushed her hair back from her face, "even the loons have called it a night." And they made their way back up to the cabin, finding their way carefully in the dark.

"Christ, it's cold in here," Jake was cursing himself for having let the fire in the stove die out. How could he have forgotten to do that? They laughed at themselves as they hustled about trying to stay warm, tearing off their clothes and letting them drop on the floor; then they quickly pulled an extra quilt onto the bed and dove under the covers. Ellie brought the folds of the quilt up to her face – it was soft and worn and smelled of cedar wood chips from the trunk where it had been stored. Jake slid the window beside the bed open wide letting the night air flow over them. It didn't matter how cool the night might be – sleeping with the window open was a tradition. Ellie could never get over how pure and untouched the air felt, here at the lake. It brought with it soft, rustling night sounds – the heavy wings of an owl as it swooped by and the sharp crack of twigs being snapped far back in the bush. She knew she would store these sounds away in the back of her mind, bringing them out later when the world became cold, and blustery and hostile. They lay facing each other, running their hands over one another, aware that this was their last night on the island.

"You know . . . the next-of-kin thing that got you down to the hospital?" Jake ran his hand down her arm. "Don't be mad, okay? I know I should have told them the truth, but I wanted to see you so bad I didn't care. I knew I should have had them call Bob, but I figured it was worth a try." Ellie didn't answer right away, and he pushed up on his elbow looking at her. "Ah, baby, tell me you're not mad."

Ellie grabbed a pillow and tossed it at him. "Would you give me a little credit? Believe it or not, I figured that one out all by myself."

Jake took a quick breath, relieved. "Smart-ass," he said, as he fell back on the bed and slid his arm under her pulling her closer to him.

"I still can't believe you're really here, El."

"I'll always be here, always, always."

SAYING GOODBYE

CHAPTER FIFTY

T his has been the best, Ellie." The sun was trying to find its way into the room through the yellow curtains that had probably hung there forever. Ellie turned her face into Jake's chest. She wouldn't let herself cry, but she couldn't talk either.

"Come on, girl," Jake pulled her tight and kissed her hard. "Red will be waiting at the marina by noon. We have to get a move on." But he continued holding her tightly for several minutes before he forced himself out of bed.

The next three hours were spent packing, and loading and closing up. After Jake had made his last run up to the cabin making certain everything was safely stored away and locked up they stood on the dock taking a last look around. The sun was brilliant, and Ellie turned her face up soaking in every last precious ray. She was dazzled by the sun dancing on the water and grabbed Jake's hand, "Look, Jake," she was laughing with the sheer beauty of it. "Our beautiful lady has found herself a whole new batch of diamonds."

Jake looked at her, his face puzzled. "Huh? What lady?"

Ellie felt her heart stumble, "You know, the Lake Lady with her diamonds. Remember? You told me about her the first time I was here."

Jake was still looking at her, confused. "Ellie, honey, I don't know what you're talking about."

Ellie felt something in her heart beginning to tear. No Jake! She rubbed her hand over her eyes. "Sorry, sweetie, I guess I was thinking of something else." Jake helped her into the boat and cast off. Ellie sat perfectly still, her blood turning to ice.

FLYING HOME

CHAPTER FIFTY-ONE

Red was waiting for them when the outboard pulled into the marina, and Abe and Arlene, the marina owners, came down to see them off. They had to be in their seventies, Ellie thought, but age hadn't seemed to have caught up with them.

"You're quiet, honey," Arlene said to Ellie.

Ellie tried to brush it off, "Too many hot dogs I guess, nothing serious," but she felt as if they were talking underwater. She watched Red and Jake joking with each other as they loaded the plane. Didn't Jake realize what had just reared its ugly head when they were on the dock? He and Ellie had spoken frequently about their beautiful lake, always making reference to "the Lady's diamonds", and she was sure that he and Jenna had talked about it over the years as well. It was an old family expression – it couldn't possibly have just slipped his mind. Ellie's own mind was reeling; her body felt stiff, her movements jerky. A milk crate lay overturned on the loading dock, and she walked over to it, grateful to have a place to sit for a minute. She sat there, staring in the direction of the cabin, rubbing the back of her neck where a headache was threatening to start. A shadow shifted, catching her peripheral vision, and she

became aware that Jake was moving toward her. He squatted on the dock beside her, peering up at her face.

"Hey, what's up, El? You look like you've just seen a ghost." Jake put his hand on her forehead, "You don't feel warm. You need a drink of water or something?"

Ellie took his hand and pulled herself up, trying to roll back the fog that was filling her head. "I'm just sad to be leaving I guess," she tried to laugh. "I'll feel better when we get up in the air."

Jake looked at her, unconvinced, and started to put his arms around her, trying to fix whatever was wrong, but Ellie pushed him away. She knew she would fall apart right now if she let him hold her.

"Come on you guys, let's get this show on the road," she forced some lightness into her voice and gave Jake a little shove.

"Whatever the lady wants," Jake was still looking at her, his head tilted to one side, curious. "Okay Red, all set to go?"

Red motioned that he was, and Jake and Ellie climbed the metal ladder onto the plane and took seats across the narrow aisle from each other. The plane was cold, and Ellie pulled her fleece jacket more tightly around herself. The air in the cabin smelled of gasoline, she noticed again as she buckled her seat belt. These small planes always smelled like this; there was no luxury here, just service. Red slammed the cabin door shut behind them, then clambered into the cockpit. Minutes later the engine roared to life and Red's scrappy little bush plane lifted off.

Ellie felt the shot of adrenaline that she had always felt back in her days with the Airline when suddenly an aircraft was no longer earthbound, that moment when it defied gravity and lifted into the sky. The small jolt seemed to clear her head slightly, and the stone that had lodged itself in her heart shifted a little. She leaned her head against the cool window, watching the land below them falling away. The trees had begun changing as the night temperatures had dropped, the evergreens now standing out boldly against the red of the maples and the copper coloured oaks. How could anything be wrong with all this beauty around them, she wondered, looking over at Jake. He and Red were pointing with great excitement at something on the ground, which Ellie finally made out to be a large buck standing next to the water. The two men were yelling at each other over the roar of the engine, making exaggerated hand motions indicating the buck's huge rack of antlers. Ellie knew they were both thinking of November and hunting season. How could anything be wrong when Jake was so obviously making plans in his head for a hunting trip?

Quit thinking Ellie, she said to herself. Just let it be. She reached across the narrow aisle and grabbed Jake's hand. "I love you," she mouthed. Jake smiled and pulled her hand toward him, kissing her palm. Ellie squeezed his fingers and didn't let go until they landed.

By the time Jake's car pulled into the apartment parking lot, Ellie had convinced herself that the moment on the dock had simply been a moment of forgetfulness. Heavens, she had them all the time: What did I do with my keys? Where ARE my reading glasses? They entered the apartment and moved through the rooms switching on lights, opening a window to let in some fresh air. The apartment already felt like home to her again. It was growing dark outside, but the lamps inside gave off reassuring pools of light. She slid down onto the couch, pulling Jake down with her, letting herself feel safe and sheltered. Nothing could touch them here. "It's good to be home," she said, as she moved closer to him and pulled his arm around her shoulders.

BACK TO WORK

CHAPTER FIFTY-TWO

Jake was up early the following morning: the company was taking on a new client, and he wanted to be in on the meeting. He had also decided that he wanted to take the rest of the month off and had a number of things to juggle around to make that possible. Ellie sat up in bed just as he was pulling on his suit jacket.

"Oh my," she said.

"Oh my, yourself," Jake moved closer to the bed. It was such an old fashioned, innocent expression, but she had such a sexy way of saying it. She had always said it like this, and it had always made him laugh. He executed a self-conscious turn. "So, do I pass inspection?"

"You look fabulous, delicious. I could eat you up," Ellie was laughing now too and grabbed his tie pulling him down toward the bed. He let himself fall on top of her, yelling that he had to go and kissing her at the same time; and then, as he managed to disentangle himself, he pushed himself off the bed.

"Oh Sheriff," she gasped, "Ah just do love it so when you flex your manly muscles."

"I'll deal with you later, Lulu-bell," he was grinning at her, straightening his tie. "Leave me alone woman, goddamn it. I have got to go!" He kissed her and sprinted

for the door, turning before he got there to remind her that they were meeting Gopher at Rosa's at seven.

"Gopher? Don't you mean Mickey?"

"No . . . remember? Oh . . . sorry, my mistake. Yeah, you're right, I meant Mickey." Jake grinned again and waved as he headed out the door. He stepped into the hallway and pulled the door shut, then walked slowly toward the stairs. Fuck! He had been sure that they were meeting with Gopher.

Ellie lay back as the door closed behind him, then plumped the pillows behind her back and settled happily into a sitting position. She reached over and pulled Jake's pillow from his side of the bed, holding it close to her. It still smelled of his after shave and she buried her face in it, breathing him in. She loved this – this waking up in the morning with Jake right here. She remembered all those mornings, especially during the first year after they had separated, when she would wake up and roll over half expecting him to still be there beside her, but of course he wasn't, and she would roll back to her own side of the bed – the emptiness of it clutching at her stomach.

Ellie ran her fingers through her hair impatiently shaking off this memory. That had been another time. She smiled to herself thinking of Jake's grin spreading over his face while he had been trying to push himself off of the bed, and she took a deep breath, exhaling slowly, feeling her shoulders relax into the pillows. She stretched her arms lazily above her head mulling over how different he had looked when dressed for work. The word "dapper" floated through her mind, but she couldn't quite envision using the word in the same sentence as "Jake." When had this happened? She remembered how he had never been able to put a shirt and tie together without her help. She was puzzling this over in her mind as she pushed herself out of bed. Now, this was worthy of further investigation.

CHAPTER FIFTY-THREE

Mickey was already seated at a table when they arrived at the restaurant.

"Well, look at you two," he yelled happily as they approached his table. "You must either be headed for a wedding or a funeral – Madison, you're wearing a tie, for Christ's sake. I'm not dying, am I? Ellie, tell me I'm not dying."

"You're just fine, Mick, you old reprobate," Jake waved at a waiter. "Bring this man a drink, he's delusional."

They settled themselves around the table, easily falling back into old familiar patterns. Ellie had thought Jake looked a little tired, or tense when they first arrived, but time with Mickey relaxed him, and he quickly seemed to return to normal. The two men discussed work for a while, and Ellie was struck again by how their stories mainly revolved around the lighter, more enjoyable aspects of their work. It had always been like this – they had never dwelt on the negative. She realized how much she had missed the banter – the light, insulting way men like this spoke to each other. Most of the friends she had found for herself in the last few years were lovely people, but, my God, she thought, they are a serious bunch.

Jake grabbed her hand, "Hey, whoa Ellie girl. I can hear the wheels spinning. Where'd you go?"

"Yeah," Mickey was shaking a finger at her, "You know the rules – absolutely no thinking allowed. Women!" he muttered into his veal parmesan.

"Speaking of women..." Jake kicked Ellie's foot under the table. He leaned back in his chair, his arms crossed, "I was sort of expecting to see your amazing, Amazonian, so-called assistant with you tonight." He was grinning broadly, waiting for an answer.

Mickey began laughing into his napkin, half choking on his dinner. "Ahhh, Jake old buddy," he finally managed to answer. "I was just messin' with you." He took a drink of water and continued. "Tiffany – that's her real name, I swear – she was only a temp. Hey, don't look at me like that. I've got a real assistant! You seem to keep forgetting what a vitally important member of the freakin' business community I really am!"

"Ah yes, the business community – it just keeps slipping my mind." Jake wasn't even trying to keep a straight face.

Mickey was also having a hard time staying serious. The success the two of them had experienced on the ice had seemed right and natural. This new success that they had found in the real world didn't seem to sit completely comfortably with either of them. "Anyway, you moron, listen up. I'm trying to tell you something here." Mickey paused for a moment, and Jake and Ellie looked at each other, wondering what was going on. "So, here it is," he continued. "My real assistant's name is Olivia and if you want to know the truth..." He stopped, changing gears. "Well, do you remember The Beverly Hillbillies?"

Jake and Ellie both nodded, and Jake broke into the first line of the old TV show's theme song, ending with a loud banjo twang. "Those Beverly Hillbillies?" he asked.

"Yeah, you got it," Mickey continued. "Well, the truth is," he hesitated for a second, "Olivia looks a lot like Miss Jane." He held up his hands to silence the laughter that he saw was about to break out, and Ellie watched his eyes going all soft. "The thing is . . . Olivia is the sweetest, most gentle, smartest person I've ever known. She has the kindest eyes – you know – they're just so . . . kind." He paused, stuck for another word, a confused smile spreading across his face. He looked at them and shrugged, knowing he wasn't sounding like the Mickey they knew. "She's probably just about the same age I am," he continued, "and it finally struck me how that is a really good thing." He took a quick drink of wine, shaking his head, and then he was grinning, "You know me, Jake. A while back I was out with this gorgeous twenty-five year old, and a song comes on the radio and so I say, 'This guy sounds like John Lennon' and she says – this gorgeous girl I'm out with, I mean," Mickey paused, looking at them, "she says, 'Who's John Lennon?' Can you believe that? John-fucking-Lennon for Christ sake!" Mickey and Jake were pounding on the table. "I mean, how is that even possible?"

"Anyway, I was telling Olivia about this the next day at work, and we were just about on the floor laughing about it, and then she was telling me a story about something like this that had just happened to her, and I was looking at her, and she seemed to change right in front of my eyes." He was rushing now, trying to get this out, "Long story short, we've been seeing each other for about three months now. I haven't said anything because I didn't want to jinx it, but as God is my witness Jake, I think I'm in love."

Mickey fell silent, staring at his hands, waiting for their reaction.

Jake and Ellie sat silently for a few seconds as well, absorbing this unexpected bombshell, and then Ellie was clapping and Jake was whistling, congratulating him, telling him how happy they were for him. Mickey sat back, his face alternating between happiness and embarrassment over the fuss that was being made over him.

"So, when do we get to meet her?" asked Jake.

"That's easy," said Ellie, "At dinner at our place – you're coming, right?

"Well, yeah," Mickey answered, "but I was only supposed to be one and now I'm two."

"Let us do the math, Einstein. Just be there," said Jake, ordering another bottle of wine.

Later that evening they settled Mickey into a cab and the two of them began their teetering walk home.

"I think I'm a little tipsy, Jake," Ellie waved a finger vaguely in his direction.

"Tipsy? Lady, you're drunk." Jake put an arm around her shoulders and began to twirl her around until she threatened to lose her dinner all over him.

"We are definitely going to hate ourselves tomorrow morning," Ellie said, having a little trouble getting out the word "definitely".

Jake tightened his arm around her, loving her soft warmth against him. This morning had sent a chill through him that even this evening had not been able to shake. He shrugged his shoulders trying to relax the muscles in his neck: this was their time, he reminded himself, and he wasn't going to let anything ruin it. He mentally ran through a list of the phone numbers of everyone he could think of, and then the names of all of his many cousins, and then grinned to himself. Nailed it. Piece of cake. He took a deep breath, feeling a weight lifting. Everything was going to be fine.

"Come on, woman. Let's get you home to bed."

TIME PASSES

CHAPTER FIFTY-FOUR

The rest of the month – the remainder of the month before their appointment with Philips – passed with barely a word said about what they were so brilliantly avoiding.

Ellie insisted that for the next while they completely avoid watching the nightly news. "We just don't need these bad vibes right now Jake," she had moaned. She had her hands over her eyes, not wanting to see any more. The broadcast had been unusually upsetting, even for the news.

"Vibes, Ellie?" They were lying at opposite ends of the couch, and he grabbed one of her bare feet and began running his thumbnail up the sole of her foot, something he knew drove her crazy. "When did we turn into a couple of tree hugging hippies, crazy lady?" Then he got into it, enjoying her efforts to make him stop, assuring her that he was certain that Gopher must know a guy who could set them up with some weed, and they could spend the news hour smokin' up, chanting, whatever turned her crank.

"Quit, quit," Ellie was screaming, trying to twist her foot away from him. Jake was still laughing at her but let go of her foot. "Alright, I agree that was a dumb thing to say," she was covering her face with her fingers. "But the news is just so depressing, and there's not one thing we

can do to help any of these people right now." She looked over at him, those eyes of hers wanting him to agree with her, and Jake knew that there wasn't a chance in hell that he wouldn't.

He leaned back against the arm of the sofa. He remembered when watching the news had become almost a rite of passage. It had happened the year he had turned thirty-two – that was the year he had begun to feel that it was time to start behaving more like his father. His father had been a miner – strong, a salt of the earth kind of a man with a moral compass that never seemed to fail him. Jake had just lost Ellie and Jenna and had almost lost his career, and he needed some of the moral certainty that his father projected. Watching the news had seemed like a good place to start. But right now the idea of not watching the news with Ellie felt like an equally good idea. "Okay, whatever you want," he grabbed her foot again. "You know, I remember when I used to get to do whatever I wanted around here," he grumbled, but then he was grinning as he sat up and laced his fingers behind his head. "Okay, just let me have the paper in the morning and keep me busy before I go to sleep at night, and I guess I'll survive."

"Jake!" Ellie threw her hands out in front of her. "Once again, you do realize I'm not twenty-five anymore, don't you? You know, I've heard there are many people out there who claim that Leno or Letterman can be equally soothing." She was laughing now, rubbing her temples. "Don't you ever want to just crawl into bed and pass out?"

"Not when I'm looking at you," he pulled her legs toward him until she ended up in his lap. "But," he added, assuming a deep, thoughtful expression while pointing his index finger in the air, "I have to admit, I do like pie. Maybe, just maybe, the beast in me could be placated with … pie. Yeah, apple, peach, rhubarb, you better watch it girl

222

– even you might someday be replaced with a huge piece of banana cream pie."

"Lemon meringue," said Ellie, jumping up. "It's a date. You, me, flannel pyjamas, David Letterman and a lemon meringue pie. Tonight. Are you in or are you out?"

Jake was in, and that night they slept the sleep of the angels.

PARIS IN TORONTO

CHAPTER FIFTY-FIVE

This one looks good," Ellie held out a book for Jake to look over. They had agreed at breakfast to pick up a few books that they both found genuinely funny and had found what they were looking for at a book store a few streets over.

Jake looked up from the novel he was flipping through and glanced at Ellie's overflowing basket. "Hey, whoa crazy lady! Any more and we'll both die of a sugar overdose."

"I'm willing to risk it," said Ellie, but she quit scanning the shelves and headed to the front to pay for the books she had picked out.

They left the store strolling slowly, soaking up the afternoon sun. It was still unseasonably warm, but there was a nip in the air and the trees along the street were showing off their fall colour. "They're reminding us not to get too sure of ourselves," Jake chuckled a little grimly. "They're saying, 'Lap it up suckers, one of these days the weather gods are going to send down a deluge of sleet, and snow and freezing rain that will freeze your sorry asses off.'"

"Well, that's just lovely – aren't you just a bucket of sunshine! Oh, hey, Jake, look." Half way down the next block Ellie had spotted an outdoor café, still open for the season. It was European-looking with striped awnings and

small wrought iron tables. Ellie stood completely still. "It looks exactly like a place I used to go to on my Paris lay-overs – look at the flower boxes." The Paris flower boxes, painted a bright blue and overflowing with petunias and begonias, could have been the same ones she was looking at right now.

She remembered finding the café on one of her first trips to France and the delight she had felt sitting at one of the tables, not quite believing that she was actually there in that sun dappled courtyard in the middle of Paris – Paris, for heaven's sake! The idea of it all had been almost too romantic to take in. In her mind there was always a mous-tached, beret-wearing Frenchman somewhere off to the side playing an accordion the way she had always heard a French accordion played in the movies. Realistically, she knew that this handsome, accordion playing Frenchman had never existed, but Ellie had always maintained that life needed a soundtrack, and she had happily included him in her memory. She remembered the coffee she had been served – rich and creamy, sometimes infused with hints of chocolate or caramel. "It's so gorgeous Jake" – she was gushing now – "come on." She tugged on his arm, pulling him along the street and through the scrolled and flowered iron gate that surrounded the patio.

Jake let himself be led along stopping to poke around in one of the flower boxes. "These won't last much longer," he gloomily predicted.

"True," Ellie admitted, her hands on her hips, her eye-brows inching toward her hairline, "but they're beauti-ful right now, and right now is what you and I are into, mister." Jake's attitude was beginning to intrude on her misty Parisian memory.

Jake grinned at her, "Coffee, Pollyanna?"

Ellie ordered for both of them, Jake almost sliding off his small metal chair, as the waiter placed two cups the size of soup bowls on their table, each filled with coffee and caramel, whipped cream and chocolate shavings. He made Ellie swear that she would never tell anyone he had ordered this. "Technically, I didn't. You did," he reminded her. "My street cred is nowhere near high enough to be able to handle the amount of static I would take if anyone found out I had been drinking this abomination."

"Abomination," Ellie repeated.

"Absolutely," Jake crossed his arms, sitting back with extreme caution in the tiny wrought iron chair. "Coffee, real coffee, is drunk black. You can add sugar as long as it doesn't show."

"No cream?"

"Oh, okay, but never whipped, no caramel, and don't even talk to me about sprinkles."

"Shavings," Ellie corrected him, being purposely obstinate.

"Right, SHA-VINGS," Jake corrected himself with great deliberation. "For God's sake, don't ever, EVER, talk to me about SHA-VINGS."

"Oh, for crying out loud, you've got way too many rules in your life." Ellie picked up the oversized cup, using both hands, and took a long sip closing her eyes in anticipation, waiting to savour the smooth, velvety taste she remembered from thirty years earlier. Instantly her eyes flew open, and she was staring at Jake. This was not supposed to be happening. The coffee, which should have been strong and rich was weak and watery, the caramel was making her want to gag, and what passed for whipped cream was leaving an oil slick on her tongue. "Oh my God, Jake! Paris never tasted like this." Ellie had pushed her cup away and was sliding her chair back.

"YES!" Jake reached into his back pocket to grab his wallet, slapped some money down on the table and reached for the bag of books. "C'mon, I'll race you to the gate." It was no race – Jake was at the exit before Ellie was halfway across the patio, but he held the gate for her and ushered her out with a sweeping gesture. Ellie walked through the opening, her hands jammed into her jacket pockets.

"What's up, babe?" Her body language had changed somehow.

Ellie looked up at him, embarrassed. "Oh, it's nothing – just me being silly, I guess." They walked for a minute and then she added, "You know how they always say you can never go home again? – I think in my case that might apply to Paris, too." Her voice had dropped to a low place, a sad note sliding through her words.

"Oh, come on, Sugar – that was no Paris! That was a two-bit, wannabe tourist trap – with great flower boxes that sucked you in! You've been dreaming about Paris ever since I first met you, and you can't give up on a dream." He put his arm around her shoulders pulling her close. "And I don't know about Paris, but when it comes to going home again I know that I'm at home as long as I've got you with me. When I crawl into bed at night and you're there – I'm at home. And that was nothing but a dream for years and years."

Ellie stopped walking and then took a step and stood in front of him; she stood on tiptoe, taking his face in her hands. Five minutes ago she had wanted to wring his neck, and now she wanted to crawl inside his shirt. She was laughing now, leaning into his chest. Jake put his arms around her, confused, but loving the sound of her laugh. After a minute she pushed away. "Honestly Jake, sometimes you kill me! Sometimes you are so sweet you literally take my breath away. It's your super power – it's your kryptonite – you leave me weak in the knees! That is the loveliest thing you have ever said to me."

"Really?" he asked. That smile she loved was twitching at the corners of his mouth. "Well then, my work here is done!" he said, dramatically dusting off his hands. "Move it, woman – this superhero needs a beer!"

"You never wanted a coffee at all, did you," said Ellie.

"Nope," said Jake.

THE CANAL

CHAPTER FIFTY-SIX

They were skating . . . it felt as if they were on a long, winding river . . . maybe the Ottawa canal. It was dark, and they were alone, the only noise the hissing sound of their blades slicing across the ice. They had been holding hands, but suddenly he let her hand drop and began picking up speed, flying over the ice as she had so often seen him do. She called out to him to wait for her, but he couldn't seem to hear her. He kept getting further and further away from her and no matter how hard she tried she was unable to reach him.

Ellie woke up, gasping for air. She reached for Jake, her hand grabbing at his arm. "It's too early, babe," he groaned, not awake, rolling onto his side.

She pulled herself against his back, pressing herself into the warmth of his skin until the panic passed, her arm tightly hugging his waist. The solidness of his body finally relaxed her letting her feel safe again, and her breathing gradually slowed as sleep crept back over her.

When morning came Ellie remembered nothing. The dream had dissolved, slipping away into the murky, shifting underworld where it had originated, but she had the curious feeling that she might have been cold during the night. And when Jake left for the gym she silently stepped

over to the dining room windows watching till he came out of the building, and then her eyes followed him as he walked down the street. She didn't want to let him out of her sight.

WHEELS

CHAPTER FIFTY-SEVEN

W hat do you think of these two bad boys, El?" Jake was leaning against the side of his car waiting for her approval. He had insisted Ellie come down to the parking lot with him – he had something to show her, he'd said, and now she was standing looking up at two bikes strapped to the roof of his car. Ellie was momentarily lost in a time warp, remembering the Easter her father had surprised her with the bike of her eight-year-old dreams. When was the last time she had been on a bike? She vaguely remembered a two-day trip with Maggie just after she had graduated high school. Could it possibly have been that long ago?

"So? What do you say – good idea, bad idea?"

"Are you kidding? This is the best idea ever – I can't wait to get on this thing."

"Not so fast, schweetheart," his Bogie imitation. "Have you ever ridden one with hand breaks?"

She looked at him in disbelief. "It's a bike, for crying out loud. How hard can it be?"

Jake raised one eyebrow, a condescending expression spreading over his face, but didn't say anything as they unstrapped the bikes and pushed them out to the path behind the apartment.

Shockingly, it was as if she had never been on a bike before. This is beyond ridiculous Ellie was thinking to herself as she fought her way out of the bushes once again and forced herself back onto the seat. She pedalled around the path, cautiously slowing as she approached Jake who was sitting with his back against a tree, applauding as she rounded the corner.

"Tada!" she yelled, stretching out her arms and legs, and then Jake was standing over her once again trying to help her up.

"The fire hydrant," he said. "It attacked you. I'm a witness." Ellie grabbed his ankle, tripping him, pulling him down beside her, and they lay sprawled on the grass.

"Just who was the fucking rocket scientist who decided to take the brakes out of the pedals?" she asked weakly as she tried to push herself up off the ground, collapsing again when she got to her knees. Jake tried to stand to help her, but he also collapsed on the grass howling and pounding his fist on the ground. At the moment, hearing Ellie curse struck him as just about the funniest thing he'd ever heard. She almost never swore – out loud anyway.

"Okay now," he said, when he was finally able to straighten up, "no sense losing your religion over this." He pulled her up and brushed her off, "One more time. This is it – I can feel it in my bones."

"Okay, okay, but you're right, this is it! If I don't get it this time I'm taking my bruised and battered body home. Kiss me for luck," she tilted her face up, pointing at her cheek and then gingerly climbed back on the bike for one last try. However, this time her brain began to get the message, and things began falling into place. She took a few cautious turns around the path and then, gaining confidence, sped up, screeching to a stop in front of Jake. Yes!

Yes! Ellie the Magnificent – able to leap tall buildings in a single bound!

"Come on, good lookin'," she called out to him. "We've got a whole city waiting to be explored."

"Not you – me," Jake grinned at a jogger who had stopped and was looking at Ellie as she sped by; then he jumped on his bike and took off after her.

Their private tour of the city began that September afternoon. They rode their bikes wherever they could, loving the way it freed them up, helping them to release the stress that was building inside them even though they would never let themselves acknowledge it. Ellie always had one of her cameras with her. Jake would sit leaning back on a park bench, his arms crossed, his legs stretched out, watching her line up a shot, making sure the light and the angle were exactly right. He loved her attention to detail, the care she put into every shot. Goddamn, he thought, laughing out loud as he realized what a turn-on it was to watch her totally immersed in what she loved to do. He insisted they make a stop at her apartment so he could see some of her work for himself.

"C'mon, Sugar, lure me up to your apartment and show me your etchings. I'm easy – I'll let you have your way with me." He tried to shove his hand into the back pocket of her jeans, pulling her beside him. "Seriously, El, I'm beginning to feel like I'm the only person in the city who hasn't seen what you do."

"Did Jenna never tell you anything?"

"Truth is, I never really let her. It was easier on me if we didn't talk about you."

Ellie had run her hand up and down his back – she had understood what he meant.

He hadn't pretended to know anything about photography, but he didn't have to know much in order to understand why her business was doing so well. He had spread several of the photos out on her coffee table, picking one up to study it more closely, and then another.

"These are really something, El," he had said. He kept coming back to a black and white shot of an elderly couple walking down a tree-lined city street. Ellie had caught them as the old fellow was talking, gesturing with his hands. The woman was looking up at him, laughing, her head tilted to the side. The sunlight streamed through the trees and washed over them, making it easy to make out the lines and wrinkles on their faces. They weren't young, but the photo was beautiful – they were beautiful. "I can almost imagine what they're saying," Jake had said. He had continued looking at the photo for a moment and then added, "You know, from what I've read, aboriginal people used to be afraid that the camera would steal their soul." He had hesitated, not wanting to sound like he knew more than he did. "I'm sure no expert, Ellie, but somehow I think you've found a way to bring some soul into every shot you take." Ellie had felt a shiver of satisfaction on hearing the pride in his voice. "You've got some stuff girl, you really do."

She had been standing back, nervously chewing on her bottom lip as she watched him. She had known this nervousness didn't make any sense. She'd had her work appraised many times before by people in the business, but at the moment Jake's opinion was the only one that mattered. When he spoke, validating this thing she loved to do, she knew she had been waiting for years for these words from him. She moved over to where he was standing and put her arms around him.

"You should be so proud of yourself," he said, into her hair. "I love every single shot." But then he bent and picked up the black and white photograph again. "I want this to be us, Ellie," his voice had become quiet. "Remember

Browning's poem, "Grow Old Along With Me"? I always liked that line. Now I'm hungry for it."

"Don't Jake," Ellie felt a burning behind her eyes and blinked rapidly, forcing it away. "No thinking. You know the rules." She put her palm firmly on his chest, and he let himself be pushed down onto the sofa. "Here," she said, "let me make this better."

KEEPING ON

CHAPTER FIFTY-EIGHT

They decided to take advantage of this free time they had given themselves and explore the museums they had never taken the time to visit (art and photography for Ellie, military and aeronautic for Jake). It was at a small gallery, one she had almost not gone into, that Ellie found what she knew would be the perfect gift for Jake – an oil painting of a group of boys playing pick-up hockey on a frozen pond. It wasn't an abstract piece of work, she knew Jake would have hated that, but it had an abstract quality that conveyed the speed and the sense of unsupervised freedom the boys were feeling as they flew across the ice, clouds of frozen breath swirling around them. It was perhaps romanticized, certainly not today's hockey world with bleary-eyed parents clutching take-out coffee cups, driving their kids to the arena way too early in the morning. But it was a piece of early hockey history, and she knew that Jake would love it. Jake was off foraging for coffee and doughnuts; he had claimed he was incapable of looking at one more piece of art – he didn't care if it had been painted by Rembrandt, himself. So Ellie was able to smuggle the painting into the trunk undetected.

"The best present ever, Ellie . . . ever!" He was grinning, looking at the painting later that evening. "Adults should have stayed out of it – this was hockey at its finest!"

The following day he bought Ellie a leather-bound collection of letters sent from service men to their wives and sweethearts during World War II. It was the most achingly beautiful gift she had ever received; she didn't know how to stop thanking him.

They took in a baseball game on one of those days that you can only find in September – one of those days so mellow it could break your heart. The Jays lost, but the day had been so perfect even Jake couldn't complain.

They played mindless rounds of mini golf and shopped buying gag gifts for everyone they knew. In the evenings they read to each other from their newly acquired stack of books that they had piled on the coffee table. They would lie on the couch curled up together, Jake's arm draped around her, her head on his chest. The books they had chosen were exactly what they needed – the various authors' quirky ways of seeing the world giving them hours of escape from the reality they were ignoring.

They rented every old movie they could recall enjoying, yelling out the best lines when they remembered them. When Jake was right he would whoop and do an exaggerated fist pump. Ellie, when she was right, would jump up, doing her stiff, jerky victory dance that she had done forever and that always left Jake laughing until he was weak. They knew that they were being unabashedly corny, but they didn't care. Sometimes the feeling – that feeling that they were adrift in a lifeboat without an oar – would overtake them. It was the same feeling that they had felt that first morning at the apartment, but they were too deeply involved in being together again to let it take root. At night they wound themselves around each other and whispered how lucky they were. Neither of them had thought they could be this happy again.

Chapter Fifty-nine

"Was it hard for you to retire?" They had pushed the supper dishes away and were into their third game of crib.

"You're just scared of losing – and there's no doubt about that, you are going to lose – so, you're trying to distract me. I'm on to your crafty ways, woman." Jake picked up the deck and began to reshuffle the cards.

"Well, that could be – I haven't had a decent hand all night. But really, was it hard when you finally called it quits?"

Jake put the deck down and leaned back in his chair. "Yes and no," he finally said. He moved forward, leaning his arms on the table. "I was tired though, El. Hockey's a young man's game, and I'd already stayed with it a couple years longer than I should have, and I think I'd finally realized that my body had taken all the abuse it could handle. But, that said, I'll always miss the feeling that being out on the ice gave me and the speed of the game – how I could completely lose myself in it. And of course I'll always miss the guys – kidding around with them in the room." Ellie knew that he meant the dressing room – players always called it 'the room'. He rubbed at his ear. "Well, it was fun if we'd won. If we'd lost, the room felt like a morgue. The best part was the feeling of being part of the team – something bigger than yourself, I guess." He rubbed his hand over his hair. "There was always something about walking into an arena, any arena, before the crowds came – there's a certain smell and that hollow, echoing sound – all arenas have that sound," He closed his eyes for a second, remembering. "No, actually it's an absence of sound – does that make sense?"

Ellie nodded and reached over lacing her fingers through his. "I think that describes it perfectly," she said, and they sat for a minute, both thinking their own thoughts. "Did it take you a while to know what to do with yourself after?" she asked. Her voice was gentle.

Jake was nodding but shrugging his shoulders at the same time. "Yeah it did. But the guys I partnered up with when we formed the company were already into it over their heads and were glad for the cash infusion. My ugly mug on the billboards didn't hurt either, so that all happened pretty fast." Jake was quiet, thinking for a moment. "It was great that Mickey and I never got traded around very much. We both loved it here – played our best hockey right here, but Gopher was traded early in his career. Man, I hated playing against him! I've seen that little bugger put a puck in the net from just over the red line. He had one Christly, wicked shot." Jake stopped for a minute, his mind travelling back to another time. "You know, El, it's the craziest thing – I can never lace on a pair of skates that suddenly I'm not sixteen years old again – it's like a time machine." He shrugged his shoulders and grinned. "And the three of us still play, every chance we get," he added. "You know what they say, 'you can take the boy out of hockey, but you can't take hockey out of the boy' – something like that – just paraphrasing." He still had that funny grin on his face.

"And then you all retired around the same time, right?"

"Yeah, it was good for us having each other," he said. "I know you think guys like us never talk, but in our own way we do. When I call Mickey a useless arse he knows that I love him. It's just the way we do it."

"I'm getting that," said Ellie. "Okay then, c'mon you useless arse. Are we going to play cards or chit-chat all night?"

"Hey, you can't do that!" Jake was laughing, shaking a finger at her. "You're still not going to win, no matter how much you sweet talk me." He leaned across the table and kissed her and then sat back down and dealt the cards. Ellie rolled her eyes as she picked up another hand of sixes and eights and nothing to go with them.

"Are you telling me that your ungodly, all-consuming love of competition, no, let me correct that, I mean your ungodly, all-consuming need to win . . . are you telling me . . . THAT had nothing to do with your regret about retiring?"

"For me? Nah, couldn't have." The muscles in his cheeks were again working hard trying to control the corners of his mouth.

LAKE WATER

CHAPTER SIXTY

Jake finished his sandwich, washing it down with tea from the thermos. "This is my all-time favourite season, El . . . right up there with play-off season." He pulled her down on the blanket beside him and then lay on his back staring up through the branches of a huge oak, his arms under his head. They were down along the river and had just finished eating lunch even though it was late in the day. They were dressed warmly in sweaters and vests – the sun was still warm, but there was a chill in the air making it surprisingly cold in the shade and Ellie had looped a long scarf around her neck. The late afternoon sun filtering through the trees painted the park golden and stretched elongated shadows across the grass.

Ellie propped herself up on one elbow, scrutinizing Jake's face. "How did you manage to get through your whole infamous hockey career without having your nose broken?" she ran her finger lightly down his nose.

Jake snorted, "I ask myself the same thing every time I look in the mirror. It sure wasn't for lack of trying."

Ellie's finger ran over his eyebrows. "Do you know that you have the most amazing eyes?" Jake looked at her, embarrassed. "No," Ellie continued, ignoring his

embarrassment, "I mean it. They're blue, but not really blue, more clean and clear like lake water. I could swim in these eyes."

"Okay," said Jake, "that's as much of that as I can take."

"I mean it," Ellie was laughing, loving his inability to accept how attractive he really was. There had never been any vanity in him. "I could swim in these eyes, for miles and miles."

"Naked?" asked Jake.

"As a jaybird," said Ellie, "if that's what you'd like."

"Yeah," said Jake slowly, rolling on top of her, not letting her up, "that's exactly what I'd like."

CHAPTER SIXTY-ONE

They had been biking all day and were tired but not yet tired enough to sleep and were propped up in bed reading.

"I used to have a witch woman who lived inside my head."

Jake peered at Ellie over the top of his reading glasses, "Really, fraulein?" The corners of his mouth were turning up. "And what do you suppose she was doing there?"

"Basically, trying to get us back together again, I think."

"Aah . . . so, a very good witch."

"Yes, a very, very good witch," Ellie said, smiling at him. She kissed his cheek and pushed his glasses back in place, and they both returned to their books.

CHAPTER SIXTY-TWO

I 'll be right back – just going down to check the mail."
"No, babe, wait. Would you come here? Please?"

"What?" Ellie turned. There was something about his voice.

"Just come here," Jake was sitting on the couch. He had his feet on the coffee table. It was dark in the room – it made it hard to see his face.

"What's wrong, baby?" Ellie closed the door and moved over to where he was sitting. She knelt on the sofa beside him and put her arms around him. "You sound sad, sweetie. What's going on?"

"Nah, not really sad, just thinking."

"Okay . . . about what?"

"Us, Jenna, everything I guess."

"We've been avoiding a lot of stuff, haven't we?"

"Yeah, we have," he put his arm around her pulling her close to him. "Look at this," he reached over and grabbed a photo album that was open beside him. "Look how beautiful she was."

"Oh God, I know! – look at her – that little hat – remember how she never wanted to take it off?"

"It's almost hard to remember her being so little," he ran his finger over the picture. "Ah, shit, El. Sometimes I feel like I screwed up so bad." He rubbed his hand over his face. "I hated not being there. You know, sometimes I'd drive by your apartment in the evening. It made me feel better . . . you know . . . just seeing your lights on."

Ellie felt like she couldn't breathe for a moment. "Don't, Jake – don't do this. We both screwed up." She ran her hand down his cheek. "Maybe if I hadn't been so stubborn . . . I just thought I was so right and that someday you'd see it." She leaned her head against his arm.

"I hated that son-of-a-bitch! I hated that he was with you and I wasn't."

"Ah Jake, I know." She tightened her arms around him. "But there is one thing I can tell you that might help. Just so you know, Jenna never did warm up to Edgar. He was always good with her – I'd never have stayed with him if he hadn't been – but all she wanted was to be with you."

"Yeah?"

"Of course! She lived for her times with you."

"I like that," A smile began moving over his face as he thought about this. He leaned his head back and laced his fingers through hers. "After I got over things a bit – knowing that you were with him, I mean – it got a little easier. If it couldn't be me, it felt good to know someone was looking out for the two of you, even if it had to be that stupid prick."

"Is this personal, or would anyone have been a stupid prick?"

"Absolutely! Anybody but me? A total prick!"

She was laughing at him and bit at his ear making him shiver. "Believe it or not, honey, you and I did okay – better than okay. Jenna is wonderful – you know that. Sometimes I don't know how, but she is."

"Dumb luck?"

"Partly, I guess," Ellie took his face in her hands. "She always knew how much she was loved. I think that was the big thing. You weren't always there," she stopped. "Now don't you make fun of me . . ."

"What?"

"Well, she always knew that your heart was there, okay? I know it sounds corny, but I know she felt that way."

He took a quick breath, and then he was smiling. The expression on his face was relieved and grateful. "That's not corny, Sugar. That's the best thing you could have ever told me about Jenna." He took another breath, a deep breath this time, and let it out slowly. Ellie could feel his body begin to relax. "Ah, babe, you always know exactly the right thing to say." He pulled her into his lap and pulled her legs around him. He looped her hair around his hand. It was crazy how much he loved the feel of her hair.

"Did you really drive by the apartment – checking on us?"

"Hell, yes!" he was laughing again. "For a while there I was a regular stalker."

"Oh God, that is so sweet and so crazy." She put her arms around his neck, "Take me to bed, Jakey – I'm tired of talking."

Hazel Young

Chapter sixty-three

Jake's appointment fell on a Monday, so as impractical as the idea had sounded at first, they planned a dinner party for the Sunday before. Jake had first suggested this on the night they had returned from the lake, catching Ellie off guard. She had not known how to respond when he had first brought it up.

"Monday could be pretty stressful, sweetie. Are you sure you want to do this?" They had been propped up in bed watching TV, sharing a beer and the last of the cashews Ellie had brought from her apartment. Ellie flipped off the remote and tucked herself up as close as she could get to Jake. He slid his arm under her shoulders, his hand gently stroking her arm. He could never get over the sweet softness of her skin.

"Yes," his voice was firm. "As of right now we don't know anything. If the word is good, our friends will just write it off as another good party. If the word is not good, none of them will ever look at me the same way again." Ellie tried to object, but Jake stopped her by putting a finger over her lips, "Don't, Sugar, you know it's true. Just in case, I want one more night with them without a cloud hanging over me."

She slipped her leg over him, pulling herself even closer to him, and buried her face in his neck. She lay there breathing in his warm soapy smell, begging a God she doubted she still believed in to take this nightmare away from them. Her mouth found his, and she licked the salty cashew taste from his lips. There were never enough words to tell him how much she loved him.

"I don't know how to say it more. You know, Jakey, don't you?" she whispered.

"I know, baby. It's okay, I know." He dried her face with his hand and pushed her hair back with his fingers, then pushed himself on top of her. Her hands cupped his face, and she forced herself to smile.

"Okay, my love, you're calling the shots here. If it's a party you want, then you are going to get one dandy party." She pulled his face down to hers. "And once again you're in luck, Sheriff, because I just happen to be the Queen of party organizers."

"That's my girl," Jake was grinning, looking relieved. Ellie turned her head away – this grin of his sometimes tore her heart wide open.

The plans for the party began the next morning with Ellie on her laptop firing off emails to everyone they were inviting, informing them of time and date, no blue jeans allowed – wear your fancy duds, and come prepared to sing or dance or play some kind of a musical instrument. As Ellie had promised, this was not going to be your average run-of-the-mill dinner party.

As the days went by they picked up everything they needed for the party, which proved to be a wonderful diversion, giving them something to look forward to. Jake immediately announced that this would be the night to serve his 'incredibly amazing, famous salmon' – his friends had christened it that because it was the only 'fit for company' thing he had ever learned to cook; they loved it, and he felt obligated to produce it at least once a year in order to repay them for the many meals to which he wrangled invitations during the rest of the year. Ellie found herself completely caught up in the dinner menu, suggesting foods that Jake had never heard of – 'Couscous? Really? Are you sure you're supposed to put that in your mouth? – Cucumbers and pears? Who dreamed that one up?' – and the menu grew until it became ridiculous, and Jake yelled that she had to stop, the table wasn't big enough to hold anything more.

"Wait! No! Dessert – we need dessert," Ellie wasn't ready to stop yet, and they agreed on a choice between a lime sherbet and a dark and decadent chocolate cake from the bakery next to Rosa's.

"If they have any sense they'll go with the sherbet," Ellie felt certain about this. "It's perfect after a meal that leaves you so stuffed you can't move."

"Yeah," said Jake, "the women will. The men? Don't count on it."

CHAPTER SIXTY-FOUR

Jake woke to the sound of rain pounding against the windows but didn't make any attempt to get out of bed. Today would be busy as the dinner party was on for tonight. He was looking forward to seeing everyone, but right now he wanted some quiet time to think. He pushed another pillow under his head, worked his body into a comfortable spot and laid back, his arms behind his head, letting his mind travel back to the rainy day he and Ellie had spent in at the lake. He remembered the sound of rain on the metal roof, the warmth of the cabin and the crackling, snapping sound of wood burning in the ancient wood stove. They had both been reading, Jake sitting on the sagging sofa, his feet propped up on an old kitchen chair, Ellie lying with her head in his lap. He remembered how she had turned her book over on her belly, saving her place, and looked up at him. "You're the magic in Whiskey Lake," she had said, smiling that smile he had fallen in love with the first time he had laid eyes on her on the flight from Boston. "Without you, it's just another wonderful lake. You make it magical." She had slipped her soft hand up under his T-shirt, slowly rubbing his chest. They had looked at each other, both feeling warm, lazy and turned on. "Just let me finish this chapter," she had said. He hadn't, but then she hadn't really wanted him to.

Jake turned on his side, watching Ellie gently breathing. What a crazy ride this month had been. He remembered the motorcycle that had hit him; the driver was just a kid really. At the hospital the next day the kid had apologized over and over again, saying how sorry he was; he just hadn't seen him. Jake grinned into his pillow. He should be down on his knees thanking that kid for running him down. If it hadn't been for him, Ellie wouldn't be in his life today; she wouldn't be in his bed – that much was certain. He looked at her face. Her thick hair had fallen over one eye, and he wanted to tuck it behind her ear the way she would have done. Fuck, he loved this woman. He didn't want to wake her, but he couldn't keep himself from reaching over and gently running his hand down her side, along the dip of her waist, over the rise of her hip.

"Jake, can you see that my eyes are still closed?" She didn't look up from her pillow but took a sleepy swat at his arm.

"Yep, and you're talking in your sleep. Don't pay any attention to me. I'll try to keep myself busy."

"Oh, you idiot, come here." Ellie rolled onto her back and stretched an arm toward him. Her arm reached under his shoulder, nudging and pulling him on top of her. They lay like this, looking at each other. She loved the feel of him: the tightness of his belly, his hands in her hair. She loved the feel of his mouth on hers, his tongue on her breasts. Gently his hands pushed her arms above her head, and one hand pinned them there while the other slowly moved over her body, down and down, finding her, staying there, slow, teasing, until at last she moaned and cried out his name. Then he was inside her, riding the wave until it crested and then collapsed beside her, groaning, "Ellie, Ellie…"

I love you, I love you, I love you… Their voices were almost drowned out by the slashing sound of rain hitting the windows.

CHAPTER SIXTY-FIVE

So," Jake was towelling off after his shower, "are you wearing your silver bracelet tonight? You know. The one you were wearing the night we met at Rosa's?"

"My charm bracelet?" asked Ellie.

"Yeah, I guess so."

Ellie paused to think and then nodded, saying yes she probably would be, and asked why he wanted to know.

Jake pulled on his jeans and jumped over to his dresser, rummaging around in his top drawer until he found what he was after.

He came toward her with his hands behind his back. "Pick a hand," he demanded, his smile playing over his face. "No, I can't wait. Here." He held up a small blue box tied with silver ribbon.

"Jake, what is this?" She oohed and aahed, turning the box this way and that, and then began carefully trying to untie the ribbon. "This is just way too pretty to rip off," she said as she slowly began to unravel the silver knot.

"Oh for Christ's sake." Jake grabbed the box from her and tore the ribbon off. "There," he gave it back to her, "now open it, woman."

Ellie screwed up her nose at his impatience but smiled at him and lifted the lid. "Oh, Jakey." Nesting inside the

velvet-lined box was a tiny silver compass for her bracelet. She picked it up, marvelling at its detail.

"It's so you'll never lose me again, Ellie." She could hear his voice growing hoarse. "I couldn't stand it if I lost you again."

"Never," whispered Ellie as she put her arms around his neck, her face nuzzling his freshly shaven cheek. Never, never.

CHLOE

CHAPTER SIXTY-SIX

Ellie stood in the middle of the living room in her
bathrobe, surveying the apartment, checking every
detail. She had just showered and her skin smelled of the
sweet, spicy lotion that Jake loved. Her hair was pulled
back into a twist but a few curls had escaped the silver
combs that were holding it in place and twisted loosely
down the back of her neck. Jake moved behind her, sliding
his arms around her. "You smell like cinnamon," he said,
kissing the nape of her neck. "We could turn out the lights
and pretend we're not home."

"Not a chance, cowboy," she hugged his arms closer to
her. "Just look at this beautiful room – it has party written
all over it." She stepped away from him and threw out her
arms, turning in a slow circle.

She had placed clusters of white candles everywhere.
Light from crystal votives flickered on the bookshelves
and on the dining room table. White candles, all different
heights and sizes, stood in crystal candlesticks on the coffee
table's marble tiles. The lights were low, the candles casting
shadows on the walls. The table was set for company: the
new, white dishes on lace place mats, the crystal sparkling,
and the silver, that had once belonged to her grandmother
glowing in the candle light. She had made a trip back to

her apartment to pick up the fine old silver and spent hours polishing it, but it had been worth it. Outside, Jake had once again laced tiny white lights through the balcony railings. Through the dining room windows Ellie could see the lights reflecting in the puddles that were pooling on the balcony, but the soft lighting in the room shut out the damp and filled the apartment with a sense of warmth; welcome relief from the cold September rain that had been pelting down on the city for the entire day.

"I love it, it's wonderful." She turned on tiptoe and slid her arms around Jake's neck, kissing his cheek.

"Now, I just have to notify our local Fire Station to be on standby, and this party can begin." He had been teasing her about the candles all evening.

"Will you quit? Believe it or not, we're all adults. I think we can handle a few candles."

"Adults?" exclaimed Jake. "This bunch of hooligans? You do realize that they're all going to come stomping in here and completely destroy all your hard work, don't you?" He wrapped his arms around her waist picking her up and kissing her. "Now go get dressed. They'll be here before we know it."

"You're right, you put on some music. I'll be ready in two shakes."

The CD racks were crammed with the music Jake loved. He recalled how totally pissed off he had been when tapes became obsolete, and he'd had to replace all of them. It had taken him a while to give in, but even he finally had to agree that CDs produced a better sound, just as everyone had insisted they would. God, he hated to admit he was wrong. He wondered what was coming next – everything seemed to be changing so quickly. Well, his taste in music hadn't changed much. He picked out some blues, some country, some Latin, sixties, seventies, and eighties favourites – but no disco. In Jake's opinion, disco had been almost as bad as rap was right now. He didn't dislike all of today's music, but there was something about rap that made him want to start throwing things or banging his head against a wall. He always maintained that if he were a secret enemy agent, an hour in a locked room with rap music blaring would have him spilling his guts. A generational thing, he decided, remembering his father yelling up from the living room couch, "Turn that damned fool record player off before I come up there and turn it off for you." He figured he and his dad would be on the same page when it came to rap.

He picked out a mix that he thought would keep everyone happy, turned the stereo down low and then glanced at his watch. Shit, he'd better hustle, he still had to get changed. He was fairly sure Ellie would be okay with what he was planning to wear. Chloe was seldom wrong.

Jake changed and checked himself out in the mirror. Not bad, he decided, and wandered back out to the living room just as Ellie reappeared at the bedroom door. She took his breath away. She was always doing that – it was a wonder he could breathe at all. She was wearing something sexy, and low-cut and blue – a blue that shot off sparks in the candle light. She had on killer heels and silver jewellery. Her charm bracelet, now holding Jake's tiny compass, jingled when she moved.

"I love it, Jake," she held up her wrist.

Jake gave out a low whistle. "Back in the bedroom," he yelled. "You're way too gorgeous to be out on the loose." His long legs quickly took him across the room, and he tried to put his arms around her, but she pushed him away.

"Just one minute, you." Her eyes travelled over him. "Who are you?" He must have changed in the spare room, she decided, because he looked entirely different than he had half an hour earlier. Jake, who had always claimed he knew nothing about clothing that didn't involve jeans and a T-shirt, now looked like something from a fashion magazine. His jeans and T-shirt had been replaced with black pants and a light grey shirt with the cuffs turned up the way she loved. A pin striped grey vest, unbuttoned, and a loosely knotted blue tie left her staring at him, speechless.

"Where did you get this outfit, for crying out loud? Do you have another woman who dresses you, locked away in a closet somewhere?" Ellie had found her voice and was running her hands over him, turning him around, loving the way he looked.

"Well, yeah, maybe in a way I do – you haven't met Chloe yet," Jake's face looked strangely smug as he sat her down on the arm of the sofa.

"Chloe? You've never mentioned a Chloe! Where the hell did Chloe come from?" Ellie was looking a little agitated.

"Calm down, girl, it's nothing like that," Jake had his hands on her shoulders. "She's my partner Hank's wife. Apparently she was a model at one time – now she owns a personal shopping service. Anyway, when I first met her she completely freaked out over my normal everyday jeans and T-shirt uniform – said I was making the business look bad." Jake rubbed his hand over his hair and laughed, "I probably was – I just never noticed."

Suddenly, Ellie wasn't too sure how she felt about this. "Is this, Chloe, still drop-dead, modelishy-gorgeous?" she asked, simultaneously feeling a twinge of jealousy and annoyance at herself for feeling it. Did you ever actually grow up, she wondered? And really – modelishy?

"Yeah, I guess she is – if you like that tall, skinny, hungry look. Honestly, she looks like she's never eaten anything more than a head of lettuce in her whole life. And she's mean – she scares the pants off me."

"She scares you!" Ellie let herself collapse dramatically onto the couch, the back of her wrist against her forehead.

Jake straightened her around and sat down beside her. "Well, she's not really mean – just sarcastic, in that British way. Did I mention that she's British?"

Ellie shook her head, not knowing what he was going to say next.

"Anyway, long story short: one night over dinner, and way too much wine – okay, so we were all pretty shit-faced – I agreed to let her take me shopping, and we've done it – shop, I mean – twice a year ever since."

"And that's okay with you?"

"You betcha! Love it! The only decision I ever have to make is, briefs or boxers. She does absolutely everything else, right down to co-ordinating my socks and shoes." Jake was sitting back grinning. "Chloe is the only person who has ever called me Jakob in my entire life – not even my mother ever called me that." He went into a hugely exaggerated imitation of Chloe's British accent: "Really, Jakob, you MUST stay away from the brown family. It's just HORRIFYING what the colour brown does to you – it makes you look, FRIGHTFULLY, like a baked potato!" Ellie was curled up against his shoulder, unable to stop laughing. "I didn't even know that colours had families," said Jake, shaking his head. "How do you get to be my age and not know a thing like that?"

"Oh, God, the things you can learn – just sitting in your living room waiting for your dinner guests to arrive," Ellie was dabbing carefully at her eyes. "Look at me – your Chloe has ruined my make-up."

"She's not my Chloe, she's Hank's Chloe, and they're coming tonight so you'll get to meet her royal-self in the flesh. All kidding aside, El, you'll probably love her. I should never have said she was mean – razor sharp would have been a better way to put it."

Jake stopped speaking, listening to the stereo playing in the background. "Listen, babe ... they've lost that lovin' feeling, again." He stood up pulling her up off the couch and wrapped his arm around her waist. Ellie shifted herself into the familiar comfort of his chest, letting the music by the Righteous Brothers move them through the apartment. This song was so filled with memories. She pulled herself even closer to Jake, feeling as if she were floating. When they had first begun seeing each other, this song had always been playing somewhere in the background. For a second she was twenty-two again; she and Jake had known each other for less than a month and were at a New Year's Eve party – it would be 1970 in another half hour with all the horns, and whistles and fireworks that a new year brings, but for the moment the party was relatively subdued and the DJ had just slipped this record onto the turn table.

"Dance with me, babe," Jake had said, pulling her into his arms. It was the first time they had ever danced together to this particular song, and it was the first time Jake had ever called her babe. Ellie was well aware that feminist rhetoric at the time disapproved of the term, but when Jake said it she couldn't begin to remember why that was.

'Dance with me babe,' and she had slipped into his arms, happier than she could ever remember being, and she knew at that exact moment, that she was in love with this sweet, funny guy who could make her laugh at the drop of a hat, and reduced her to a puddle of candle wax just by holding her hand. She wouldn't admit it out loud for months, not even to Maggie, but at eleven thirty on December thirty-first, 1969, she knew that she wanted to spend the rest of her life with this lovely man. Ellie felt a sensation like champagne bubbles in her chest as she recalled the moment so clearly. How did music have the power to do this – erase years and take you back like this, she wondered? She tightened her arm around Jake's shoulder and snuggled into his neck.

"Mmmm, your aftershave is giving me goose bumps," she said in his ear.

"You don't want to hear what your dress is giving me," said Jake. "In fact, if these yahoos don't show up in about five minutes, you may not be wearing a dress at all."

"Wonderful," said Ellie. "An oldster's orgy! I'm sure Jenna will be particularly pleased."

"Oldsters, my arse! Shut up and dance with me, smart-ass." He tightened his arm around her waist and deftly manoeuvred them around the dinner table.

GOODNIGHT GRACIE.

CHAPTER SIXTY-SEVEN

Everyone turned up: Jenna and Ron, Bobby and
Claire, Gopher and Shelly, Mickey and Olivia, Red
and Glenys, and, much to Ellie's delight, the mysterious
Chloe and her husband Hank – Henry, as she referred to
him. They trooped in with dripping raincoats and umbrel-
las, Bobby with his guitar. The laughter started the minute
the first guest entered the room and didn't stop till the last
cab arrived to ferry them all safely home.

They all agreed: the apartment looked fabulous; everyone looked magnificent, all dressed in their finest; the food
was divine; the wine absolutely perfect. It was a night for
hyperbole, a night when everyone was out to have a sensa-
tional time and everything meshed like magic.

After Jake's salmon, which had now become, Jake's
'Incredibly Amazing, World Famous Salmon', and every
scrap of the main course was only a happy memory, the
dishes were cleared away and more wine was poured.
Bowls of nuts and platters of fruits and cheeses were
spread across the table, and the entertainment began. They
laughed and cheered and were occasionally almost brought
to tears as when Mickey's Olivia stood, at first a little self-
consciously and then losing herself in the music, forgetting
herself. She began the first line of that wonderful old song

they were all so familiar with and held everyone mesmerized, taking them on a trip down the yellow brick road, her strong, clear voice swooping and soaring, filling the room. When she finished, the entire table sat totally silent for a few seconds not quite believing what they had just heard – then they were on their feet clapping and whistling as Mickey proudly held her chair as she sat back down. "She sings lead soprano with a choir here in the city," Mickey proudly explained. "You'll have to come and see them sometime."

Ellie leaned across the corner of the table, "I think our boy really is growing up," she whispered in Jake's ear. Jake was shaking his head, still not quite believing it.

Gopher and Mickey did a hilarious, "Who's on First", after which Jake proclaimed, "I've been watching you guys do that routine for thirty years, and every time you do it, it gets better."

Shelly sang a funny little song from another era that her mother had sung to her when she was small. It was a tale about a Sergeant Major kissing his sweetheart under a tree, scandalous at the time, and it left everyone recalling and retelling their own childhood memories. "Oh my God, your father didn't really tell you that!" – and explosions of laughter.

Jake looked over at Bobby and began to laugh, "Then there was the time that Bobby was convinced that Dad was going straight to Hell because he had grabbed our mother's sanctified bottom."

"Oh, you poor baby," all of the women were hushing, and "aahing" and telling Bobby how sweet he was, and the men were tipping back in their chairs, their hands pounding drum rolls on the table.

"Please tell me you straightened him out about this," said Ellie. "I can't believe I've never heard this story."

JAKE & ELLIE

"Hell no, I just let him believe it," said Jake as he slapped his hand on the table. "I told him that he'd be in the same boat if he ever tried it with a girl. Okay, okay," he held up a hand, "in Bob's defence you can't really blame him – he was only about eight years old and holier than the Baby Jesus, himself – but man, it was funny!"

Bobby balled up his napkin and threw it at Jake. "And that, ladies and gentlemen, is why, thanks to my jackass of a brother, my wife of twenty years has never had her beautiful ass pinched – I continue to live in a state of constant terror over the fate of my immortal soul!"

"Here's to guilt," said Mickey, raising his glass. "If we didn't have Catholic guilt, and Jewish guilt, we wouldn't have any stories to tell at all." They all agreed, happily drinking to this, and for the next little while the stories continued to flow.

A bottle of wine later Jake tapped his fork against his wine glass and loudly cleared his throat. "Show time, folks!" he said, throwing out his arms, "and I think I'm up." He pushed back his chair pulling his harmonica from his pocket, but before he could begin Gopher jumped up on his chair, and sounding exactly like the French Canadian CBC announcer after an NHL game, proclaimed loudly, "And now Mesdames et Messieurs, le troisième étoile, DA TERD STAR . . . JAKE MADISON!!" and the whole table clapped and roared, sounding like the crowd at a game. Jake turned his back on them, covering his head with his arms, laughing till he seemed ready to fall over. And then he and Gopher were hanging on to each other, slapping each other on the back. When things calmed down Jake put his harmonica to his mouth. After a few false starts caused by the laughter that continued to break out of him, one of the bluesy tunes he had played for Ellie that night on the dock began to move slowly through the room . . . a sultry torch singer

273

running her seductive fingers over everyone seated at the table. Ellie felt a sweet shiver running through her as she remembered that evening at the lake. When he finished, the table applauded wildly, and Jake profusely thanked all of the wine that had been drunk. Ellie slipped out of her chair and hugged him, kissing him loudly, leaving lipstick marks on his cheek.

"I can't believe that all it took was a dinner party to get me da terd star," said Jake, bowing one last time to his still applauding dinner guests, bringing on a round of boos and hisses.

Chloe stood and slunk to the head of the table with that slinky model's walk that she still maintained and performed a song so bawdy even Gopher looked shocked. As she finished, they all solemnly swore that none of them would ever throw another party without inviting her – with or without Hank.

And so it went. Bobby tuned his guitar, and far better than Ellie would ever have imagined, gently plucked the strings, coaxing from it the song, 'Pussy willows, Cat-tails', – that Lightfoot melody so wistful it always touched off something deep inside of her, leaving her longing for some intangible thing. She glanced over at Claire and knew from the far-off expression on her face that she was feeling the same way. Jake accompanied Bobby, blowing softly into his harmonica. After they finished, the brothers abruptly changed gears and with an exuberant 1-2-3 went into a boisterous version of 'The Hockey Song', maybe the high-light of the evening. Stompin' Tom would have been proud.

It continued on until everyone had done their piece, everyone exclaiming over how well they all had done. Then suddenly Jake was on his feet yelling, "Ellie, you little minx. It's your turn."

Ellie covered her face, peering out from between her fingers, and then stood up. "Okay, here goes. No, wait, I need a prop," she yelped, as she dashed for the bedroom, returning in seconds cinching a belt around her waist and then rolled the waist of her dress around it until her skirt reached mini length. "This one's for you, Sweetie-pie," she said, pointing at Jenna, and then she twisted a loose curl of hair around her finger and with a tap dancer's flourish sailed into her version of Shirley Temple, singing about ships and lollipops in the little entertainer's oddly deep voice. She pranced and pouted, dipping and bobbing as she tapped her way around the living room, finally finishing it off with her index finger deeply imbedded in an imaginary Shirley Temple dimple and a low sweeping curtsey. She brought down the house; Jake could not stop laughing.

"Mamma!" Jenna was on her feet, clapping, "I haven't seen that in years." Then, trying to explain, "Mom and I used to watch old Shirley Temple movies when I was little, and we'd try to imitate her." And then they were both up tapping, doubled over laughing until Jenna yelled, "Stop, stop! This pregnant lady is going to pee her pants!" and everyone attempted to settle down.

They all began drifting off into little groups, loving the fun the evening had brought with it, smiling at each other across the room - old friends who hadn't been together in far too long and new friends feeling welcome and connected.

Jake stood up and moved over to the stereo, turning it up just as the opening chords of Roy Orbison's "Pretty Woman" came hammering out of the speakers. "Ellie, come dance with me." He was yelling at her from across the room. "This is Roy's revenge - it may be the only song where he ever gets the girl." Ellie stood up, flinging out her arms, and Jake crossed the room, threw his arms around her and danced her through the crowded apartment. Almost everyone in the room had grown up with this song, its lyrics and pounding guitar riffs virtually winding their way throughout the DNA of an entire generation, and they sang, and stomped, and clapped until the light fixture above the table vibrated along with them.

"Someone in the building is going to call the police," Ellie screamed at Jake over the noise.

"I told you they were a bunch of hooligans," he yelled back as he pulled her closer, and she realized she really didn't care if the police did turn up at their door.

The song reached the climactic moment in its storyline when the question loomed as to whether or not the girl would turn around. Jake was holding Ellie's hands, backing away from her, moving to the repeating guitars – his knees easy, his eyes on her face. An image crept into Ellie's mind of all the times she had seen him on the ice – skating backwards with no obvious effort, loose, only his mind seeming to move his body, his eyes never leaving the player he was watching. She suddenly realized how all the difficulties had blurred the memory of how much she had loved watching him move on the ice. "They're so incredibly fast – and, I guess, graceful at the same time," she had once said to Maggie. "Sometimes it's almost like ballet – ballet on Speed." She had been joking but not completely.

But, then, the music blaring from the speakers brought her back to the present as those lines that no one expected to hear coming from a Roy Orbison song were wailing out again, thirty-five years after everyone had first heard them... She was walking back to him ... Roy was actually going to get the girl ... Pretty woman ... and Jake grabbed Ellie and spun her around until they fell backwards into a chair.

"Oh, ya gotta love a happy ending," Jake was laughing, leaning back in the chair, his arms wrapped tightly around her. "It's an oldie, but this one's ours, Sugar," he said in her ear as she leaned back against him.

As the song ended, the noise in the room became overwhelming. Ellie watched as Jake and Bobby exchanged glances across the room. They were shaking their heads and shrugging, loving this, and then Bobby gave a shrill whistle calling a time-out before they were all evicted from the building. The party slowly began to quiet down, still erupting every once in a while in residual laughter. Ellie and Jake eased themselves out of the chair they had collapsed into and slipped into the kitchen, returning shortly with coffee and dessert. They discovered that they had both been wrong; everyone opted for cake. The mood was too high, everyone feeling a little too good to let a few calories spoil the evening.

Eventually people began to reluctantly gather their things together. Cabs were called, thanks said, hugs and kisses exchanged and promises made to get together again soon. Couples lingered at the door, not wanting the warmth and closeness of the evening to come to an end. It was after two when the door finally closed for the last time, and Ellie and Jake dropped down onto the sofa.

"Thanks, babe," Jake's voice was easy sounding, light. "That was exactly what I wanted."

They crawled into bed too tired for much more than a good night kiss, and both had almost drifted off to sleep when Ellie sat bolt upright. "Jake," she hissed, "do you realize that Gopher's real name is Malcolm?"

Jake threw a pillow at her head, "Yes, you screwball, but only his mother and Shelly are allowed to call him that." He leaned over and kissed her again, "Say goodnight, Gracie."

THE APPOINTMENT

CHAPTER SIXTY-EIGHT

The alarm clock on the dresser read six thirty-two when Ellie opened her eyes later that morning. Her first thoughts were of last night's party: what a good time it had been, how much she had loved seeing everyone again. The laughter had been so contagious. She didn't remember the last time she had felt so relaxed and connected to a group of people. She turned her head to look at Jake, and instantly, like a light being switched off, the magician of some black art snapped his fingers, and she felt the fog that had filled her head at the lake begin to roll in again. Something cold and heavy began growing in the pit of her belly as she realized what today was. So this was it: it was actually here. This was the day they had been putting up barricades against, trying to pretend would never really arrive. Her finger began worrying the small furrow between her eyebrows, and she felt the sting of tears behind her eyes. Time. Fucking, goddamned, son of a bitching time. Where had this month gone?

Ellie pushed her covers off and quietly slipped out of bed. If she stayed here she knew she would never be able to hold it together. The fear of what might be coming today was filling her entire body, and she knew for Jake's sake she was going to have to man up, put her game face on,

whatever expression he would use. Today was going to take more courage than she thought she had. She remembered being in labour with Jenna, screaming at Jake that she had to stop, she couldn't take it anymore, and Jake rubbing her back, or letting her fingernails rip into his hands, saying over and over, "You have to, Ellie. There's no stopping now, you just have to do it. I'm here, baby. I'm right here."

They had just begun to let fathers into the delivery room back then, and Ellie remembered how grateful she had felt knowing Jake was going to be with her, not that he would have known it at the time. As the difficult labour progressed, the pain found her cursing at him, screaming at him that she hated him, that he was never getting near her again. But then at the end of it all there had been Jenna, beautiful, perfect Jenna. Ellie recalled the look on Jake's face the first time he had held Jenna, how he had whispered to her so softly, promising to always be there for her. He had said the same things to Ellie after the nurse had taken Jenna away to the nursery. He had held her hands and kissed her sweat-soaked hair, telling her how beautiful she was, how proud he was of her, how much he loved her and how he would always be there for her.

She had begun to reach for her robe on the hook on the back of the bedroom door but stopped, leaning her head against the wall.

Oh, Jakey, no. Please, God, no, not now.

She had to get out of here before the screaming in her head became loud and vocal. Today wasn't about her or whatever she might be feeling. At least for today she had to keep all of this wrapped up tightly inside herself – today was about getting Jake through whatever was coming. Ellie pushed her arms into her robe and moved silently out of the bedroom and into the kitchen.

Oh Lord, the kitchen was still such a mess. Methodically, moving as quietly as she could, she began removing dishes from the counters, filling the dishwasher. She rinsed out the coffee pot and started a new pot, breathing in the aroma of freshly brewed coffee as it filled the room and wondered, as she always did, how anything that smelled this good could taste so bitter. The coffee maker gave its last gurgling sigh and she poured herself a mug, stirring in teaspoons of sugar. She wasn't hungry yet, so she picked up her mug and stepped over to the low windows in the dining room, settling into the cushions on the window seat. They had built this window seat the second year they had been married, Ellie remembered. She remembered the smell of sawdust and saw herself sitting at her sewing machine sewing the cushion covers.

In the winter, in their first years in the apartment, there had been a skating rink across the street – it was a parking lot now. The winter she was pregnant with Jenna she would often curl up here at night, a quilt pulled over her. She loved to watch the experienced skaters glide across the ice, all confidence and grace, and the newcomers, shuffling with great determination from one end of the rink to the other, falling down and picking themselves up, brushing snow from their backsides and dusting off their knees. She would cheer them on, mentally willing them to make it down the rink without a fall. Jake would often go out on the ice after everyone had left for home. He would race around the perimeter of the rink, backward and forward, stopping in that instant, shocking way that he did, sending ice shavings flying in front of him. He would perform for her, clowning and doing pratfalls, his arms waving wildly in the air, pretending to stumble and then catching himself. He would be laughing – she could see his laughter frozen in the air. When he would return to the apartment she would pull him under the quilt with her and rub his icy hands and press her face to his cold cheeks.

Somehow, it all seemed like only yesterday.

Ellie could see the light from the sun beginning to appear on the horizon – the rain had finally stopped during the night. She pushed a window open a crack and let her senses fill with the cool, rain-washed smell of the city. She slid her knees up to her chin and hugged her legs close to her, watching as the sky took on shades of pink and gold. The bedroom door creaked as it opened, and she looked over to see Jake standing in the doorway. He was wearing sweats and an old black T shirt; he was watching her, a smile working on the corners of his mouth.

"I always loved the way you looked sitting there," he said. Then he laughed, "Hell, I always loved the way you looked sitting anywhere."

Ellie was so happy to hear him laugh she felt as if her heart might crack wide open. "Hi, sweetie," she smiled and wiggled her fingers at him, "there's fresh coffee if you want some."

"Not right yet," he walked over to the window seat and pushed himself into place behind her, pulling her close to him, his legs around her. "Did I tell you how funny your Shirley Temple was?"

"Yes," Ellie laughed. "Have I ever told you how much I love dancing with you?"

"Yeah, but you can keep telling me." She could feel him smiling into her hair. "I love you Ellie – bigger than the sky – that's what my mom always used to say."

"I love you so much Jakey, more than all the words in all the books in all the world. That's from a Hellman play, I think . . . I'm not sure . . . I forget." It bothered her that she wasn't certain. She pressed her face against his arm.

"It's alright, babe. Let's just get through today, okay?"

"Okay." Ellie focused on breathing – shallow breaths, in and out through her nose.

DIAGNOSIS

CHAPTER SIXTY-NINE

They had some time to kill as their appointment wasn't until one, so they filled in the morning as best they could. Jake went for a run while Ellie showered and did her hair. Jake came home and showered, and they finished cleaning the kitchen, setting the apartment back in order. They made themselves some toast and marmalade and mugs of tea.

"I hate marmalade," Jake said, picking a piece of orange rind off his toast. "I've never been able to make up my mind about it, but as of right now I officially hate marmalade."

"Good to know," said Ellie.

"I was parked in front of Rosa's, Ellie"

"What do you mean?" She put her mug of tea down and waited for him to explain.

"A few months ago – before we saw Philips. I never told you about it – I didn't want to think about it." He paused, rubbing his forehead. "I was driving home from work. I was supposed to meet Mickey, and I thought that somehow I had gotten lost . . . but I hadn't . . . I was right there in front of Rosa's, looking at the restaurant, but nothing looked familiar – it was so weird, like something from *The Twilight Zone.* I was right there, El, and for what felt like forever I didn't have a clue where I was."

"Oh baby," Ellie pulled herself into his lap and put her arms around him, holding him as tightly as she could.

They left the apartment at noon, pulling into the parking lot where Dr. Philips had his office at twenty to one. Jake turned off the engine – "Zero hour," he said. "Let's do this thing." They were ushered into the office as soon as they arrived and sat in two of the four chairs that were placed around a coffee table in the centre of Greg's office. There was no intimidating desk, just a table with a computer that sat in front of a window overlooking a busy street.

At exactly one, Greg entered the room. They all smiled and shook hands. This is barbaric, thought Ellie; I want to rip this man's eyes out. She grabbed Jake's hand. Greg didn't keep them waiting; he understood how stressful this was for them. He looked from Jake to Ellie with such a flood of empathy in his eyes that Ellie heard herself uttering a low moan, and then Greg took a deep breath and began.

He was so sorry he couldn't give them the news they needed to hear. He had put Jake through every possible test, and the results all pointed to the same conclusion. Jake was in the very early stages of a form of dementia. He gave them all the technical terms and details, but he knew it was impossible for them to absorb these details right now. He was so sorry. There were drugs that Jake could take that might help delay the disease for a while, but there was no cure.

"The concussions . . ." said Ellie.

Greg looked at her, his eyes sad, and gave the smallest shrug. "The cause of dementia is very hard to prove, but we are beginning to see a higher percentage of it in athletes who have played contact sports," he stopped and grimaced slightly, "and even though there are still no absolute connections, in my personal opinion I don't doubt it for a minute."

Jake sat in his chair, unmoving. He looked over at Ellie and then back at Philips. He made an odd motion with his hands and then moved one hand to his head, rubbing his hair, and Ellie felt scalding tears running down her cheeks. This funny, familiar motion had broken her. This doctor, this so-called healer, had just ripped out her heart.

"How long?" asked Jake.

"I think you can count on two or possibly three good years before the disease really starts taking hold," said Greg. "Nothing's written in stone. It could be longer." Ellie knew that he was trying to give them hope, and hated him for it.

Greg wrote out a prescription for a sedative, and told them he would like to see them again in two weeks when they'd had time to digest things. He gave them an email address where he could be reached. He said again how sorry he was.

Jake looked at Greg. How could this person be telling him this? – This person who didn't even look old enough to vote. He felt his hand curling into a fist, and he frantically looked at Ellie. Her eyes were as wide-open as Jake had ever seen them. His mind flashed back to a word test he had been given at the beginning of the month:

"Now, quickly, Mr. Madison – can you name your favourite shade of blue?"

"The colour of Ellie's eyes," he had answered. It wasn't a question he even had to think about.

Now he kept her eyes locked in his until he felt his fist begin to relax. He looked over at Greg; he knew Greg had seen his fist clench. "I'm sorry," he said. "I know this can't be easy for you either." And then Jake held out his hand to Ellie and without another word they left the office.

SHOCK

Chapter seventy

Jake was walking so quickly Ellie almost had to run to keep up. "Jake, honey, wait. Slow down a little."

"I have to get away from here," his voice was ragged.

"The car's just over here."

Jake was in the car with the motor running minutes before Ellie was able to get to the door. He pushed her door open from the driver's seat. "Get in," he said, not meeting her eyes.

He paid the parking attendant, not waiting for his change, and the car leapt out of the lot onto the street. Jake drove in silence, his face stony. They reached the river quickly, and he drove toward a park that he knew was down this way. When it appeared the park was stark and naked, yesterday's heavy downpour having stripped much of the colour from the trees. The late September sun felt weak and watery as if it too had been washed out by the rain. The thought that overnight the world had become a grainy black and white photograph seeped unwelcome into Ellie's brain.

Jake slammed on the brakes, parking the car half in a parking spot. He lowered the windows, letting the cold air fill the front seat. Ellie watched as his head slowly dropped onto the steering wheel, and then finally he was crying,

not trying to hold anything back, horrible primal sounds escaping from his chest. She was out of her seat belt and beside him within seconds, cursing the console, half kneeling on his seat, trying to hold him, telling him how much she loved him. She stroked his head and his back, "It's going to be okay Jakey, it's going to be okay, we'll make it okay," she kept repeating, knowing that everything she was saying was sliding into a deep, bottomless hole.

His ragged crying finally stopped, his breathing became more regular, and he raised his head and leaned back against the head rest. He looked over at Ellie and gently pushed her back into her own seat.

"Well, that's it then, isn't it?" he said quietly.

"What can I do, Jake?" Ellie's voice was hushed and broken. "You know I'll do anything, just tell me."

Jake cleared his throat, wiping his face with the back of his coat sleeve.

"This is a game changer, Ellie," he stopped, staring straight ahead. "I honestly didn't believe it would turn out this way, but there you go. It's like when you've got the game all tied up, only seconds left to play, and some asshole finds a hole and slides the puck into the net, and the horn blows and that's it, game over."

Ellie was weeping now. She tried to stop herself, but she couldn't.

Jake turned in his seat, meeting her eyes for the first time since they had left the office.

"You have to go now Ellie."

Ellie was screaming now, "No!" Just no, over and over, crying, wailing. He couldn't be saying these words to her.

Jake's voice had become completely calm. They both knew how ugly this could get, he said, and he wasn't going to have her diminished to the role of nursemaid, cutting up his food, helping him get dressed, changing his diapers. This last he spat out with disgust, turning away from her.

"Jake, you don't mean this. This is my choice to make, and it's not a choice at all, it just is. I love you," she was sobbing and stuttering. "Don't make me leave. Please Jake, don't say that."

Jake stared out the front window not saying anything; he barely seemed to be breathing. Then he turned toward her, his face twisted in an expression Ellie had never seen before. His voice was low, "Yeah, Ellie? What happened the first time? You walked out on me then, didn't you? You'll do it again. You don't stick around when things get tough, do you, pretty girl? I shouldn't have trusted you then, and I don't trust you now."

Ellie was shaking. This couldn't be happening. She opened her mouth, trying to find some words that would help, and Jake slammed his hand down hard on the steering wheel. "Shut up!" He was almost snarling, his voice low and menacing, "Don't say one more fucking word!" He turned on the ignition, "I'm taking you back to your apartment. I'll call Bobby when I get home. He'll get your car and your stuff back to you by tomorrow. End of discussion, girlie." His lip turned up in an ugly sneer, "I can't say it hasn't been fun."

Ellie slumped in her seat, her back to Jake, staring out the side window. She felt like a noose was around her neck choking her. She couldn't have spoken if she tried.

FACING IT

CHAPTER SEVENTY-ONE

Bobby and Claire showed up at Ellie's apartment that night. Claire had pulled Ellie close to her, whispering words of comfort like one would to a small child.

"What can I do, Bobby?" Ellie laid her head back on the sofa, still clutching Claire's hand.

Bobby looked as devastated as Jake had. The brother he idolized was horribly sick and there was nothing he could do to help him. He looked at Ellie and shrugged, "I don't know, I just don't know. It makes me crazy - at work I always know what to do. Here, where it matters, I don't have a clue." He stood up and walked to the window, kicked at a pillow that was lying on the floor then returned to his chair beside the couch. It tore at Ellie's heart to see him so sad.

"I got his prescription filled and made him take one of the sedatives before we left. He fell asleep in a second - he should be out till morning. Claire and I are going to stay at the apartment for a few days then we'll try to talk him into coming home with us till he gets things sorted out - if he's ever able to get things sorted out." Bobby put his head down in his hands, and Claire moved over to the arm of his chair and began rubbing his back. "I'm sorry Ellie..." His

voice died out. He didn't know what he could possibly say to make things better.

Jenna was at the door minutes after Bobby and Claire were gone. She sat on the floor dumbstruck as her mother, as gently as possible, explained what was going on. The two of them sat on the living room rug, pulling afghans around themselves, crying and speaking in whispers. Eventually, they moved to the bedroom, and Ellie held her arms around her daughter until she finally fell asleep, her breathing still coming in little sobs.

THE DECISION

Chapter seventy-two

J ake wandered around the apartment shoving things into a duffel bag. Bobby would be back in a couple hours, and Jake didn't want to hold him up. The last three days had passed in a medicated stupor, but he hadn't taken anything today. He had decided when he woke up this morning that if there were going to be a time in his life when he was completely addled, and it sounded like that wasn't too far off, then for this part of his life he would be as alert and lucid as he possibly could. He moved into the bedroom, picked up a pile of books that was sitting beside the bed and was sorting through them when a bookmark fell onto the floor. He squatted to pick it up, a chill shooting through him as he realized it was a photograph. His mind went very still, sensing danger, and he cautiously turned it over. And there she was, standing on the dock at the lake laughing up at him, the lake shining behind her. Jake raced for the bathroom, throwing up everything he had eaten for breakfast.

When he was finally able to return to the bedroom he threw himself down on the bed. What the fuck was the point anyway? The depression he had been trying to fight off earlier folded itself around him, making it feel as if his arms and legs were too heavy to move. The need for sleep

filled his head with a fog that he didn't try to resist but accepted almost gratefully. He slept for over an hour: his sleep deep, drugged-feeling, and he would probably have gladly remained in this semi-comatose state forever but gradually became aware of a noise making its way through the fog in his brain, bringing him back to the present. Groggily, Jake pushed himself up, his face tracked with lines from the rumpled sheets he had been lying on. What was going on? Had he forgotten to give Bobby a key?

Moving as quickly as he could, not to keep Bobby waiting, Jake hurried through the apartment, throwing the door open for his brother.

"Hello Jake." It was Ellie standing in the hallway. When she spoke her voice was barely audible. "I used my key to get into the building," she held up her key chain as if to prove something. "Can I come in ... please?" Her voice was pleading. She looked like she hadn't slept at all in the last three days, her skin blotchy, dark lines under her eyes. Jake stared down at her, wanting to grab her and hold her and knowing that he couldn't.

"What do you want?" He was fighting to keep his voice level, not wanting to let anything show that might give him away.

Ellie stood in the doorway looking up at him, twisting her hands together. "The things you said ... I just don't ... I just can't believe you meant them," she stammered. "Could we just talk?"

Jake tried not to look at her, "There's nothing more to say Ellie." He looked down at the floor, his voice low and rough. "I think you'd better leave."

Ellie leaned against the wall, putting her hands over her face. Jake knew she was fighting not to cry. "I can't believe it. That wasn't you. Please ... just tell me why you said those things." Her control was gone now, and her sentences were punctuated with gasps as she tried to get her words out through the ragged grief that filled her chest. "If you don't love me, if you can't trust me, then I'll just have to accept that, but Jake, I've been over it and over it, and it doesn't make sense, I just don't believe it. I know you. My heart knows you. Please," Ellie knew she was begging, but she didn't care, "please, just talk to me."

"Oh God, Ellie," Jake could feel his knees going weak. He loved this woman more than his own life. How was he going to make her understand? He took her hand, pulling her out of the entrance, and pushed the door shut, then led her into the apartment. They stopped at the couch but didn't sit down, standing there awkwardly, their arms half reaching for each other and then dropping limply to their sides. Jake laced his fingers behind his head and twisted from side to side, trying to fill his lungs. It felt as if there weren't enough oxygen in the air. Finally he lowered himself onto the sofa, keeping his eyes on the floor. When he began to speak his voice was cracked and low, so filled with sorrow that Ellie could hardly bear to listen to him. She sank down on the rug beside him.

"Ellie, this is how it is. This is how it has to be," he began, so quietly she could hardly hear him. "I have to go through this, I have no choice, but I can't stand the thought of you going through this too." He again began to reach for her but pulled his hand back and leaned back in the sofa. His big hand covered his eyes for a second, and then he dropped it and looked down into her eyes, pleading with her to understand. "I can't stand the thought of you being chained to me through some sense of duty. This will get really bad, Ellie." He stopped, knowing he'd blown his cover completely. "I thought if I could make you hate me you might go away and forget about me." He hesitated, reaching for her again, and this time he finally did grab her hand. The room was silent for a minute, and then tears began welling up in his eyes. "Ellie, remember the loons?" he asked. She was nodding, tears streaming down her face. "I couldn't stand the thought of you calling out to me and me not being able to answer you because I wouldn't really be inside here anymore."

Ellie took a ragged breath, and her head fell against his knee. She stared down at the floor and then, hardly daring to form the words, she whispered, "Jake, are you saying that you still love me?"

"Oh baby, it killed me to say those things to you." He kept wiping at his eyes with the back of his arm. "I was just trying to make you want to get as far away as you could from me and this fucking disease."

"But that's it, Jake," Ellie was stammering, trying to make him understand her. "What happens to you happens to me too. You can't go through this alone because you're part of me. You can't escape it, but neither can I. Maybe it's the glue factor thing. Do you remember that?" Jake nodded, remembering that moment before the door had slammed behind her.

Ellie moved a little, looking up into his face. She wiped at her face with the back of her hand and then wiped her hand on her jeans. "I think there's really only one question here, Jake," she paused, taking a shaky breath. "If we turned the tables – if I were the sick one – would you stay?"

Jake laid his head back on the couch. The laugh that came from him was hard and dismissive. "I can't believe you would even ask me that. You know I would never leave. You know that, Ellie."

"Well," she said, "I think that takes care of it, doesn't it. Are we done with all this nonsense, then?"

Jake stared down at her, something in his eyes changing, a small bit of the pain shifting. "But, Ellie, there's so much really bad, ugly stuff that can happen here," he hesitated, not wanting to let go of the lifeline she had just thrown him but afraid for her, not wanting to drag her down into this pit with him.

"Shhh, Jakey," Ellie moved up on the couch beside him, gently putting her hand over his mouth. "For me, the only thing worse than you being sick is me not being able to be here with you to help you through it – can't you see how that would just about kill me? I love you so much – this is the only place I can ever be – right here, no matter what. And, Jake, there are so many people who love us," Ellie began listing them off, "Bobby and Claire, Jenna and Ron, Mickey, Gopher, Red, you know how loyal these guys are, they'll be with us every inch of the way." Ellie's hands rubbed up and down Jake's arms. "Please, Jake, just say I can stay – we won't have to do it alone, they would never let us." Her eyes never left his face, begging him to say yes.

Jake continued to stare at her, agonizing over what to do. The room was silent, neither of them knowing what more to say, and then Jake began to nod his head, finally hearing what she was telling him. She was right of course; they would never let them do it alone. He and his friends never talked about it much – that wasn't the way they did things – but if one of them needed help there was never any question that the others would be there to help in any way they could.

Mickey had labelled it, 'circling the wagons', and that was what they had always done for each other when things got rough, as they had done during the terrible year after Gopher's son had died, or the year Red had been injured when his plane had gone down. How could he have forgotten this? They wouldn't hesitate for a minute: they would be here in any way he needed them. And more importantly, they would be here when Ellie needed them.

Jake knew how strong Ellie was – she had almost sin-gle-handedly raised Jenna and had made a life for herself without taking a penny from anyone; but it was her heart that he was thinking about. She had just let him back into her heart and he knew how fragile it was. He knew that no one could ever make this right, or even okay, but he knew that his brother, and his buddies, and their wives and their families might be able to make it bearable. Jake took the first deep breath he had taken in three days and felt the oxygen flowing through him. Ellie would be safe with them – he knew this – and the relief he felt moving through him was a visceral thing flooding every cell in his body.

He pulled her toward him, burying his face in her hair, and slowly began to let some of the fear and pain fall away from him as her words loosened the grip the diagnosis had tightened around him. He cupped his hands behind her head, bringing her face to his, kissing her again and again; tasting salt on his tongue. For the briefest moment the ancient connection between salt and life nudged at the edges of his mind – something he had once read but forgot-ten until now.

Ellie was crying again, but now it was with relief and a sweeping sense of gratitude that they had overcome this first hurdle. She stroked his face and said his name over and over again. She loved him, she just loved him …

Finally, Jake straightened up, wiping his arm across his face. "Okay then, El," he said, gently pushing her hair back from her face as he tried to regain control. "Since it looks like we're going to do this, let's make it official, right now. What's it called?" he paused for a second, thinking. "Renewing our vows, that's it. Let's do that."

"But – it's not that easy, is it? Don't you have to prepare for that kind of thing?" Ellie's eyes were coming alive again, but her voice was still halting and shaky.

"Give me your ring. I know what I want to say to you."

She looked at him for a long moment and then began twisting her ring off her finger. "Yes," she said, "I know what I want to say to you, too."

They exchanged rings and sat very still for a minute, wanting to get it right.

"Ready?" asked Jake.

"Yes," said Ellie.

Ellie took Jake's hands, rubbing them gently, trying to compose herself. She looked across the room and then back at him. "Jake," she started and then stopped. There was so much she wanted to say. "Jake," she said again, "I have to say this in two parts – the part that I need you to know – and the part that I want you to hear."

He squeezed her hands lightly. "You do it however you want, El."

She took a deep breath and began again. "Jake, I need you to know, with every fibre of your being, that we are going to go through this thing together. No matter how bad it gets, I will always be here. Always, always, always! Do you know this, absolutely, without a doubt in your mind?"

Jake could only look at her and nod, his heart so full that for a moment he felt unable to speak. Ellie was nodding too, and then her body seemed to relax and she took his face in her hands. "And this, my love, is what I want to say to you," she said, briefly touching her forehead to his.

"Jake, I love you. I've loved you from the first moment I saw you, and I will love you forever." She squeezed his hands, locking his eyes in hers. "If the day ever comes when you can't, I will remember for you. I will remember how you could skate like the wind, how you could soothe a baby with just the sound of your voice." She stopped, wiping at her eyes with the heel of her hand. "I will remember your laugh, and I will remember how your love was so strong and unconditional. Trust me, Jake, I will always remember you, the real you, and if someday you can't, I promise I will remember for you." Ellie leaned toward him, kissing him softly, and then slipped his ring back on his finger.

Jake pulled her hand toward him, kissing her palm. What she had said was so beautiful. He searched his mind, looking for the words that could give her a moment as beautiful as the one she had just given him.

"Ellie," he said, "just when I think I can't love you any more," he stammered for the words, "any bigger, greater – you do something like this, and I do." His voice was becoming strong again, and he slid his hands up her arms. He took a minute, just looking at her, and then he began.

"Ellie," he said, "I love you more than life. I love the way you care, the way you laugh." The words were right there; he didn't need to search for them. "I love your eyes, and your hair and your body. I love everything about you. I always have, and, Ellie, I will continue to love you every minute of every day until I can't love you anymore, and when that day comes, I trust you to know that deep inside my heart, I still do." Tears were again streaming down Ellie's face as Jake slipped her wedding band back on her left hand where it belonged.

He dried her eyes with his hands and kissed her face. "There's still time, Sugar," he whispered to her. "We'll make it count – you and me." And then he stood, pulling her up with him and wrapped his arms around her waist.

"Dance with me, babe," he said.

- THE END -

EPILOGUE

W e fooled 'em, bud," Mickey reeled in his line and laid his fishing rod in the bottom of the boat. "Who?"

"Everyone - the team, the Corporation, hell, even the fans."

Jake looked at Mickey, trying to understand what he was talking about. He wasn't grasping it, but the sound of Mickey's voice made him feel good.

"That night at try outs when we were talking in front of the pop machine, remember? We were laughing, and I asked you how long you thought it would take them to figure out that we were just a couple of rink-rats from back in the bush – do you remember that?"

"Yeah, yeah," Jake was grinning. He did remember. He had no trouble remembering things from thirty years ago – it was yesterday that baffled him.

Mickey was laughing. He had a great booming laugh, "And you said you wouldn't tell them, if I didn't." He was still chuckling as he reached behind him, pulling two beer from the ice cooler on the floor of the boat. He twisted off the caps and handed one to Jake. "Remember when we had to use an opener to make this kind of magic happen? I think the inventor of the twist-top should win a Nobel prize."

Jake was laughing now too – both Mickey and Ellie could do this to him. He jerked around, checking the back of the boat, "Where's Ellie?" He slammed his beer down on the seat.

"Hey, buddy, calm down. It's okay. She's at home with Claire, it's all good." Mickey put his hand on Jake's shoulder and kept it there until he felt his friend begin to relax. "Come on, drink up – it's time to get back to the cabin anyway. Bobby said he was making some chili – since there are obviously no fish left in this goddamned lake, I could use some of that. How about you?"

"Yeah," said Jake. Suddenly he wanted to get back to the cabin – maybe Ellie was there – no, Mickey had just said she wasn't, but maybe Mickey was wrong . . . no . . . things started coming back to him, but it was like a kaleidoscope that kept changing, and the patterns were all splintered shades of grey.

******

Greg had been wrong – they had four years before the disease rose up on its hind legs and ripped into them tearing everything apart; but they were four wonderful years that Ellie would hold onto forever.

They were remarried in a Catholic ceremony – they had both suddenly felt a pull to return to the faith they had known as children though neither of them could completely explain it – maybe it was just the comfort that old familiar ritual brought with it. Ellie wore a silky blue dress that floated around her feet when she moved, and her hair was done in a loose braid that fell over her shoulder. Jake had insisted that she wear baby's breath in her hair like she had done the first time, so, for him, she had woven the tiny white flowers into her hair, and when Jake saw her he had taken her in his arms and kissed her and told her that she was even more beautiful now than she had been back then. Jake wore a black tuxedo. He had laughed when he had tried it on, saying that it was still a monkey suit but a vast improvement over the one he had worn to their first wedding.

"You look like James Bond, only better," Ellie had whispered to him as they had stood at the front of the church.

"And you look like an angel," Jake had whispered back.

"In the name of the Father, and of the Son . . ." the priest had begun.

They had spent the day before the wedding with Bobby and Claire on their property outside of the city. They stayed in their guest-house for a week after the wedding as well; they had no desire to go anywhere – they just wanted to be with the people they loved.

The day before the wedding they had spent the morning tramping through the trees behind the house. Bobby really had hit the big-time Ellie realized as she and Jake had hiked around his piece of land. A creek with tangled bushes on either side wound through his property, and there was a stand of maples, most of the colour now stripped from the branches, that Bob tapped for the sap that rose up through the trunks in the Spring. Jake told her how he loved coming up here at that time of year – sugaring-off time – they would come back out here in February or March, he promised her. They stopped when they reached a clearing at the top of a hill and let their eyes take in the view below them. It was the end of October and the land was quiet, the way it gets as it prepares for winter.

"It's so beautiful . . . it's just all so beautiful." Ellie felt the tingling in her chest that she always felt when she was touched by the wonder of a thing. "Bobby must feel like Robin Hood, maybe the Sheriff of Nottingham," she was laughing as she slid down onto a log letting herself soak up her surroundings.

"No, I think he just feels like a kid who grew up loving the bush – and now he's lucky enough to be able to bring the bush to him." Jake was kicking at the ground a few yards from the creek. "And the really great thing about Bob is that he knows how lucky he is." He was still kicking at the dirt. "Right here," he said.

"Right here, what?" asked Ellie.

"I'll show you this afternoon," Jake lowered himself onto the log beside her and wrapped his arms around her, squeezing her, a sideways kind of squeeze.

She nuzzled her nose into his cheek. "My nose is frozen," she said, and Jake pulled her face into the fleece of his jacket.

"You're always frozen. Are you sure that they actually HAD weather in Saskatchewan?" he asked, and then he had to wait till she quit laughing, hunting through all of their pockets to find a Kleenex to wipe her face and blow her nose before they could head back down the hill to the house. There was still nothing that could make him happier than being able to make her laugh. Later that afternoon Jake hustled all four of them into the truck that Bobby used on the property, and they drove up the gravel back road to the spot beside the creek. A hole was now dug at the spot where he had been kicking at the dirt.

"Out, out," he yelled, and they all piled out of the truck, looking at him, wondering what he was doing. He went around the truck and heaved a jagged piece of concrete from under a tarp in the back. It was an ugly thing the size of a large cinder block with the remains of an angry message spray painted across one side – only the F and the U still visible. Jake placed it close to the hole and stood there kicking at it with the sole of his boot. "I found it at a construction site," he said. "It's been in the trunk of my car for a few days – I've been planning this for a while." He moved over to Ellie, putting his arms around her, "We need some kind of a symbol, or ritual, baby – Voodoo maybe – who knows? Whatever . . . we need something." He stepped back to the piece of concrete and stood looking at them. "You all know what this ugly piece of shit represents, right?" They all nodded, now understanding what was happening, and then Jake was screaming and kicking the concrete into the hole. "AND I'M BURYING THE FUCKER!" he yelled, triumph in his voice, and then they were all on the ground, pushing dirt into the hole. They fell against each other, the moment filling them with emotion that none of them were ever completely able to put into words.

And for four years it worked. The disease stayed buried, or at least went into hibernation. Greg was at a loss to try to explain how the disease had gone into such a steady holding pattern. "Just keep doing whatever you're doing," he told them every time he saw them. "We, so-called experts, are wrong all the time. Nothing could make me happier than to be proven wrong again." Both Jake and Ellie had developed a tremendous fondness for this young looking doctor – his kindness, patience, and basic human decency had won them over. Jake still often referred to him as, Baby Doc, but it had become a term of endearment. Greg insisted that they drop the "Doctor" and just call him Greg, and they loved him for it. It broke down a wall and let some light filter through the fear that surrounded every office visit.

Their apartment building became a condominium that winter. Both Jake and Ellie loved their corner of the city and had no desire to move, so they bought their apartment as well as the smaller one next to them, and renovations began immediately with Ellie photographing every step; from that first day with Jake grinning and swinging a sledge hammer at the adjoining apartment wall, to the last day with all of the guys posed leaning against the pool table in the new games room, the gigantic wide-screen

TV in the background. There were other slightly off-kilter shots that Jake had taken of Ellie in their new kitchen with its large island and breakfast bar and built-in stainless steel appliances. Ellie had made sure that Jake kept the swinging kitchen door, though. She would always love that door. And then there were shots of Ellie's new studio – everything state of the art. Jake had poured his heart into building this office space for her.

And as the reno wound down, a steady stream of Jake's friends began filling the apartment. It became unusual not to have an extra body at the dinner table, and Ellie loved it. Seeing Jake so at ease and preoccupied was all she needed to make her happy. Baby Jake was born in April and became the light of Jake and Ellie's lives; Mickey and Olivia were married the following September; Jake was feeling great, and life was good. It was better than good. Every moment was precious, and they never let that get old.

Mornings would often find Ellie awake early, lying on her side staring at Jake, loving the way his eyes moved beneath his eyelids, loving every line in his face. Some mornings Jake would wake to see her watching him and would smile his slow smile and run his finger down her nose. 'It's alright, babe, I'm still here,' he would say. Some mornings he would push himself on top of her, asking her if she wanted him to show her just how here he really was. Tell me, he would say, his mouth against her ear . . . tell me.

At first it was impossible to put it all aside, but after a while they both began to relax into their new normal. Jake's memory continued to annoy him, but it was nothing they couldn't deal with, and everything else seemed to remain constant. Maybe everyone really had been wrong they told each other, or maybe this was the mildest of all cases, and their denial made everything feel normal and possible.

On an evening shortly after the diagnosis, Jake and Bobby had met with Mickey and Gopher at Zack's. Jake had known that he had to tell them, but it was hard. Talking about it gave the disease substance and validity. He hated that. His two friends had sat stunned while he and Bobby tried to explain this unexplainable thing to them. God, they had been friends for a long time, Jake had been thinking as he watched them trying to process what they were hearing. Finally Mickey had yelled, "Stop! I can't breathe!" and then awkwardly pulled Jake into a rough hug, hitting his fist against his back as he tried to hide the fear behind his eyes. "It's going to be okay, Madison," he kept saying. "Somehow it'll be okay." Gopher grabbed Jake's arm across the table and said the same things – trying to find the right words. When all the words had been said Mickey and Gopher stood to leave, not wanting to leave him but not knowing what else to do. Mickey hugged him one more time. "We know how to do this, bud," he had said. "How many times have we said it? One game at a time – we'll play it out one game at a time." It had made them laugh – how many times had they repeated these words to the press? The words had held power in them back then, and they still did. They gave them room to focus on the present and let tomorrow take care of itself.

That was the night that Jake had given Bobby a letter to give to Ellie – "just in case," he had said. Bobby had put a hand over his eyes and shook his head, saying that Jake couldn't think about that, but Jake insisted and Bobby finally took the letter. He had started to reach for his wallet to settle the tab, but Jake put his hand on his arm stopping him and signalled the waiter to bring another round. "There's more to say, Bob," he had said.

*****

309

The three men filled their bowls with chili, wandering down to the lake to eat and then returned to the cabin for seconds, all the time berating Bobby's cooking.

"No, it's good, Bob," said Jake. He was afraid his brother's feelings might be hurt – somehow this year had found him more sensitive to other people's feelings – to everything. He felt embarrassed thinking of all the times Ellie had caught him blubbering over something as sentimental as a commercial involving babies or puppies. He tipped his head back as he felt Bobby trying to wipe something from his chin.

They built a fire and hunkered down around it, Mickey and Bobby keeping the conversation to stories from when they had all been young. Jake could sometimes keep up with them if they kept the talk in the past. A loon wailed far out on the lake and Jake looked up, startled, and then covered his face with his hands. "Ellie," he said, and Bobby roughly rubbed his hand up and down his back.

"She's okay, Jake. You know that we'll always make sure that she's okay." Mickey looked at him strangely, not understanding why he had said it like that. Jake stood and said he was going to bed, but then he grabbed Bobby, and they hung on to each other as if they were drowning. Mickey didn't like it – something was wrong here, and he jumped up yelling at them to cut out the love fest, and Jake hugged him and clapped him on the back and headed inside.

"What the fuck was that about?" Mickey felt his stomach churning.

Bobby turned away from him, the crook of his elbow wiping across his eyes, "Just the disease – sometimes it breaks my heart." His voice was quiet and sad.

"Ah, yeah, I know . . . something about it just felt off. Sorry, Bob, didn't mean anything."

"I know," Bobby picked up a pail and went down to the lake to fill it. When he returned he doused the fire and the two of them headed inside to bed.

The next morning Jake was gone.

******

Bobby was at the picnic table, his head buried in his arms when Mickey flung himself out of the cabin door. "Where is he?" Mickey yelled. "Where the fuck is he?"

Bobby shook his head and looked out at the lake, and Mickey, realizing what he was saying, started screaming, "No," over and over. He was bent over at the waist, and then he was hitting at Bobby's shoulder demanding to know what was happening.

"He must have swum out past the point," said Bobby, his voice barely there.

"No way! He would never have done that – you can't make it back if you swim past the point. He knows that!"

"Yes," said Bobby, "he did. He's always known that."

"No!" said Mickey as what Bobby was implying began to sink in, and he slowly sank down onto the bench. He wiped his arm across his eyes. "Why?" he asked. "Why now?"

Bobby didn't say anything for a minute as he wiped his arm over his face, "it just got too hard, Mick," he groaned, "it's just all got too fucking hard. You were there – you know how terrible everything's become over the last two years. Most of the time he seemed to be blundering around not really knowing how bad it was getting, but every once in a while he would look at me, and he was so sad and lost behind his eyes, and I knew that he knew. It killed me to see him like that," Bobby had to stop as he tried to find some control . . . "and then, two days ago . . . he hit Ellie . . . he couldn't live with himself after that." Bobby put his hand up to his forehead, rubbing furiously – wanting to erase it all. "Mainly," he said, his voice filled with a pain that he would live with for the remainder of his life, "mainly, he was afraid that he might hurt her again . . . he couldn't let that happen." His voice tapered off.

"No!" Mickey was swallowing hard. "Fuck, not Ellie . . . how?" He slumped against the table.

"Ah, Mick, it was the disease, not him. You know it would never have been him." Bobby quit speaking, just staring down at the table. "It's hard to know exactly what set him off – you know how scrambled everything is," Bobby choked and had to stop and breathe, "I mean – was – for him. From what Ellie said, they were disagreeing about what colour to repaint the bedroom. It was all pretty normal, I mean for Jake right now – you know how impossible it is for him to stay on topic." Bobby stopped, realizing that he was again speaking in the present. He shook his head and let it go and then continued. "But suddenly he just flipped out and whirled around, and Ellie saw his fist inches from her face, and then a split-second before he hit her he opened his fist. She's pretty badly bruised up, but he could have killed her if he'd really hit her."

"Fuck, no! Fuck! I can't believe it – Jake loved Ellie more than anything!" Mickey was almost mumbling to himself. He didn't say anything as he tried to absorb this, and then he raised his head, "What happened after that?"

"He made Ellie get into a cab and come to our place, and then he phoned me."

"What did he say?"

"Catfish," said Bobby.

"Catfish?"

"Yeah, that was a kind of code that he came up with six years ago, that night at Zack's." Bobby's voice had become monotone – just droning it all out. "He didn't tell me all the details, but it didn't take much to figure it out. He said he'd fight the disease for as long as he could, but if the day ever came when things got completely out of his control he would call me, and "catfish" meant I should get a hold of you and come up here." Bobby paused, rubbing his hand over his eyes, "I can't believe that he was able to remember it, but he did." He looked down at the table. "He said he didn't care if it was summer or winter, he'd find a way. He said that it was his life, Mick, it had to be his decision – he said it over and over again."

Mickey didn't say anything; he just sat there letting tears run unchecked down his face, wondering how Jake, in the state he had been, had been able to do this. But then he thought about how much he had loved Ellie, and he knew. "You did the right thing," he finally said, putting his arm over Bobby's shoulders. They stared out at the lake, and Bobby handed him a piece of paper that had been on the table, weighted down with a rock. On the paper was a note written in the cramped, spidery hand that Jake's writing had been reduced to.

'Gon for a swm', was all that was written on the page.

"Officially, no one has to know what really went down here – you okay with that?"

"Yeah, of course, no one," said Mickey. He put his head down on his arms and when he spoke again his voice was slow and heavy. "Christ, Bob . . . what are we going to do without him?"

******

Ellie sat curled up in a corner of the couch. It had been a month since Bobby and Mickey had pushed their way through Claire's back door. Ellie had known, without knowing, that something terrible had happened just by looking at them, and had felt her knees turn to water. Mickey had jumped forward, literally leaping from the doorway to the stairs where she was beginning to crumple, and caught her before she hit the floor. She knew she would never have been able to get through the weeks that followed without all of them ready to grab her and hold onto her before she was pulled under too deep. But now it was time to try to return to normal, some kind of normal, and she had insisted that she come home. She looked around, missing him in every corner of the apartment; in the couch cushions, in the window panes. She rubbed at her eyes – she had cried so many tears in the last month that her eyes had become red and raw. She took a sip of tea, now cold, and pulled Jake's letter from her sweater pocket. She had memorized it weeks ago, but her heart needed to see his handwriting – it was strong and bold – it would be the way she would always remember him, she knew that. She ran her fingers over her name on the envelope. He had written it – Ellie – he had written it.

Oh Jakey. She unfolded the paper and began to read it again: 'My beautiful Ellie,' it began, and then the words she had read over and over again: 'You are my heart. I have always loved you. I will love you forever.' Ellie buried her face in the sofa.

******

Jenna let herself into the apartment with Little Jake trying to push himself ahead of her, rushing to get into the room. His eyes caught his grandmother curled up on the couch. He felt as if his young heart might burst he was so happy to see her back home where she belonged, and he ran toward the sofa, hurling his sturdy little body at her. Ellie sat up, wiping at her face, and then Jake was yelling: "Mommy,

Mommy, come fast!" His grandmother was sad; he could see that – his mother had to fix this. Ellie held out her arms and pulled her grandson into her lap. He was five now – he wouldn't fit into her lap much longer, but for now he still did, and she tightened her arms around him fitting his head into her shoulder.

Jenna watched them, her own grief pulling at her. But she knew that Ellie's grief was so much greater, and she also knew that right now her son was the only comfort that she could offer her mother. She slipped down onto the floor beside the couch. "He loved you so much, Mamma."

"Oh, Jenna, I know," Ellie took several shaky breaths trying to steady her voice. She wiped at her eyes and ran her hand over Jenna's hair. "He loved all of us so much. I never doubt that for a minute, not even for a second – it's just that I'm missing him so much . . . I've been missing him, little pieces of him, every day for the last two years . . . you know, the way he's been slipping away from us, just inches at a time," she paused, rubbing her cheek over Jake's hair, "but now it's all so final." She pulled Little Jake even closer, "I just have to let myself be very sad for a while . . ." Her voice faded off, and Jake straightened up a bit and looked at her closely. He had his grandfather's clear eyes – his lake-water eyes.

He patted at Ellie's face with his small hands. "Knock, knock, Grammy," he said.

"Shhh, not now, sweetheart," said Jenna, but Ellie put up her hand. The ache that filled her heart let up slightly as she felt a smile forming at the corners of her mouth .

"Who's there, little guy?" she asked.

Jenna leaned her head against Ellie's knee. She reached for her mother's hand and laced their fingers tightly together.

Somehow they would get through this.

ABOUT THE AUTHOR

Hazel Young grew up in Island Falls, Saskatchewan and taught school in the north after attending university in Saskatoon. She was diagnosed with Multiple Sclerosis in 1985. She has lived in four different provinces and now resides in Airdrie, Alberta, with her husband. They have two children and three grandchildren.

CPSIA information can be obtained at www.ICGtesting.com
Printed in the USA
LVOW10s1245250815

451457LV00001B/80/P